IT'S A MATTER OF MATTER OF TRUST

MARY MICHAELS

Published in Australia by Sid Harta Books & Print Pty Ltd,
ABN: 34632585293
23 Stirling Crescent, Glen Waverley, Victoria 3150 Australia
Telephone: +61 3 9560 9920, Facsimile: +61 3 9545 1742
E-mail: author@sidharta.com.au

First published in Australia 2021
This edition published 2021
Copyright © Mary Michaels 2021
Cover design, typesetting: WorkingType (www.workingtype.com.au)

The right of Mary Michaels to be identified as the
Author of the Work has been asserted in accordance with the
Copyright, Designs and Patents Act 1988.

This book is a work of fiction. Any similarities to that of people living or dead are purely coincidental.

All rights reserved. No part of this publication may be reproduced, stored in a retrieval system, or transmitted, in any form or by any means without the prior written permission of the publisher, nor be otherwise circulated in any form of binding or cover other than that in which it is published and without a similar condition being imposed on the subsequent purchaser.

Mary Michaels
It's a Matter of Trust
ISBN: 978-1-925707-44-1
pp368

About the Author

Mary grew up in Melbourne, Australia. She has always loved reading books because they transported her to exotic places, introduced her to amazing characters and piqued her interest in page-turning narratives. She left Melbourne and travelled to London, Europe and the US, and eventually settled in Adelaide. Her love of books inspired her to teach English Literature so that she could bring books to life for her many students. Writing has always been an irresistible force for her and she thrives in the joy of creating stories.

To Nick and Thean

For Emilie,
My long distant friend!!
Love
Mary Michaels

1
...

There were too many unexpected, unresolved differences now between Princess Alia and Alex. She did not want to think of them at present. They were pushed to the back of her mind as she thought of her father once more.

King Johan the Third ruled for forty-six years, until his demise on the 17th of November 2014, in a just succession as a Constitutional Monarch. Succession was not always smoothly achieved. Over the nine hundred years of ascensions to the Royal Reign of Rubinia, many rose to the throne through bloody battles and brute force. In the last two hundred years, intrigues and plots were cleverly planned, but in recent times it was with much gratification to observe that the sensitivities of humanity sharpened the intellect to take peaceful and justified control of the throne by divine right and absolute primogeniture.

Queen Sylvia sat silently in a carriage with her daughter Princess Alia, her son-in-law Alex and her grandson Prince Stephan, while the transport ahead carried her husband, her monarch to his final destination. Alia brought the blanket up closer to her waist. She felt the warmth of the autumn sun around her, yet she was cold. As she looked longingly at her husband of nine years and at her son sitting opposite her, contently next to each other, she naturally slipped into reflection. From the day of her son's birth and over the eight years of his life, an obvious and intrinsic bond developed between father and son. At times she felt excluded. Yet, since his grandfather's death, her young little man displayed acts of kindness with some hugs and kisses towards her and she knew he sensed her silent ache. It was more than she could say for Alex.

She knew her father died from a massive stroke and sadly lingered for two months in a senseless suspension approximating life. Alia thought, for all the intricate and efficient medical technologies that graced hospitals to extend the breathing process of a patient, it would be best, at times, to let nature take its course. The endless days and nights waiting anxiously for a positive result pressed heavily on their hearts with each disappointment that occurred. At last logic prevailed as the queen, Princess Alia and Alex stood motionless by the king's bedside while the life support system was switched off. An unexpected cry escaped the queen's lips as her head lowered and kissed her husband on the forehead. Princess Alia felt numb; she could not cry nor show tears of painful emotion. She would mourn her father in private. As her mother dabbed her teared eyes with a handkerchief, Alia came and stood close by her, yet without touching – she

1

was in public and from a young age she was taught not to display any form of emotion in such an arena. This made her mother's tender expression of a short punctuated outburst surprisingly unfamiliar, but she recovered quickly and stood reposed by her monarch's bedside.

The memory of that day was emblazed in Alia's mind and more acutely so, as Alex stood quietly beside her with only a few words of comfort and just a slight touch on the shoulder to let her know of his presence. There was opportunity to say more with a soft touch of a hand or a warm arm around her shoulders, when doctors and staff left the royal family alone for quite a while, after the support machine stopped its slow persistent hum. Alia took her mother's arm and softly encouraged her to leave the room. Alex went to the door and opened it for the queen and Princess Alia to walk out. Instantly, one of the bodyguards was swiftly on the scene and held the door open for Alex to pass as well. His silence engulfed Alia's heart, as Alex walked a few steps behind her and the queen.

It relieved Alia's mind to know that her mother was to ascend the throne. She could not bear to think that it might have been herself at this young stage of her life. There were too many other things to consider without having to think about the responsibilities of the Crown.

Her thoughts were jolted as the horses came to a sudden halt in front of the Castelneuf Cathedral. The carriage ahead of them had already stopped and eight military guards prepared themselves in absolute precision to carry the casket off the bier in unison and efficiency. The royal family was helped out of the carriage by the military guard in attendance. Behind them officials of the country, which included the Prime Minister, began to take their places for the procession into the church. Firstly, the queen entered the cathedral, followed by her family and the small procession of officials to Bach's Requiem Mass, which imbued the congregation with the saddest Gregorian chant melody ever composed. This was compounded even more so as the queen cut a solitary and sad figure all in black attire with a hat of fine tulle lace which fell from the brim just covering her eyes and gently touching the bridge of her nose. Everyone in the cathedral stood with bowed heads as the king's casket passed by.

2

When the Liturgy Service concluded in tranquillity, reflection and an expectation of destiny, the casket with the monarch's reposed body began to make its way out of the cathedral, followed by the queen and her immediate family. Pew by pew was emptied as people began to follow the bereaved silently.

Everyone filed outside and all felt the cold, crisp air touch their very bones. Even the sun's rays had a losing battle; the wind whipped into corners and groups of people who huddled together as they talked waiting for the Daimler vehicles to carry some of them to the next destination. The king's limousine slowly wove its way to the main street where people still waited patiently to see the casket to its final journey at the Abbey and find its permanent home in the royal vault.

Eventually, the farewells to the extended family were made, the handshakes and kisses dutifully performed, and at last the royal family found themselves alone. The limousine took them to the palace where the queen wearily made her way to the apartments with two or three of her chambermaids. Likewise, Princess Alia, Alex and Stephan were glad to be surrounded by their familiar environment. There was little exchange of words between the parents. Their focus was to address the needs of their son, so the conversation by-passed each other and found the focal point on Stephan. Both mother and father were saved from their charade as Susanna, the nanny, arrived to take Stephan to his bedroom.

Alia moved uncomfortably in the chair and focused intensely on the cup of coffee and tray of sweets. She could not confront Alex's eyes.

'Alia, are you all right … do you want me to stay in your apartment tonight?'

'Do as you wish.' She continued staring at the cup and occupied her hand by unnecessarily stirring the coffee so quickly that some of it spilled onto the saucer.

Alex walked up to her and gently placed his hand over hers which was still trying to stir the coffee. 'Please look at me … please.'

Slowly her gaze eventually fell upon his face, but not directly on his eyes. He brought the chair from the table next to Alia and sat on it, making sure he faced her. 'Look, I know you're going through a very sad time losing your father … I know we've gone through very hard times, to say the least, and it is not easy for you nor for me.' He drew in a hard breath and exhaled with a deep sigh. 'It is not the time nor place to discuss our situation …' He leaned forward and touched her hands that were now tightly clasped together on the table. 'I will stay here with you and Stephan until things calm down a while.'

'You can use the double bedroom ... I'll call for someone to set it up.' Her hands were still cupped by his.

'There's no need ... I can organise that.' He released her hands and, as he stood, bent down and kissed the top of her head. 'Goodnight, Alia.'

'Goodnight,' was all she could say.

She laboured out of her chair, flipped the shoes off her feet and aimlessly walked towards the bedroom. The light-headedness she felt only served to make her movements slower. One clothing article after another came off and she went to the ensuite bathroom. As she stood under the shower with the stream of warm water washing over her, Alia realised that trickles of tears were also running down her cheeks. She covered her face with her hands and began the copious tears with intermittent sobs, as if those tears could expunge the pain and hurt that had settled, excessively, in her soul. Unaware as to how long she had remained in the shower, she was shaken only by the sudden cold stream of water that began to flow onto her tingling body. Quickly, she turned off both taps, stepped out and reached for the towels that were warmed on the bath rails. She pressed the warm softness to her face and body until she felt dried. As she looked into the long elongated wall mirror, she saw the noticeably puffy skin around her eyes and the red rims that had formed. Automatically, she reached for the skin toner and various creams that were normally used; and lastly, she felt the dryer's warm air rustle through her thick chestnut hair until it was silky dry.

As she walked into her bedroom, she came to a sudden halt, startled to see Helena, her personal chambermaid. Desperately, she turned in the direction of the walk-in closet-room to cover the state of her countenance. Her thoughts were quickly arrested. 'Your Highness, I have put out some nightwear. Would you like anything else?'

While still in the closet-room, she responded, 'Thank you Helena. I'll manage myself. Goodnight.'

'Goodnight, Your Highness.'

She heard the bedroom door softly close and she moved out of her hiding place. The nightwear and other accessories were strategically placed on the bed. She slipped into her nightie, took an aspirin, switched off all the lights in her bedroom and tucked herself deeply under the bedclothes.

3

...

As daylight broke, Alia hesitantly attempted to move out of bed. Her eyes scanned the ceiling idly. She rolled on the left side, then onto her right, and she could see that the pale gold cornice on the ceiling had an angel at each corner. As her eyes skimmed down the wall opposite the foot of her bed, she noticed a hairline crack on the right-hand side of the wall, which began from the cornice and slowly wove its way down to the middle of the wall and then magically disappeared behind the plaster. It was so fine, in fact, that it had never been discernible until that very minute. Instinctively, she made a mental note to inform Helena and let the plasterer know.

'No, I won't tell Helena.' She looked at it again. 'I think I'm warming up to its intrusive likeness on my wall. There it shall stay to keep me company and ...' A firm knock on the door diverted her attention. 'Come in, Helena.'

'It's not Helena – who were you talking to?' Alex approached the foot of the bed. 'Were you on the phone?'

'No, it's nothing. I should get up. What time is it?' She

pushed the bedclothes to the side and slowly considered getting out of bed.

'It's nine.'

She looked at Alex and her eyes widened as she responded, 'It's so late. I better get up,' and with a stronger effort forced herself out of bed.

'Do you want breakfast up here?'

'No, I'll be down shortly.'

'Stephan and I will be in the dining room.'

Alex made his way to the door of the room and Alia disappeared into the bathroom. As he began his way into the hallway and found the top of the staircase, he stopped suddenly and remembered when they had met after eleven years' absence. He was at the bottom of those stairs and Alia stood exactly where he was at this moment. For a second or two he found his heart beating quickly and his chest heaved at that inextricable love that was between them. He clearly realised nothing could rival that initial love they had for each other. He soon recovered and quickly made his way down the staircase and into the dining room.

'Stephan, do you want a hot chocolate? Mummy will be down for breakfast. I think it will be nice to keep her company while she has her breakfast. I'll get a cup of coffee for myself.'

'Okay, Papa.'

Father and son sat cosily at the dining room table talking and laughing together. 'Pa, where's Basco today? I haven't seen him for a couple of days.'

'He's with Hans who's looking after all the dogs.'

'But he's my dog and I want him here. Can I have him here?' Stephan pleaded with disappointment written all over his face.

'*May* I have him here, Stephan.'

'May I have him here?' repeated his son.

'After breakfast.' Alex looked at his son's downcast face and said, 'Hey, Stephan. Do you remember when we bought Basco? He was only two years old and you were…?'

'Six, Pa. You're checking up on my math.'

'Yes, I am. Do you remember when we brought him home? We went to the small room off the laundry area and fed him with dried food and water in bowls that sat on the floor? Little did we know by doing that, a Saint Bernard of his size will also gulp a lot of air. We left him for an hour or so and when we returned – wow, the whole place stank from smelly farts.'

'You said that it "stank of gas warfare"!'

'I did, too.' Both laughed heartily. 'Just as well, the dog handler bought him the food-stool for his bowls to sit in. That helped a lot.'

'It sure did Papa,' and then they laughed some more.

Just at that moment, Alia opened the door and entered the room.

'Good morning, Stephan. What's all this laughing about?' Alia walked up to her son and gave him a long hug and a kiss on the cheek.

'We're talking about when we first brought Basco

home, how he stank out the little room next to one of the laundries.'

'I don't remember that, Stephan. Was that on the first day you brought him here?'

'Yes, Mummy ... but it doesn't matter.' He looked awkwardly at his father, but Alex smiled at his son and nodded his head. 'Would you like me to get your breakfast?'

'No, thank you, Stephan. I'll get my own. I am so pleased we are having breakfast together.' She went to the chiffonier buffet and chose a toast with marmalade, some goat's cheese, crackers and a few thinly sliced pieces of pear. 'So tell me, what have you been doing and learning? It seems I haven't seen you in a little while.'

'I've been building a rocket with my Legos and Pa's helping me – it's sooo much fun. I didn't think we could build it so high, but we did! Can I show you after breakfast? You'll love it!'

'I would like to see it very much. How is school?' Alia asked him eagerly.

'You know how much I love math – I can just do it all day long, but I also like reading, that's second best. I'm reading *Super Snoops*.'

'What's that all about?'

'It's about three boys who go into the forest to find the wizard's cave and he can do lots of magic. I love it!' Stephan's eyes sparkled with excitement as he rattled off some of the adventures the three Snoops had in the forest.

'Tell Mummy about the small alien spacecraft that the boys found,' Alex prompted his son.

'A spacecraft! Wow, that's exciting.'

'They were lost in the forest and they used the spacecraft as a shelter to protect them from the cold ... but then they discovered some precious things in the spacecraft, like a non-ferrous metal detector.'

'Hey, what's a non-ferrous metal detector?' Alia prompted Stephan to continue with his explanation.

'It detects non-magnetic metals ... and you know, Mum, that was important so they can find their way to the wizard's cave.'

It was the first time her son called her "Mum". It was always mummy or mother. A shadow of a smile passed her lips and as she looked up, there was Alex smiling at her, and she knew that he understood. It dawned upon Alia that she had missed out on precious time with her son and somehow she had to rectify this.

There were twelve national days of mourning for King Johan, which meant there would be no national duties for Alia or the queen, and Alia was determined to productively use these days to become better acquainted with Stephan and his small world. Instinctively, Alex turned to his son. 'What do you say we ask Mum to come and help us build our rocket?'

'That's a great idea, Pa!' He suddenly stopped and looked intently at his mother. 'Have you got the time to help us?'

'I do.' She went to her son and brushed his face with her silky hands and kissed the rush of fair hair that tumbled onto his forehead. 'Why don't we go now?'

Stephan's parents took him each by the hand and as they walked towards the staircase, they lifted him up high and allowed him to land a few feet in front of them. The squeals of delight echoed around the palace as they also made play of going up the stairs in attempts to catch their son as he bounded up with full energy and some to spare.

Hearing the ruckus, the queen came out of her office and went towards the stairs to see what the commotion was all about. She stared at the happy threesome and placed her hand over her heart, sighed and softly said to herself, 'It's about time!' She moved in the direction of her office again and faintly felt a small spark of joy ripple through her whole being.

In the playroom, they continued to build the rocket. Alia found herself in all kinds of positions — on her knees, on her back as she attempted to place the blocks under the rocket's wings. Stephan played a supervisory role as he handed his parents various blocks for different parts of the rocket. 'Mum, you put this right on the tip of the wing ... under it ... just there. Pa, put this on the very top to the right ... a little more to the right ... that's it.'

As Alex completed his task, he tried to move his feet and in the process tangled them with Alia's legs when she began to come out from under the wing. He fell flat on top of her and remained as such, laughing loudly. Alia was instantly taken by surprise, but quickly saw the funny side of it. Stephan stood on the side and viewed the pile-up and began to roar with laughter. In the seconds that it took for this scene to occur and as the chaotic jumble began to lessen, it was Alex who first wound down his merriment and still lying over Alia, he took her face in his hands and gave her a thorough kiss on the lips. She lay motionless as her heart quickened. Suddenly, Alex realised his son's presence.

'Okay Mum, this is for doing such a good job on the rocket and this is for helping us have such a fun time altogether,' and with that, Alex pecked her forehead with a kiss, scrambled up and stretched his hand out to help Alia off the floor.

She stood in something of a daze and as she was straightening her clothes from the tumble, Stephan came and hugged her so hard that it almost reduced her to tears. She was not used to his demonstrative affections. 'You're the best, Mum!'

'Thank you, Stephan. We should do this more often.'

'I agree!' Alex quipped as his eyes met Alia's.

Alia felt confused and helpless, and her only recourse was silence. Her eyes locked with his and she was lost in the past. She was saved by a door knock. She blinked involuntarily and in a stronger voice than she'd normally answer in called, 'Come in.'

Susanna walked into the playroom and made a quick curtsy. 'Your Highness, it's time for Stephan's pony ride lesson.'

'I'm too old to ride a pony. I want to ride a horse!'

'We'll see what your riding instructor has to say,' Susanna urged him.

'Stephan, you do exactly as your instructor tells you. Are we clear on that?'

'Oh, Pa,' he uttered disconcertedly as a frown spread across his forehead. He took the nanny's hand and reluctantly walked out of the room with her.

Alex swerved to face Alia, he exhaled as he uttered, 'Alone, at last.' He noticed Alia's tentative glance, but he was determined to approach her. This had been the closest he had gotten to her in too long a time. 'Alia, let us talk, right here, right now … while we have the opportunity.'

'I'm not sure … I think I want to go and change.'

'There's no need to change, Alia. You look fine.'

'What is there to talk about that has not already been said?'

'I want you to understand why I won't accept a royal title. I have never sought or asked for one. I cannot be less than who I am.'

'How can you be "less" by accepting a title? I …'

'Because I have not been born into it, nor have I earned it. I'm a self-made man and I'm happy with just the title of Doctor. Do you realise how hard I've worked in the last eight years? Do you know how far I've come in the aerospace industry to date? My work is not only for my own personal advancement. It's for our country, as well. The inroads we have made in this industry, physically and technologically, are mind-boggling. This could not have happened if I hadn't put in a hundred percent of my focus.'

'More like two hundred percent. I have hardly seen you since Stephan's birth. I understand that at the start of your company you had to be physically there, you had to get it off the ground, but you have not let up for eight years.' She sighed heavily, looked at the floor and spoke softly. 'Do you realise people think we're about to get a divorce?'

'You shouldn't take notice of gossip mongers.' Alex tried to dispel her fears.

'I don't. I take notice of the facts that are in my life. I can count on one hand the number of times you have supported me in my royal commitments. It's no wonder people stick the knife in my heart and twist it with sarcasm.' She then imitated the tone of a voice used. '"And where is Alex again? No doubt working late – alone — of course!" Do you think that people can't read or see what's in the news? You and your personal assistant looking very cosy in a dozen different places!'

'Where else would I be but with her. She *is* my assistant. That's her job,' Alex blurted out with some force in his voice.

'And what about the restaurant and the boat on the river … and God knows how many other places you were together.'

'You have to believe me. I asked her to help me host some business events at the restaurant and on the boat … and that's all it was. How can you believe the paparazzi? You know very well that we started drifting apart because I could not fit into your world and you could not fit into mine. The truth is … we're both too stubborn,' Alex stated adamantly.

'Well, nothing then has changed, has it?'

'Yes, it has. After eight years, the company has gone public. I am still the controlling shareholder with fifty-five percent of the shares, I've got a Chief Executive Officer and many of my responsibilities have lessened.'

'So what exactly are you trying to say?' Alia felt puzzled.

'Are you willing to compromise a little? Before you answer this, let me explain. I need someone by my side at times, when I have to entertain new clients, when organised events occur, when you just simply appear next to me as my wife.'

'I guess I can do that. I'd have to get permission from the queen.'

'Fair enough,' Alex added reasonably. 'I know your father wanted me to eventually take the title of king, but I could not do that. It pains me to think how much I had hurt him.' Alex looked soulfully at Alia. 'It saddened me that he, too, withdrew his affections from me. There was nothing I could do about it. But what hurt me most of all was you, Alia. Your cold distancing was unbearable.'

'I wanted you by my side, as well. Were you at the Children's Hospital when it was opened and gifts were handed out to the children? Where were you when the President of America visited our country? Every royal and statesman was there, except you. And do you know what hurt the most? That little imp of a man King Gregory, with his stings and stones he thrust at me, cut me to the core. Once, he had the audacity to approach closely and whisper in my ear, 'You should have married me. I'd be by your side, always. Where is that husband of yours anyway? As if we didn't know.' He then walked away with that triumphant sinister grin on his face and began talking and weaving his black web with others. I wished the floor had opened up and swallowed me.' Tears began to trickle down her warm cheeks. She turned her back so Alex could not see them.

Within seconds she felt his warm breath on the back of her neck and his arms had encircled her tightly. He slowly turned her so they were face to face, and with the back of his hand he wiped away her tears. He pressed her tightly to his chest and with that same natural urge of long ago, Alia lifted her face to his and their lips met inextricably. He suddenly disengaged himself, took her hand, and together they walked quickly out of the playroom and down the hallway to Alex's apartment. He opened the door and ushered Alia into the lounge area. Swiftly, he locked the door and swept her into his arms where soon they were both lost in the cravings for the love of each other.

4
...

In the ensuing five days Alia and Alex found time to be with their son and with each other. It was Stephan that preoccupied them the most; he was their focal point. He did not go to the Palace International School during the days of mourning; however, tutors were provided to keep him abreast with the curriculum. When he wasn't learning, he was playing games, or going for walks with his parents. Most of all, Stephan spent an inordinate amount of time with Basco. They romped around out in the cold, chased each other, played hide-and-seek and generally were inseparable, until it was time for dinner. His parents placed their own personal problems on hold. Ultimately, on the sixth day everything came to an abrupt halt.

Alia was with her son in the playroom, working on a massively large picture puzzle. Both were seated on the floor and the child's table was covered with pieces to the puzzle that began to fit into each other, yet not quite discernible as to what the images were, exactly. Other pieces were strewn

4

on the floor and they assiduously concentrated on finding the right one. At times, Alia would choose a ridiculously wrong piece to see her son's reaction.

'Oh, Mum, no. I've just got to teach you how this works. Try and find the rounded corner pieces first and then the straight edge pieces and work from the outside in. I'll show you. Here's a rounded corner piece with blue and a bit of gold on it. It's probably the sky – see the picture? There's no other blue for a pond or water. So ... we'll put it up here.'

'Well that's very clever, darling. I've learned something today.'

Alex stood at the door's entrance and followed the whole process. 'So, is Mum a good pupil?' he asked as he stepped into the room.

'Oh, yes Papa.'

'May I borrow Mum for a moment?'

Alex gave Alia his hand to help her off the floor and together they left the room as Susanna arrived to supervise Stephan. They both went into the private lounge and sat opposite each other. Alia leaned forward with hands on her knees. 'What's up?'

'I just got a call from work and it seems that there is a glitch with one of the events that's coming up. I'll need to go in and sort things out.'

'Oh, what event is that?'

'I have some international clients coming in and lunches and dinners and a hundred other things need my okay.'

'And is Ebba organising all this?' Alia's tone rang with suspicion.

'Of course,' was her husband's laconic response.

'Well then, you had better go.' She looked down at her tightly clasped hands and noticed the knuckles were quite white.

'Don't say it like that Alia, I have no other choice.'

'Just go.' The resignation in her voice did not miss its mark.

Alex looked at her momentarily, but Alia did not shift her gaze from her hands. He stomped out of the room without another word. He thumped his way down the stairs, picked up his briefcase at the door and smartly found his car with the door open and the driver by the side. 'It's okay Trent. I'm driving.' He didn't wait for his driver to answer. He got in by himself and blazed off. His mind raced to the speed of his car. 'She's a stubborn fool! I can't understand her anymore.' His mutterings continued in the same vein all the way to his destination. When he parked the car, he collected himself a little and walked towards his office. The doorman tipped his hat as he opened the main door, other employees ventured a 'good morning' here and there. He reached his office and without acknowledging his personal assistant and he snapped, 'Come into my office.'

Ebba Nilsson picked up her iPad and followed him into his office, closing the door behind her. Alex still bristled over Alia. 'Bring me up to speed, will you? What's happening?'

'Jacob Einheimmer wants a personal conference with you

before you see anyone else, but the snag is that our CEO wants to be a part of it.'

'How does he know about it?'

'I was on the phone with Mr Einheimmer when Mr Fischer entered my room and caught part of the conversation.'

'Don't worry, I'll deal with that. Get Einheimmer on the phone for me.'

'I have coffee for you. Would you like this now?'

He looked up and in a calmer tone said, 'Yes, please.' He watched Ebba Nilsson walk to the door, wearing a straight black skirt that hugged her hips, not too tightly, just sufficiently so it discerned her curves. Her white blouse opened to a point where no revelation of a cleavage was detected. Her gold tresses were straight, but with a few loose curls at the ends. Her powers of concentration emanated from wide blue eyes that accurately discerned people and situations.

Alex was shaken from his thoughts as Ebba entered. She brought the coffee with a couple of dark chocolates that were his favourites. 'Mr Einheimmer is in a conference. He will ring you within thirty minutes.' She leaned over and left the coffee with the chocolates on his desk and as she did so, her blouse billowed a little revealing just the upper supple rounded softness of her breasts. She realised that Alex noticed it. Swiftly, she straightened up and with a professional serious face asked, 'Is there anything else I can do for you before I go to my computer?'

'Nothing else for now, Ebba.'

As she closed his office door, Alex leaned back into his brown leather chair and sighed. How long had he noticed her, other than as his personal assistant? Far too long. She had been recommended for the job four years ago by a colleague, Jacob Einheimmer, after Alex bought out his small company. Ebba's credentials, experience and intellect were irreproachable, and her impeccable conduct towards the clients was invaluable. At first, he saw her as a worthy employee and felt fortunate that she worked for him. Certainly, the clients were impressed with the calm and professional disposition she always revealed. Mr Einheimmer trusted her implicitly as his initial employee. Ebba Nilsson had a natural ability to say only what was necessary, while allowing the person with whom she spoke to tell her all *she* needed to know. Apart from her obvious attractiveness, her dress was always understated in her workplace. Not even the events she organised and attended for the company saw her in anything more than the classic black dress, pearls and an occasional hairstyle swept up on her head. To this, there were variations with only minor differences. Careful never to take the limelight, she nonetheless did so. She addressed her employer and the clients in the appropriate and proper fashion, by their title, and always stood at a suitable distance between them. Should she need to gain someone's attention, she always waited a little to the side and at the exact moment would softly call his or her name. A tallish woman, but never towering over anyone, she exuded an instinctive attraction that was wholly her own to command.

4

His thoughts wavered in a different direction. As far as Alia and Alex were concerned, after the magical first year of their marriage and the birth of Stephen, their life together began to go downhill. The problems were usually the same with variations on the theme. Alia complained he was never with her, neither at home nor at her royal duties. He resented that she did not understand how hard he worked to make the company a pillar in the eyes of the aerospace industry and for their country. She called him selfish, insensitive and who-knows-what under her breath, but never allowed their disagreements to progress to a blown-out argument. It usually ended with either one or the other tramping out of the room. Then there was the deathly-silent treatment of each other, only speaking if they had to, but the exception was always when they were in Stephan's presence. Then, everything appeared normal.

Alex's stubbornness was an exact replica of Alia's. There were so many opportunities for one of them to cave in and extend an olive branch, but some stringent sinew in their being held them back. Several times he recalled approaches he made to her only to be snubbed with a swift turn to face him and arms in the air allowed to drop to her side in despair. 'I give up,' she'd say. 'I can't find a middle ground here.' It had become her stock retort. His was no better. 'Stop being a princess for once and start being a wife.' He knew this cut her to the quick and a few times he resented saying it. 'I'm sorry I had to say this, but you're making it impossible for me, Alia.' He could see the pain he inflicted in her eyes, but it was now too late to reclaim a single word he uttered. Then with resignation she'd say, 'Why don't you go to your work ... that's more of your home than here!' What made that statement so harsh was that it was softly spoken, and it rang true in his heart. At that point, his only recourse was to walk away.

The few times he joined his wife at an official function, they both smiled at each other, walked arm in arm and projected a proficient public face. There were, of course, times when both of their guards were down, especially when they were outdoors and ran into each other on walks; or he'd find Alia in the garden helping his father plant some flowers. It became her means of escape, without being answerable to anyone, not even to Robert Glandore, but on that score, she was fooling no one. To Robert, it was obvious from the outset that his son's marriage to Princess Alia began to deteriorate from its infant beginnings. Neither he nor she ever vented their problems and that brought limitations for opportunities to discuss or just listen to their difficulties. As he watched Alia digging with the trowel, the amount of energy expended to dig a small hole in the dirt, place the plant in it, cover the roots with more soil, pat it down to steady it, and then water it, appeared to be more of a project of gigantic proportions, as if it were a fully grown tree to be transplanted. 'Your Highness, if you are getting tired, I'm happy to call young Jimmy to come over and help me.'

'No, Mr Glandore. I'm just fine,' and with that she'd pound the ground around the plant with all her might.

4

Robert epitomised all things that were professional; never interfered in their lives; always spoke with a demeanour that was appropriate to all the royals in the palace. As for his son, there were words of wisdom, often ignored but not forgotten, and he always had a way of revealing the truth to him. 'Look Alex. See those weeping cherry trees? They can be self-sustained for quite some time, but neglect to water them and sooner or later they'll dry and die.' He'd pat his shoulder and say, 'Think about it.' He had thought about it and knew exactly what his father meant, but what was that adage? "It's easier said than done."

It was not always that bad and he tried to remember the idyllic honeymoon on a private island in Greece. It was owned by an industrial magnate, Les Frombourg, who owed King Johan some favours over the years. There were very few people on the island at that time of year, but plenty of staff and they couldn't do enough for Alia and Alex. Their days were spent in each other's company, relaxed with the occupation of knowing all they wanted to do was to please one another. The hikes up the hillside with the eternal olive trees dotted along the way transported them to ancient times. He helped Alia climb up higher than they wanted to go, but they talked and laughed about everything and anything. Alia related to some classical studies she had done at university and quoted Socrates as saying "An unexamined life is not worth living." Alex offered his hand and helped Alia to sit upon a boulder and soon sat beside her. He was quick with his retort, 'Oh, I believe in the examination of life, especially in the examination of you ... those beautiful eyes, those ears, those cheeks and especially those cherry lips.' No sooner had he kissed each and every part of her face when he finally settled on those sweet lips. If their day was not spent on the hillside, it was dedicated to the calling of the Mediterranean waves as they frolicked like a couple of seal pups in and out of the frothy waters. They sunbathed by the swimming pool and read; usually, Alia had a novel in her hand and Alex had a newspaper. 'Hey, Alia. Do you realise there's a world out there?'

'I don't care. I don't want this to ever end.'

'Whatever happened to us?' he thought. 'Perhaps I should examine my life with more determination and evaluation. But damn it all, it takes two to make a relationship work. Why isn't Alia helping with this?' He was shaken from his deep thoughts as he heard a far-away knock on a door. He heard it again and this time it crystallised loud and clear that it was his office door. 'Come in,' he called out.

Ebba entered. 'These documents require your signature. I'll leave them here.' She left as quietly as she came.

The last thing Alex wanted to do was read these dry documents, but it was essential.

As he came towards the end of the documents, his cell phone rang. It was Alia. 'Alex, King Gregory is coming to visit tonight and obviously I had to ask him to stay for dinner. Will you *please* be here by seven – I really need your support tonight. I'm sure he's up to no good.'

He glanced at the documents in front of him and quickly

thought of all the other essentials he had to do. 'I can't promise, but I'll try.'

'I've heard that line so many times before and it usually means no. Either you can or you can't!'

'I *said*, I'll try!'

'Goodbye.' The conversation came to an abrupt end.

'How predictable can she be!' he muttered under his breath.

He was not going to let this interruption get the better of him. He concentrated on the paperwork piled on his desk and pushed everything else to the side. Then, he needed to read his emails from Lars Gilmar outlining the computerised technological upgrade of all the systems in the company's latest supersonic invention. Although he had the staff who could deal with most of the issues, at times it became necessary to accept outside assistance. This was a crucial endeavour and Gilmar's proposal seemed to lock into the problem in an informative and, more importantly, suggestive way for resolution.

Alex did not know him very well, but his enquiries proved to find the man favourably. He would not hesitate a moment to employ him, except that his project was so secretive, he took a risk in the admission of an outsider. While he was considering all of this, Ebba returned to his office.

'Dr Glandore, Mr Einheimmer is on the phone. Shall I put him through?'

'Yes, thanks.' He waited a few seconds and soon Jacob Einheimmer's voice was blaring in his ear. 'Mr Einheimmer, this is a pleasant surprise. How can I help you?'

'Don't you think it's about time you started calling me Jacob?'

'If you wish.'

'Now, I've heard on the grapevine that Lars Gilmar might be working for you. If I were you, I'd look a little closer at his track record ... what kind of a man is he? I've had many more years of experience in this industry than you and Gilmar combined. So, what I'm proposing is that you do your background homework in greater depth and meet me to discuss the situation.'

'Mr Einheimmer, I've ...'

'Jacob.'

'*Mr Einheimmer*, I have no idea where you've obtained such unfounded information. But I can assure you that even if it were true, I'd never employ anyone without a thorough check.' He paused for a moment and thought carefully. 'I realise that part of our deal, when I bought your company, was for you to receive a good-sized sum of shares in my aerospace company in lieu of receiving full cash.' Again he stopped and thought with some caution how to respond. 'With all due respect, this does not give you the right to tell me how to run my business.'

'I see I've offended you and that was not my intention. All I'm saying is don't rush into anything. I hope we shall be able to meet soon. Goodbye, Alex.'

Alex stared at the phone in his hand with astonishment. He placed it back on the receiver and tried to replay in his mind the whole conversation that just happened. Fortunately, he had taped it and played the whole thing over a couple of times. Try as he might, he could not work out from where his information was gleaned. As he pondered on this turn of events, Ebba knocked and entered.

'Dr Glandore, it's eight o'clock. If you don't need me for anything else, I'll get ready for home.'

He looked at her in a slightly distracted manner, but simply responded, 'No there's nothing else. Good night.' She gently closed the door and he waited until the outer door was shut. When he was certain she was gone, he entered her office. Going to her computer, he tried to log in. She had changed the password. He could not do anything for the present, but that prompted him to return to his office and check his computer. Nothing seemed out of the ordinary. Before he logged out, he changed his password and sat in the chair contemplating the unusual events that had unfolded that evening. The word "evening" echoed in his head. 'No. It's a quarter to nine. She's going to be livid with me.' He locked the drawers of his desk and made certain everything was secure in his office. He switched off the lights, dashed down the hallway and quickly acknowledged the night watchman as he rushed by.

The speed with which he drove was unlike him. He veered left and right, overtook cars and trucks alike and when he caught a red light drummed his fingers on the steering wheel, willing the green light to appear. Eventually, he came to a sudden halt at the front steps leading up to the palace. As he clambered out of his car, the door opened and there stood Parkinson, as dutiful as always, while King Gregory brought Alia's hand to his lips. Gregory's descend was sprightly as he made his way towards Alex. There was a Cheshire cat grin on his face which annoyed Alex considerably. 'Well, old man, you're home at last, are you?' With his hand outstretched to shake Alex's, it was impossible not to reciprocate. It would be considered the height of ill manners. What Alex really wanted to do was to knock that grin off his face. However, he simply gave a faint smile and said nothing. Alex followed Gregory with his eyes as the door to his car was opened and he disappeared inside the black limousine like a warlock in modern transportation. The car began to vanish down the long driveway as dust puffed up around its rear wheels.

Alex looked up and saw Alia standing in the door's archway with Parkinson beside her. He climbed the steps three by three until he reached his wife. He gave her a perfunctory kiss on the cheek and took her by the arm and went inside. When Parkinson left in a different direction, he steered Alia to their private lounge. The minute the door was closed he carefully scrutinised his wife's face and he knew she was angry. 'Before you say a single word, I want to apologise for my absence ... but it was truly unavoidable – something quite serious occurred.' Alia didn't utter a word. She sat in the armchair with arms folded on her chest and stared up at the man who was referred to as her husband. 'But first tell me, what did he want? I wanted to knock his block off with that supercilious grin on his face.'

4

'Well, you were too late to do that. What did he say to you at the bottom of the steps?'

'The usual drill that people dig when they want to get at you. It doesn't matter ... what did he want?'

'He didn't explicitly say but insinuated that we will be better off if we do what he does. I did not understand what he meant, but apparently it will all be clearer to us in a short time. He will return to do this. Would you know what it's about?'

'No clue at all.'

'What was this *serious* thing that occurred?' Alia asked with some annoyance.

'We have a spy at work. Don't know who it is, but secret information has been leaked out. I don't know how serious or how much information has gone missing, but everything will be double and triple checked.'

'It's strange that this has happened to you at the same time as Gregory appeared cloaked in some mysterious meanings. I don't like it!'

'Time will tell. We can't worry too much about it. We need more information.'

He looked over at Alia who was up and now stood by the window, absently staring out. He walked over and stood closely behind her. 'Was he really very awful tonight?'

She turned to face him and found herself in close proximity – too close. He wrapped his arms around his wife and drew her close to him while he buried his face on the side of her neck and whispered, 'I'm really sorry I wasn't here tonight.'

That was all Alia needed for her to melt in his arms. They held each other like this for quite some time and were suddenly surprised by Parkinson's voice. 'Ma'am, sir, is there anything I can do for you tonight?'

Alex composed himself and responded, 'No, thank you, Parkinson. Goodnight.'

Alia drew in a deep breath and exhaled heavily. 'I think I'd better go off to sleep as well.' As she approached the door, she turned. 'Alex, I think we should keep each other informed as events occur. Goodnight.'

'Of course. Goodnight, Alia.'

5

Alia snapped shut the book and placed it back on the pile by her bedside table. As she sat up in bed, desperately attempting to read a novel without much success, she succumbed to her troubled mind, which was filled with what had transpired that evening. Gregory unsettled her and on top of all that Alex never appeared at the dinner. Things had not been well between them for too long a time.

She allowed her mind to wander to her wedding. It was the happiest day of her life. It was in spring on Thursday, eighteenth of May two thousand and six. The daffodils and tulips made an array of gold, red, and orange colours almost everywhere the eye could wander. The sun added warmth and smiles on everyone that day. The palace was bathed with crispy white ribbons, scents from a variety of flowers and music whirled around columns and glided upstairs in every room. Two quartets had been hired, and they played all day long until the carriage was ready to take the bride to the cathedral. Alia could still remember the whiff of aroma that pervaded the palace nine years ago.

Her wedding dress was designed from the House of Paolo Ruscetti, an internationally acclaimed designer from Castelneuf, the capital of Rubinia. The silk off-white dress had a fitted bodice with a sprinkle of miniature diamantes. From the waist down, the skirt flared with a trailing hemline at the back and a grand border right around the entire skirt, embroidered with lily-of-the-valley, which was the national flower of Rubinia, and a loose application of diamantes. The dress train of silk tulle fell from a two-hundred-year-old royal tiara that belonged to the Casteler family. Alia's bouquet of flowers included lily-of-the-valley and the gold Sylvia rose named after her mother. This particular rose was propagated by Robert Glandore in the palace gardens.

The carriages were resplendent with brightly polished brass and clear glass so everyone could view the Princess, the queen, Alex, and other family members, not least of all Alex's best man Isiah Cumberbatch, groomsmen Dave Malloy and Jonathon Levinson. Alia's Matron of Honour was Christy Cumberbatch, the bridesmaids Princess Carlotta and Rosalind Landers, now Princess Rosalind. All of her attendants wore deep cream outfits which reflected partly the bride's dress in that the bodice was fitted and the skirt slightly flared. She recalled how handsome Alex looked as he turned to see her walk down the long aisle towards him; it was the beginning of their new life. When she arrived right beside him, she looked up and he whispered, 'You look beautiful. I love you.' She gave him a glowing smile from a love that abundantly emanated from her heart.

    The reception was held at the palace ballroom for about four hundred selected and intimate guests. The remainder of the people who attended the cathedral ceremony were invited for drinks, cocktails and hors d'oeuvres. Naturally, Alex, Alia and the bridal party attended and for practical reasons, Alia's dress train was removed, but the tiara reinstated. Although it was a formal occasion, an air of casualness accompanied with a friendly atmosphere graced the event as they eventually made their way to the palace ballroom. To the newly married couple, everything around them glittered and everyone glowed, as all the food courses were elegantly consumed while champagne incessantly bubbled in crystal fluted glassware. The dance floor only heightened their elation as they swayed closely together and twirled to the light-headiness of music as it swirled around them. It was a day that nothing could spoil Alex or Alia's effused joy.

    Even the speeches were worth the listening with some hilarious anecdotes of years past and present. Isi was more than happy to reflect upon their university years at Cambridge and in particular, Alex's determined efforts during one regatta race against Oxford. Alia still recalled Isi's words. 'We know how well we were all fed at Cambridge, but that did not help our rowing team. A week before the race, Alex, as captain of the team, got everyone to weigh in. The discovery was quite disturbing; the crew weighed an average of one point nine kilograms per rower heavier than their opponents from Oxford. Having considered all possibilities, Alex consulted the kitchen staff at the main dining hall and each rower was given a more stringent and healthier diet than the rest of the students, much to the rowers' discontent. But that wasn't all — exercise time was doubled. Needless to say, Cambridge won the race on the river Thames that year.'

Alia found herself smiling. She thought, *Even back then he survived on raw determination. Nothing really has changed; he simply cannot wind down.* She glanced askance at the digital clock on her bedside table which read one seventeen. How was she going to get up by six-thirty? She flicked off the light switch and tried to nestle under the bedclothes but found it hard to turn off the constant flickering thoughts in her mind. It was not surprising that when the chambermaid woke her the next morning, her head throbbed and pounded alarmingly.

'Good morning, Helena. Will you please give me a couple of Disprins? The quicker the better. '

'Yes, Your Highness.' Helena quickly curtsied and went to the ensuite bathroom and retrieved the Disprins. 'Here's the water and the Disprins.'

Alia swallowed them gratefully. 'I'll be all right on my own. Thank you. Uhm, just put out navy pants and jacket and a white striped blouse.' She disappeared into the bathroom and sometime later when she emerged, it was a relief to find the hair stylist was in attendance. Somehow, she could now face the day with some confidence.

5

By the time she went down to the dining room for breakfast, Alia was informed that Alex had already left for an emergency meeting at work. She gathered it probably had to do with the problem they had briefly discussed the previous night. It disturbed her to think that such devious things were happening at Alex's plant and office. She tried to think of something more pleasant and he arrived in the dining room at her very thought. 'Stephan, good morning, my dearest boy.'

'Mummy, can you spend some time with me today?'

'Of course. I'm at your beck and call. Say what you want, and it shall be done!'

'If we go up to the playroom, we can try and finish making the rocket. That will be a surprise for Papa.'

'Right. Let's get you some breakfast and we'll start.'

Mother and son sat together and talked about things that Alia knew nothing about, except that they all interested Stephan. She knew that he was a whiz at maths and reading. Books about adventure, dragons and wizards were his favourite, but what she didn't know was that he loved playing the piano. 'Is it possible,' she thought, 'that in the eight years of my child's life I have been unaware of this?' She looked at him as he devoured his breakfast and drank milk.

'Stephan, before we go up, will you play something on the piano for me?'

'Sure Mum, I will.'

Hand in hand, they went into the drawing room and she noticed a small raised stool under the piano so a child's feet could rest on it. Stephan opened the piano stool where he kept all his music and got out two or three pieces to play. Among them was Beethoven's *Fur Elise*. Alia asked him to play this piece for her and in quite a professional manner, he placed it on the piano's stand, straightened his back and placed his fingers appropriately on the keyboard. With confidence and dexterity his small fingers glided over the keyboard and played the entire piece. Alia's amazement was evident as she clapped loudly and went and gave her son a warm hug and kiss. 'When did you learn all this? You've only been playing for one year.'

'I started just before I was five. You know that, Mum. I love music.'

'So I can see. Just over three years and you play like this. You're wonderful, darling.' Then he surprised her with *Twinkle, Twinkle Little Star*, but he had placed such a variation on the theme that Alia could not help but smile at his imagination.

As they walked together towards the playroom, Alia's mother appeared coming down the staircase. 'There's Grandmama ...' Before she could say anything more, he dashed forward and ran towards her.

'Grandmama, did you hear me play the piano for my mum?'

'I did and you play so well. Stephan, I need to speak with your mum for a moment and she will be with you shortly,' the queen urged him gently.

'Go up to the playroom and Susanna will be there. I

won't be long.' Alia saw Susanna at the top of the staircase as Stephan climbed the steps.

'Let's go to our private lounge.' Queen Sylvia looked at her daughter and saw how her face shone with pride. 'You did not know that he played so well, did you?'

'I can't believe that I didn't know. Where was I?'

'My dear girl, you buried yourself so much in work, afraid to look right or left in case someone might notice the pain that you carry so deeply in your heart. But, Alia, I am your mother and I can see past that exterior. You know, my dear, you've always had a passion for art and I advise you to look up Titian's *Woman with a Mirror*. We have two faces, darling girl. One we project to the public and one we carry inside of us. I just don't know how much longer you are going to bear this, before the mirror cracks.'

'Is this metaphor related to me?'

'You know it is. Ah, here we are.' Alia opened the door and both women went in and sat comfortably in separate armchairs. 'Alia, I can hardly tell you how pleased I am to see you spending time with Stephan. He needs you, you know. But I am not here to discuss Stephan. Why didn't you tell me that Gregory approached you about joining some "Order" or other?'

'There was nothing much to tell. He was not forthright and appeared to be mysterious about such an "Order". But tell me, how did you find out?' Alia's curiosity was piqued.

'I received a visit from Prime Minister Yallenski of Borovia, who presumed I had knowledge of this "Order". I said to him I knew nothing about it. Then he told me in a very thick voice, "Ah, Your Majesty. Your country was the first we thought of. Speak to your daughter ... she knows." Then, as he was leaving, he took my hand and before he kissed it said, "It will be regrettable if you are not with us."'

'My knowledge of it is as much as yours. I think I'll contact Gregory and see if I can extract more information. Show that I'm interested, yet not committed,' Alia firmly stated.

'Do this Alia, and report to me. Once I know more on the matter, I'll have to have a conference with our own Prime Minister.' She sighed as she stood and saw her daughter take her cue and do likewise. 'Go now and get to know your son better.'

'Thank you, Mother, I will.'

As Alia left their private lounge, she churned around in her head the strange conversation with her mother. What in the world was happening out there? She felt the urgency that this group was pressing upon them, yet they revealed nothing substantial. She made a mental note to contact Gregory as soon as she could.

As she opened the playroom door, Stephan ran towards her. 'Come and see what I've done to the rocket. We still haven't got the wings right. Will you work on that, Mum?'

'Of course I will. Now, let me see where all the blocks are and which ones I need.' Alia found a pile of blocks and sat on the floor cross-legged and began to sort out the various shapes that would fit under the wings. As her hands worked proficiently at the task, her mind revolved around the conversation with her mother and as to what she should say to King Gregory when she meets him. Intermittently, Stephan broke that train of thought which occupied Alia and automatically wavered between the notions in her mind and Stephan.

6
...

Alex arrived early at his office and found there was no one else in sight. He sat in his leather armchair and stared out of the large corner window. Seeing the tops of trees swaying to the tune of the breeze helped him to harness his thoughts. Initially, he considered convening a full executive staff meeting as he mulled over the situation of the previous evening on his way to work that morning. However, thinking things through as he sat in his office, he knew that was not the avenue to take. If there were spies in his corporation, then it would be best to retain a secretive state of operation. The less known by everyone in the company, the better chance of getting to the bottom of everything. He unlocked the drawers in his desk and took out some relevant documents. As he read through these, he heard his personal assistant's front door open. He immediately went to her office. 'Ebba, I'd like you to log into your computer and while you're at it, give me your new password.'

'Of course, Dr Glandore.' She sat at her desk and soon the computer screen glared with its infinite blue light.

'It may be a good idea if you go to the staff room and have a coffee while I work here for a while. I'll let you know when I need you.'

'What seems to be the problem, sir?' Ebba was mystified by Alex's demand.

'Nothing, at present.' He followed her with his eyes as she left the office and disappeared in the hallway.

'Now, let's see what's in here.' He scanned all the files connected with Einheimmer and Gilmar but the rigorous search revealed nothing – nothing at all. He looked at file after file without any sign of success. *There must be something I'm missing.* He ceased the futile search and tried to bring the state of his emotions into some form of equilibrium. As he looked at the monitor filled with files, he noticed one marked with "EN". Naturally, it had a separate password. He picked up his cell phone and rang Ebba Nilsson. 'Ebba, return to your office, immediately.' She did not tarry. She was there within seconds. 'I have found this file here and I need you to open it, please ... also give me your password.'

She came around and viewed the monitor. 'But, Dr Glandore, this is my private file.'

'If this, or any other file, is found on a company computer, it is *not* private. It is the property of this company.' He saw her distraught face. 'Open the file now.' He stood to allow her to sit in the chair.

She typed in the password and clicked on the file and all

was revealed. 'Now write down the password and allow me to sit in the chair.' Ebba did precisely as she was told. Alex began to read:

Dear Ms Nilsson,

Your mother's multiple sclerosis is taking a turn for the worse. We now have medication which will improve her condition and perhaps enable her to enjoy periods of time at home, in a considerably comfortable state.

If you wish to expedite this procedure, please inform us so we can commence proceedings for a positive outcome. The price for this modern 'miracle' drug is eight hundred American dollars per month's prescription. Mrs Ohlson will require one syringe application administered by a district nurse who will arrive weekly to perform the procedure.

We look forward to your response and await your instructions.

Yours faithfully

Eric Hammerstrom

MD, RFPh

There were several other letters and signed documentations that related to Ebba's mother's condition. There was nothing else revealed in relation to Alex's espionage problem in his corporation.

'So, this is all about your mother's MS condition.'

'I told you it was private,' Ebba reiterated emotionally.

'Yes, you did. But I repeat, nothing is private on company's computers or any other property connected with your workplace.' He examined her concerned face and asked, 'Tell me, how well do you know Jacob Einheimmer?'

'Fairly well. He was my boss and I worked for him.' Her low voice sounded flat.

'You've not had any dealings outside of work with him?'

Her face was ashen by this time and she swallowed hard. 'No ... why would I have any dealings with him?'

Alex scrutinised her carefully. 'Take a half-an-hour off and compose yourself. I'll be at my desk.'

'Thank you, Dr Glandore.' She left promptly without a second thought and retreated to the staff bathroom. There she splashed some water on her face, freshened her makeup and left for the staffroom. She desperately needed another coffee. Ebba Nilsson took the thirty minutes given to her and contemplated her situation. It was time for her to pull herself together. She felt relieved with her ultimate decision. She stood and tidied the well-fitted skirt around her thighs, poked the blouse further into her skirt and tightened the black belt with the gold buckle around her slim waist. She found the sink, rinsed her cup and placed it carefully in the dishwasher. She straightened her back and walked confidently towards her office.

Ebba went to her desk and saw a pile of letters that arrived in the morning neatly placed by her computer. Carefully she began to open all the appropriate ones. There was one marked "Private and Confidential" and left that to be opened by her boss. She noticed the dictaphone on her desk as it compulsively blinked its red light at her. She placed the earphones over her head and began to word-process all the letters and instructions onto her computer. There were never enough hours in the day for all the work she needed to complete, but she ploughed through it all.

Eventually, Alex came out from his office and stood by her desk. He decided to say nothing further to Ebba. He could see she felt uncomfortable with the questions he asked, but for now any of his employees could be under suspicion. He felt the quandary that surrounded him. Who really were his employees?

Ebba removed the earphones. 'This letter is marked "Private and Confidential" and gave it to Alex. 'All the other letters are here.' She handed a small tray filled with opened letters and gave them to her boss.

Alex took them to his desk and firstly opened the one marked "Confidential".

Dear Dr Glandore,

You do not rightly know me, but I would like to fix this right now. I have some important information that you need to know and I request that you, yourself, ring me at this number 0900 111 678 030 to make an appointment at a particular place and time.

Yours

Blake

He set his office phone to record the conversation with the writer of this inexplicable communication. The number supplied was operable and the ring tone rang only twice when a male's voice answered. 'Yea.'

'I'd like to speak to Blake.'

'Yea? And who's calling?'

'Someone who wants to make an appointment at a "particular place and time".'

'Just wait!'

A few seconds later a different voice sounded over the phone. 'Is this Dr Glandore?'

'Yes ... and who are you?'

'Blake will do at present.' He breathed deeply, as if he was asthmatic. 'Meet me Tuesday at twelve noon at Victor's Café. It's north of the city in the Cortesta district. We'll talk then.'

Alex was left with a shrill buzz in his ear as Blake at the other end had hung up. He was pleased he made a copy of his voice and the next step would be to have it analysed by someone. He knew going to the authorities was not an option at this stage. He needed to choose someone he trusted completely. In his own mind there was only one person, Bob. His record was impeccable in the twenty-nine years that Alex knew him. If his memory served him well, at some stage of his career he was in the Secret Service in the US, albeit for a short time. Undoubtedly, he would have contacts that could examine and analyse this situation. He placed the letter in the safe and secured it with a secret digital password and locked it.

Time was precious to Alex and as he looked at his watch, he quickly realised that the unwelcomed events that had occurred in the morning squandered several hours. Somehow this must be resolved as soon as possible.

He browsed through the rest of the mail and set forth to respond and dictate more letters. He made a mental note to also look into Ebba's mother's situation and see what he could verify. In the midst of all that was running through his mind, he received a call from the workshop hangar in regard to the latest project. It was from his Chief Engineer. He immediately left for the workshop.

'Hey Mack, what's up?'

'Have a look at this? Someone has mangled this part of the delta wing. It appears to have been done in haste. Look at the flaps ... so essential for lower speeds.'

'When did you discover it?'

'Early this morning. What worries me is if they've messed with the engine. I haven't had a chance to look.' Mack climbed up onto a platform and examined the engine. Nothing seemed to be disturbed. 'It seems okay up here ... but that doesn't mean that photos and videos have not been taken of the engine.'

'Blast that! It's so annoying. We did more research and work on this particular prototype to especially reduce the sonic boom. I was looking forward to going to the US and demonstrate that we've now overcome this barrier. They've got to lift this prohibition of supersonic flights over land.' He looked up at Mack. 'Did you find something up there?'

'Yep ... tried to pull at the duralumin to expose the engine better... definitely scraped about in here. I must've interrupted him.'

'How do you know it's a "him"?'

6

'I don't, but you'd have to be really strong to try and pull the duralumin away from the engine to get a clear view of it.'

'Let me get up there and have a look.' Alex also climbed up to the platform and confirmed Mack's assessment. 'At what Mach level did we get it to work?'

'Definitely at Mach 2.2 and headed towards a top speed of Mach 3.6. At this speed it will travel at two thousand, six hundred and sixty-four miles per hour and if you want it in kilometres, almost four thousand three hundred kilometres per hour.' He scanned Alex's face and saw the worried expression on his brow. 'Alex, don't worry. This civil aircraft will have to cruise continuously at speeds above the speed of sound. We have here an engine with turbofans and afterburners to reduce the heat generated by friction as the air flows over the aircraft.' He stopped suddenly, knowing fully well that Alex was the master of this engine.

'Let's go down, Mack. We need to talk.' They began to descend from the platform and Alex ran the palm of his hand across the aircraft's streamlined body as he went past it. 'It's a beauty, isn't it?' Alex confirmed what Mack was thinking.

'It sure is ... now tell me, what's going on?'

'As you can see, we're being sabotaged.' Alex stated urgently.

'I can see that, but why?'

'This is highly confidential. What transpires between us stays between you and me. At this point I'm not exactly sure, but someone wants us out of the way. I think they smell our near success and want it for themselves. Do you know what this means to our company if we come out as the first ones to overcome all these challenges in the aerospace race?'

'I have an idea.'

'Make it a hundred times that. Our target year is twenty-twenty, and I am thinking that whoever it is that's trying to ruin us will also know our target year. So, I say let's foil them — we'll bring out our perfect model well ahead of time. Say twenty-eighteen — no later than early twenty-nineteen.' Are you up for it?' He stared at Mack to see if he could determine a response.

'You know I like a challenge. Let's do it!' They sealed their hardy intentions with a strong handshake.

7

Back at the palace, Alia began to learn more and more about her son. She saw how much the dog meant to him and thought, 'Why hadn't I paid closer attention to my son's growing years? Perhaps my mother is right. I am that woman with the mirror.' She continued to admire the boy with his dog as she looked out from the window and smiled at the antics they got up to. It amazed her how gentle the Saint Bernard was considering his massive size; he could knock Stephan down, as if he were a balloon in his way. They both stood next to each other and walked at an exact calm pace towards the garden; the foolery was over, and that precious time together sealed another layer of love between them. Alia's lips formed a ready smile and when they were both out of sight, she wondered why she had never had a dog of her own. Then her smile broadened. She did have someone she could play with, someone she loved very much, when she was just a little older than her son. She sighed as she recalled those tender years between Alex and herself which were never to be repeated again.

There was a knock on her door, which startled her. 'Come in.'

Her personal assistant, Jillian, entered the room. 'Your Highness, King Gregory is in the waiting room to see you.'

'Thank you, Jillian. Will you make some tea and coffee for both of us? Strong coffee – I think I'll need it today.'

'Yes, ma'am.' She quickly curtsied and left the room.

Alia went to her bedroom and pulled out of her closet a different jacket – one more professional that said, "I'm not putting up with any nonsense". She marked her pace with control and breathed deeply to remain calm and patient. As she entered the waiting room, King Gregory stood immediately. 'Your Highness.' Alia proffered her hand and he raised it to his lips.

'Please come into my office.' She turned to Jillian. 'Is the coffee and tea inside?'

'Yes, ma'am. Would you like me to pour?'

'Please.'

Alia asked Gregory to take a seat and soon was offered tea. She sat behind her desk with the strong cup of coffee and waited for Jillian to leave. They proceeded to make some small talk about nothing in particular and Alia felt it was incumbent upon her to start the conversation for the real reason Gregory was there.

'So, Gregory, let's begin to discuss this "Order" you feel is essential for us to join. Tell me everything you know. Convince me.'

7

'You don't mince your words, Alia, do you?' He looked straight at her and he knew she meant business. 'Okay then. You and I know that Europe is fragmented – even with the supposed union which managed to draw-in some nations. The East, culturally, politically and economically is enormously different to Western Europe. There is hardly a topic about which every nation can see eye to eye. Take Russia, a massive nation in size with such a diverse population, culture, economy, and politics that although it's operating under a "democratic" banner, we all know that that is a ruse. Take central Europe, those poor divided countries scarred with centuries of wars and devastations have never recovered to see a new improved life in the twenty-first century. Take our nations, just on the border of Central and Western Europe. We are quickly becoming buffer states between the East and West. We need to climb out of the mire and make a stand for social and economic independence.'

Gregory took a sip of his tea and looked over at Alia. She had her hands clasped on the desk and appeared relaxed. 'You may very well want to ask, how are we going to achieve this? And this is the great thing I am about to explain. Simply, we gain force and power from each other – as one. Although there are differences between us, each of these member countries will be united and act in secrecy. This is the key factor – secrecy. The heads of these states will know, and they *will* make sure that a law is passed and control of civil authorities is in their hands, as well as integrating the cultural differences. Sooner or later, no one will know whose cultural practice belonged to whom. All as one, without any squabbles. Economically, we will retain twenty percent of the Gross Domestic Product of each nation that joins the WSO. When we have accumulated sufficient funds, we shall join forces as one stronghold that neither East nor West will be able to break. Forget about America, Canada or the UK, we will be invincible.' Gregory stopped suddenly and looked benevolently at Alia. 'Perhaps I've been speaking for too long. Is there anything you'd like to ask at this juncture?'

'What exactly does the WSO stand for?'

'The World Secret Order'

'And how many are in this ... WSO club?'

'No Alia. We are not a club. An Order – a civilised, enlightened Order.'

'But why secret. Why not go through legal channels and present your views by forming a political party?'

'We need to be covert, otherwise it will cause a revolution. We don't want that. Too many ugly things happen – too many lives are lost.' He then added seriously, 'I don't know about you, but I respect my life.'

'And how, exactly, do you intend to control parliaments and governments of all kind?'

'Ah, and here is the brilliancy of it all. We will install our people in the guise of representing existing political parties for various seats of power and infiltrate senate, legislature, and local government, but very slowly. Before anyone knows what has happened, we will have control over all political institutions in each member nation, or should I say state. The teaching of our principles and ideas has already begun – but as I said, slowly.' With infused enthusiasm Gregory continued. 'From infancy, early learning centres, kindergartens, junior schools, high schools will be indoctrinated with our beliefs, cultural, political and economic. Every man will have a job, it will be his right, every woman and child will have opportunities to join our various clubs within our Order and made available to all members in a family. The family is important, and we must look after them.'

'When you say "very slowly", what is your time span?' By this stage Alia was more than inquisitive.

'We hope it will all work out over a five to ten-year period. If it requires a bit longer, so be it.' Suddenly, his concentration fell seriously upon Alia and added, 'The WSO has been in existence over twenty years. We're not a fledgling group.'

'How do you know these people you endorse will get the vote to "infiltrate" the political system?' Alia was determined to dig deeper and find out what Gregory was refusing to say.

'Oh, don't worry about that. We have ways to make sure it all happens.' Gregory could see that Alia was not convinced. 'It is, perhaps, too much for you to digest all this information. I am sure you will come to understand our way of thinking. It's going to be a perfect new world.' He looked around him and the office had begun to get dark. The sun had set and only the after-light was left to poke through the windows. 'I shall leave you now, Alia. Think carefully about it.'

Alia stood and offered him her hand and he graciously

kissed it. She came around from behind the desk and walked him to the waiting room door where Jillian promptly held it open. As he was about to go out, he turned and gave Alia a dazzling smile. 'I ran into your son – Stephan, isn't he? He was with his dog outside. My, how he's grown. Our children are the most precious things, don't you think?'

'Of course.' Alia frowned as he disappeared down the hallway with Parkinson beside him.

'Jillian, did you tape this whole conversation?'

'I did. The tape is directly under your desk.'

'Will you come in and get it for me, please.'

'Yes, straight away.'

They both went into Alia's office and Jillian approached the desk, placed her hand under it and immediately produced the digital tape. As Jillian left her office, Alia sank into her desk chair, still reeling from everything she had heard.

8

It was well after dinner time when Alex arrived at the palace. Parkinson greeted him as the faithful retainer that he was. 'Where is everyone, Parkinson?'

'Sir, you'll find Her Highness at her office and the queen is in the private lounge.'

'Thank you.'

He went straight up to Alia's office. Her office door was locked. 'Alia, are you in there?'

'Oh, it's you Alex. I'll open up.'

'Why have you locked yourself in the office?'

'Come in and take a seat.' She went around the desk and sat in her chair. 'How did work go today?'

'You haven't answered me why your office door was locked?'

'I just wanted to be alone to think without interruptions.' She placed her elbows on the desk and allowed her chin to sit comfortably on her clasped hands and said, 'I had a visit today from King Gregory. To say it was interesting would be an understatement. He came and sat in the chair you're in and told me all about the WSO.'

'The what?'

'World Secret Order. Evidently there exists such an Order where countries, mainly from central/western Europe have already joined. Their aim is to create a secret world Order, with its beginnings in central Europe, and spread their philosophy and from what I understand, it is compulsory to join. This WSO will see to it that every *man* will have a job, that the family will take precedence and children can become indoctrinated with their ideas, and politically, there will be a covert infiltration in Parliament by members they endorse to spread the Order's philosophy.'

'In other words, yet again, another Utopia. And how is this going to evolve?' Alex's voice rang with sarcasm.

'By extricating twenty percent of each member's Gross Domestic Product to accumulate enough wealth as a united front and become the power that these countries deserve. Their ideas have incubated for quite a few years and now they are ready for it to hatch and act on it.' There was a scowl on Alia's face. 'I am sure that they will stop at nothing to achieve their goal.'

'Have you any evidence as to what transpired between you today? Have you looked at the CCTV film?'

'I have taped the entire conversation and I was listening to the tape to gauge his meaning between the lines when you knocked on the door. I must put it in the royal vault where no one can get their hands on it. The CCTV system is

8

installed only in the main parts of the palace, not in offices.' She picked up the tape and placed it in a small box ready to be stored in the vault. 'Are you any nearer to the spy at your work?'

'No, but we discovered damage to an airplane, a prototype of its kind and I'm sure it was photographed and/or videoed. The CCTV shows nothing. I checked the film and there is a space of ten minutes where it is blank. These people are pros, they know what they're doing. Tell me, how well do you trust Bob?' There was exasperation in Alex's words.

'After today, I'm not so sure. How can anyone know what goes through their private thoughts? But we have to start from somewhere. Why do you ask?'

'I want someone to thoroughly investigate Ebba Nilsson, my Chief Engineer and CEO, which means there are very few people left in control. I can't leave anything to chance.' Alex paused a moment and asked, 'How old is Bob now?'

'I was ten when he started here at the palace … that's about twenty-nine years ago. I think he would have been around twenty-seven years old; he was quite young, but to a ten-year-old, he was ancient. Why is his age important?' Alia asked curiously.

'In case he has to wrestle with anyone at the plant, but first I need to get permission to use him from the queen.' Alex knew it was not straightforward. 'What do you think of the possibilities?'

'I know he still has connections with some of the most sophisticated secret services in the world. He originally came from the US. I recall when I was in America seeing him with some of his old cronies — so I'd imagine he's the kind of person not to let connections lapse altogether. As a matter of fact, now that you bring this up, I think it would be a very good idea if he also looked into this WSO business.'

'I agree. It's a bit late tonight, we can talk to him tomorrow morning, but first,' Alex paused there and went towards the desk, 'do you want to come with me and discuss it with the queen?'

'Of course.' Alia stood and said, 'We can go now, but I'll lock this tape in the vault first.'

'You should get Bob to do a complete check for any bug devices in your office area and your PA's.'

'Yes, I did think of that,' Alia answered.

While Alex and Alia considered consulting the queen, Her Majesty continued to work in the private lounge with documents that required her signature. She was more than careful these days and King Gregory came to mind immediately. Queen Sylvia could not comprehend what in the world was happening around her, but she needed to persevere.

Sylvia Amsler Gilland learned early in life to persist towards her aims, which did not include becoming a queen. Her family's history was one of expectations. Although from nobility, her father was one of the lesser nobles, being the last child of five sons. Had she been the daughter of the first son, who traditionally inherited all of the estates and wealth that the Gillands owned, then life for her would have been different. As it was, fate gave Sylvia a father who was the last son to be born and forced to make something of himself.

Her grandfather was not totally heartless; his fifth son, Luca, did inherit some lands in the mountains, which were considered worthless at the time. This, however, did not deter him. He had learned to accept the traditions of his country and held no ill will against his family. With some foresight he realised the value of tourism and began to build one of the most luxurious ski resorts in Europe. The borrowed money from the banks was paid back quickly and as he prospered, so did his chances of marrying into a "good" family. The Duchess of Catalonia was not only beautiful, but very rich. Although they encountered some opposition, his cultivated demeanour, charming good looks and, of course, his obvious wealth, albeit nouveau-riche, won the day.

The world was changing in the twentieth century and the "new money" made it possible for this class to access the aristocracy and high nobility whose fortunes were quickly being usurped by heavy taxes and constant restorations to mansions and palaces. It was not unusual to find actors and actresses, businessmen and CEOs rubbing shoulders with the established old order. Queen Sylvia remembered clearly the first day she met Johan, her future husband and monarch. She was nineteen and he was twenty-four. Her father Luca and her mother Marianna were visiting Luca's oldest brother at the family home estate. Sylvia naturally went along with them and when they entered the drawing room, there was Johan, all resplendent in his military uniform. The brass buttons worn smartly on both sides of the double-breasted jacket reflected the lights in the room and the gold epaulettes on his shoulders revealed his rank according to the length of the fringes, which fell distinctly over the end of his shoulders and made him look broader. His obvious good looks did not make Sylvia's heart flutter, as they shook hands. She already had her life planned. In her mind she was going to go to university and study Medicine. The idea of helping people to get well was ingrained in her soul. Her final school grades were top in every subject she took, especially in the sciences. It was her heartfelt secret and she told no one. This charming man was not part of her equation, plans or thoughts in her life. Actually, she was more than pleased when the visit was over. However, she could not understand why a feeling of alarm seemed to pervade her, as if she was losing control.

Queen Sylvia returned to her paperwork but could not concentrate on the blurred words. She recalled the day she entered her father's office and gave him her application for the study of Medicine at Zurich University.

'What's this, Sylvi? An application for *Medicine* at Zurich? This is the first I hear of it, and what makes you think that I would sign such an application? I can tell you this, Sylvi, no daughter of mine is doing Medicine.'

Although, she loved it when her father called her "Sylvi", somehow, today it left a sour taste in her mouth. In fact, her reaction was so severe, her throat so dry, that try as she might, she could not swallow or utter a word. Her only recourse was to run out of his study room and go straight to the bathroom where she threw up the little she had in her stomach. She was nervous enough all day to approach her father, but never in her wildest dreams did she expect this kind of reaction from him.

Finally, her mother, the peacemaker, promised Sylvia that she could go to university and do something in the Arts. Perhaps music or art – she was an excellent artist (which she mainly used to sketch anatomical bodies). Finally, it was settled she would do art, politics and economics and she pleaded to do honours in art. By her twenty-fourth birthday she was out of university studies. Again she thought she'd work in one of the large art galleries and her dream was to be at The Louvre in Paris. This was not meant to be either. That very same summer, she was reintroduced to Johan and she eventually understood that the two families had organised for both of them to be married in May of the following year.

She did not dislike Johan, but neither did she love him. He, on the other hand, adored her. She was intelligent, beautiful, cultured, a virgin and with the sweetest demeanour he ever encountered. To this end, his endeavours were to make her fall in love with him. Sylvia smiled when she thought about how hard he tried to please her and eventually, in their third year of marriage, he succeeded. She saw his love and kindness when Alia was born and she knew without a doubt that her battle was lost to fate, irrespective of personal wishes and desires.

Queen Sylvia was still smiling to herself when she heard the knock on the door. 'Come in,' she said sweetly. 'Oh, what a lovely surprise. Alex and Alia, come in.'

'Mother, are we disturbing you?'

'No, not at all. Come and sit down.' They sat together on the sofa which was directly opposite the queen. 'What keeps you up at this time of the night?'

'If it's too late, Mother, we can talk to you about it tomorrow.'

'No, no. I'm fine. What is it?'

'Now, just before we start,' Alex motioned with his finger to his lips not to say anything. He got up, switched off the lights and looked to see if a red or white light was reflecting from somewhere. He couldn't see it, so he began a manual sweep of the room and felt under the coffee table, checked the light stand and lights on the ceiling, stood on a chair to check the top of the book case against the wall. He took a little longer than his search in the other areas of the room. Suddenly, he pulled at an object, brought it down and disconnected the spying device. 'Now we can talk.'

Alia and the Queen were amazed to see such a device in their home. Queen Sylvia stood. 'Are there any others?'

'I don't think so. Not in this room.' Alex reassured her.

'What is going on?' The queen looked concerned and unsure of what to expect.

'Your Majesty, this is what we are here to tell you. Please take a seat and Alia and I will explain.'

The queen settled in her armchair and tried to regain a

8

measure of composure. Alia went to the tray where water and teas were at the ready and poured a glass of water for her mother. 'Thank you, darling.' She drank much of the water and then quietly asked. 'Will you please tell me everything you know?'

9

King Gregory got ready to attend a most important meeting for the WSO. He was the President, and it was imperative to set a standard of punctuality. He arrived at the country house of his Vice President's estate near the borders of Switzerland and France. He was particular about driving his automobile himself, and everyone else at the meeting did exactly the same. There was no staff at the holiday house, not even a gardener, to be seen. The car reached the long straight narrow road that led to the *Prairies Maison*. As he approached the closed black wrought-iron gates, he took a small remote control from the glove compartment of the car, clicked it and the gates began to open. He drove his car through and parked it next to a silver Rolls-Royce that he recognised as his Vice President's automobile.

As he got out of the car and began to walk up the steps, the front door opened and there stood Antony at its entrance. 'Gregory, always well ahead of time. Come in.' The men shook hands and together walked across the reception hall and towards the dining area. Everything was in place. An iPad was placed on the table in front of each of the six chairs. A screen was rolled down, ready to be used. A computer was set up for several presentations during the day and Gregory sat at the head of the table, ready in anticipation of everyone's arrival for a prompt start to the proceedings. When all six were present and seated, Gregory rang a small gong that was beside him. 'The one hundred and twenty-sixth meeting of the WSO is now open for discussions. Before we begin, apologies from Heinrich. He is overseas drumming up business of trade for his country. Soon it will be for all of us.' A firm, but low murmur came from the others around the table. 'Hear, hear!' This had the effect of imbuing the President with confidence and he continued. 'First on our Agenda: Palace of Rubinia. Gentlemen, as you can see from your iPads, I visited the Palace of Rubinia and spoke to Princess Alia. Now, although her mother is the queen, I can assure you that it is she who can persuade Her Majesty to relent to our wishes. However, although she asked many questions, there was no definite commitment. I had the whole conversation taped, the princess projected a passive-aggressive attitude, albeit in a calm state. I don't think we have her in our pocket as yet. I fed her what she wanted to hear and there were many truths in what I said to her. It is best that she slowly discovers who and what we are really about. I will approach her again when she has absorbed the conversation that transpired between us. As for the husband, there is such a rift between them that it makes him inconsequential. We are now open for questions. Yes, Marcus?'

'How can he be so inconsequential when he's running an industry worth billions of dollars?'

'Can you not see? Once we have the people in authority and infiltrated the politics of the country, *all* industries will also be ours. All it will need is a little persuasion. We aim high and then catch the lower fish. Gunter, you have the floor.'

'There is something in what Marcus says. We can't allow him to monopolise this industry. Eventually, we will be in need of its products and services. I, for one, am not going with cap in hand for anything he produces, even though we will need them. We should act now and make sure it comes under our control as quickly as possible.'

'Gunter, have you heard of the word patience? To swat a fly, you have to quietly, slowly and patiently get close to it and then SWAT.' As he loudly catapulted the word "swat" from his mouth, he simultaneously slammed his hand hard on the table, which made all the iPads and computers shake in their intellectual casings. Suddenly, his voice returned to the softly-spoken manner that everyone was accustomed to. 'Leave this important case to me. They will bend to our will, I am sure.' He looked around the table with an air of indulgence and magnificence. 'Now, what I want to hear from each of you are your successes. So without further ado, we'll begin from my left and go around the table. Vassili.'

'I had some success, but not complete success. The

people in my country have experienced many wars and destructions. They've had the occupation of Communism and for a large percentage of the population, this remains quite fresh in their mind.' He looked at the others who sat in a nonchalant manner, then turned to Gregory who was rod-straight in his chair without his back touching any part of it. 'You see, Gregory, my country is ensconced in the belief of God, one of the first countries to embrace this religious euphoria from its beginnings. It is rooted deeply in culture and deeply in society. I'll not hazard to say in politics, but even there, there are elements of it. It has comforted them through wars and Communism. People gain strength in their beliefs and in miracles.'

Gregory had heard enough. 'Vassili, what is your solution? That is what I'm interested in, not in fanciful fairytale beliefs and miracles. We know what Karl Marx meant when he said that "Religion is the opium of the people". But what do *you* recommend?'

Vassili promptly answered. 'To proceed according to our Constitution and infiltrate all educational institutions with our principles of no form of religion of any kind, which should take care of the younger generation coming up. In the last few years, we've had many immigrants from all around the world who brought with them many different religions. Their house of prayer could be a church, a mosque, a temple, a hall – any form of building where devotion to a supreme being is conducted. We must all be *one* in all aspects. No religion, but *one* culture. As for the older generation who has been brainwashed with such nonsense, we will slowly begin to disallow religious meetings anywhere and everywhere. To do this effectively, we will have to bring them under some form of disrepute and officially close down any scrap of evidence that they ever existed. In the process, we'll endeavour not to make martyrs of any of them. There's nothing more powerful than a martyr!'

Gregory leaned back into his chair and chuckled to himself. 'You've done well, Vassili! I couldn't have done better myself.' He appeared gratified as he settled comfortably in his chair. 'Now, Mr Vice President, let us hear from you.'

Antony looked around him with an air of primed confidence. 'Gentlemen, as you well know, my life is ingrained in politics. I have been a member of my country's senate for many years. As a matter of fact, my illustrious family line has lived, breathed, and represented the political arena for decades. Already, the infiltration has begun. There are two senators, whom I will not name, at present, but who have shown an enthusiasm for what I described as our "new world" of the future. Mythical obsessions do not only lie with religion. In the realm of politics, democracy has played its powerful hand in places where it was not welcomed, and gentlemen, we know the cruel devastations and outcomes of the wars it has produced. It must be accepted that democracy, as it stands, is over-rated and definitely has no business in some countries – impregnable and impossible to be accepted. This makes *our world* an alternative welcome change. My strategy, as my research and experience show, is that people, deep down and at times not so deeply, really want to be controlled, want to have all the heavy thinking done for them. As long as they have work, earn a living, have interests in life – whether it's sport, or any other endeavours, let them make *that* their religion; or the extraordinary arts, which, by the way, we will have influenced to present themselves according to *our* Constitution, then we have won them over. We must use the *softly, softly* method and before they are aware that any change has occurred, they are ours. Too many good ideas over history have rotted away through brute force. I believe my machine is in motion.'

'Antony, I can always rely on you. Let's see how many more you can win over by our next meeting.' Gregory looked at the last member at the table. 'Jude, what have you to report from the cultural area of the Arts?'

'I quickly discovered that the use of flattery towards the artistic realm of my country, or indeed any country, is incredibly useful. There is no one better than an artist in any endeavour, be it theatre, cinema, music, authors, journalists, playwrights, comedians, singers, young or old, it matters not, to win them over with some form of compliment, be it sincere or not. Those who were willing to hear what I had to say, became quite enthused. The more difficult ones went on their high horse and proclaimed that this will limit their artistic freedom of expression and cripple their artistic genius. I allayed their fears by reminding them that they are the artists and whatever their genius produces is naturally from their own brilliant intellectual artistry. What we offer are the practicalities of their art. First and foremost, the financial advantages that *our world* will offer; the marketing benefits of their artistic works, and last but not least, the number of people that will form their audience, spectators, patrons, viewers, readers and the list went on. Many quickly changed their mind and easily saw the benefits.' There, Jude stopped, and a flicker of a smile came over his face. 'Of course, they do not need to know that their future artistic endeavours will have to conform to the WSO's approval.' There were a few sniggers and 'well said' around the table. He continued. 'A few foolhardy individuals persisted with their own personal rant and wanted nothing to do with such a "world". This was to be expected and I will remind you all of the old adage: "Slowly, slowly catchy monkey".'

Gregory stood in front of his chair and enthusiastically commanded: 'This deserves a round of applause for everyone. Give yourselves a clap.' He began and everyone else followed in a thunderous applause.

When they subsided, the Vice President added, 'For our good work, there is champagne, and a pre-prepared dinner will be served buffet-style by us, at the second dining room table. Let us proceed to the drawing room.' They moved out from their chairs and in warm camaraderie of handshakes and backslapping, they disappeared from their one hundred and twenty-sixth conference meeting.

10
. . . . . .

A lot had occurred which needed to be disseminated. Alex and Alia were first down in the dining room for breakfast. Stephan was to have breakfast in the nursery and by way of recompense, Basco was to eat with him. This very rarely happened so it was more than acceptable to their son. Alex was anxious to speak with Alia. He informed her that he had spoken to Bob early that morning and he took a selected crew to sweep the entire palace for any spying devices. 'I don't know if this has been done yet.' Alex indicated with his hand meaning the dining room. Before they entered the room, Alex quickly rang Bob. 'Is the dining room done?' He listened astutely with 'Hmms and Uhhs' as his response. He turned to Alia and nodded his head and put one thumb up to indicate this room was bug-free.

Alia settled at one end of the table while Alex chose to sit a little further away. At that very moment, Parkinson entered. 'Is there anything I can do for you Your Highness, sir?'

Before Alia could respond, Alex interjected, 'No, thanks,

Parkinson.' As he slowly and quietly left the room and they heard the door close with a click, Alex spoke softly to Alia. 'Come and sit here next to me.'

As she moved and sat in the chair on the right side of Alex, she whispered, 'Surely not Parkinson?'

'At this stage, I suspect everyone – with the exception of you and the queen.'

'Hmm, that's nice to know,' and Alia gave him a wry smile.

'It's for your protection, Alia.' He looked at his full plate of breakfast and then turned sideways to view the door. 'I want us to go and sit at the other end of the table so I can see whoever comes in through that doorway. It's no good having the door behind you.' Together they went and sat at the advantageous position where the door was easily visible. 'Now, straight after breakfast, I'm going to work, and I'll be taking Bob with me. Mike is staying here with you, but if there is any problem – any problem at all, ring me immediately.' Alex sounded concerned.

'What I'd like to know is this: why did you tell the Chief Engineer about your sabotage suspicions? That only alerts him to be more careful. It might be him. You really don't know.'

'Firstly, it's obvious it was sabotage and secondly if he has anything to do with it, he'll be pressed to cover his actions. Whatever his goal, it must be accomplished sooner rather than later if it is to be a success.' Alex observed Alia's enquiring face as she placed the cup to her lips to drink coffee. 'I need to be … we need to be at least one step ahead of them.'

10

'The problem is that spying devices can be replaced at any time. How do we keep up with them?'

'Daily morning and evening searches. It won't be easy. Have you thought of placing a CCTV system in every room?'

'I will *not* have it in my bedroom. This is not a prison. We need some privacy. It's bad enough that the cameras are in the main parts of the building, let alone bedroom and offices.' Although she was frustrated, Alia could see the sense of it.

'Right you are. I don't have them in our offices at work either. These guys are really professional.' He noticed her worried countenance. 'We will beat them. You have my promise on that.' He gulped the remaining coffee in his cup and stood. 'I need to leave and hope that nothing worse has occurred at the workshop.'

As he walked to the door he turned. 'Alia, you know that I love you, even when you drive me crazy at times.' He didn't wait for her response, he just left, which was just as well, because Alia struggled to know what to say to him. She wanted to believe him, but her head was filled with doubts and question marks. As she sat there staring at the door and thinking, *He'll need to prove it to me*, the queen entered the dining room.

'I'll have a cup of tea with you, Alia.'

'Sit here, Mother. We can observe the door better,' Alia suggested.

'So it has come to this, has it?' She poured her tea and sat next to her daughter. 'I see Alex and Bob are on the move.

Mike is just outside making sure you're all right.' She went up to her daughter and touched her hair which had strayed onto her forehead and face. 'I must say, Bob and Mike have been with us quite a long while.'

'Mother, that doesn't mean anything these days. According to Alex, everyone is suspect, except you and me.'

'Just as well.' The queen sipped her tea. 'What are you doing today?'

'I'm staying here to spend more time with Stephan.'

'Have you heard from Gregory? I would have thought he'd be on your case again quickly.'

'Oh, he'll be around – sooner rather than later. What surprises me is how he thinks this hair-brain scheme of his is going to work.'

'There are many times in civilisation when all it took was one man, only one, to brainwash people's minds and change the course of history.'

'And there have always been those who were willing to fight and die against them.' Alia stopped and ran her fingers through her hair. 'And they shall do so again.'

'Let's hope, my dear, that it shall not have to come to this — if he can be stopped at this early stage of madness. You are a fortunate generation. You have not witnessed first-hand aggression or war of any kind. War is an ongoing disease and Europe has had its belly full of it; World War One, World War Two, Communism. My uncle Paolo died at sea during the Second World War, my great-grandfather was injured so badly in the battle of the Marne during World War One

10

that he would've died in those mud-sludge infested trenches as he lay face down, half-drowned in this putrid trench, had he not been found by an unknown soldier who picked him up and forced him to vomit a stench full of muck he had swallowed.' The queen paused as she pondered her story.

'Vivid description, Mother.'

'I still have the letter that he sent to his father.' The queen realised the crassness of her comments over breakfast. 'Not the right moment to mention it, but when is the appropriate time, when the wolf is howling at our door?'

'Quite right, Mother. Don't distress yourself. We'll sort it all out.' Alia stretched her arm across the table and placed her hand on hers.

'I must go, Alia. I have work to do and a meeting to attend.' Please, take care of yourself and keep a close eye on Stephan.' She left the dining room with many thoughts running through her head.

Alia sat at the table and replayed in her mind all that her mother said. She could not even begin to imagine what it would be like during a full-scale war, and although her mother was born three years after the Second World War had ended, she would have witnessed the devastations it had caused, both the physical and psychological, as she was growing up. It had taken many years for countries to rebuild and work towards recovery. This was made a little easier with the Marshall Plan that was instigated by the United States to help Western Europe. She knew this through her studies at university, but somehow, it only came alive as she listened to her mother's description of her family's involvement during World War One and Two.

Her thoughts were interrupted when the dining room door slowly opened and Parkinson appeared. 'Your Highness, may I send in the staff to clear the table?'

'Yes, thank you, Parkinson. Is Stephan still up in the playroom?'

'No, Your Highness. He is outside with his dog and Susanna.'

Alia pushed herself away from the table and walked towards the door. Parkinson was already halfway down the hallway. It seemed impossible that someone like him would be involved in a covert life outside the palace — a gentle soul, such as himself. She went on one of the back balconies to see the whereabouts of her son. It soon became obvious when her eyes followed the sounds that echoed in her ears; she saw Stephan as he romped about with Basco, while Susanna and one of Mike's assistants followed closely by him. Alia decided to go down towards the terrace and soon came upon the group of four. Basco ran up to her but knew to gently approach her. Immediately behind came Stephan. 'Mum, you're here! Do you want to walk with Basco and me?'

'Of course. That's why I've got my walking shoes on and am ready to go.' At that very moment, she made a sprint down the pathway and called out, 'Catch me if you can.' Quickly, Basco was right on her heels and soon Stephan came right behind his mother, laughing as he ran.

'I got you,' he cried out as he clasped his mother by the waist. 'I'm glad you're with me, Mum.'

'So am I, my dearest boy.' She ruffled his hair and ran again. Susanna and Mike's assistant kept up with the pace and Alia thought, 'I must find out this assistant's name.'

When the pace slowed down, they considered returning through the upper pathway which ran closer to the palace. Basco didn't leave Stephan's side for a second and he walked according to his master's stride.

'So, you are Mike's assistant?'

'Yes, Your Highness.'

'What is your name?'

'Nat Bolland, ma'am.'

'I detect an American accent. Where do you come from?'

'Minnesota, one of the coldest States of America.'

'I'm glad you're used to the cold. It gets very cold here, come heart of winter. You'll see the difference in a month.'

'Yes, ma'am.'

Susanna walked just behind Stephan and Nat kept guard behind all of them. When they progressed along the pathway for a few minutes, Nat went beside the princess and quietly spoke. 'Your Highness, there's a car approaching the palace from the main entrance. Remain here and give me a few minutes to investigate.' He didn't wait for Alia's response. He quickly disappeared among the trees and was out of sight instantly.

Alia turned to her son and softly spoke to him. 'We need to quietly stay here until Nat returns. Make sure Basco doesn't bark.'

Stephan turned to his dog and hugged him around his neck. 'Be nice and quiet Basco,' and he placed his forefinger to his lips with a 'Shush.'

It felt to Alia an interminable time before Nat returned and as she saw him make his way back to them, she felt a great relief and exclaimed as he approached, 'I'm glad to see you here.'

'It's King Gregory. He has asked to see you, Your Highness.'

'I don't have an appointment with him, but I'll see him.' The small group left the cover of the tree-lined pathway and walked towards the clearing at the front entrance to the palace.

Parkinson was dutifully at the grand door as they entered the palace. Alia noticed that Nat remained outside, and she turned to speak to him. 'Nat, I'd like you to come in.'

'Your Highness, Mike is inside, and I'll have to be outside. I'll come in if you specifically want me to.'

'No, that's all right. Mike will do.' Alia turned to speak with Susanna.

'Will you take Stephan up to the playroom?'

'Ma'am, he needs to do his piano practice.'

'Leave it for now and I'll let you know when he can do that.' She turned to her son and spoke to him softly. 'Stephan, I have a meeting with someone, and I want you to stay upstairs with Susanna until my meeting finishes.'

'Yes, Mummy.'

10

'Susanna, remain upstairs until I send word that you can come down.'

They began to make their way upstairs and when they reached the top landing, she addressed Parkinson. 'Where is His Majesty?'

'He's in the drawing room, ma'am.'

'Thank you, Parkinson.' Alia quickly walked towards the library and rang her assistant to meet her there. Jillian was already in the library before Alia arrived. 'I need this meeting taped.'

'I've got it all here.' With skill and deftness Jillian placed the digital recording apparatus under the desk.

'Jillian, His Majesty is in the blue drawing room. Will you escort him here, please?'

Alia sat behind the desk and patiently waited for Gregory. As he entered the library, she stood and went towards him. He charmingly took her hand and kissed it and when all the preliminary salutations were performed, he sat in one of the armchairs opposite the desk. 'So, Gregory, I presume that there is something important you wish to discuss with me in this impromptu visit.'

'Naturally, it is about the WSO. Now that you've had a bit of time to process everything that transpired at our last meeting, I'd like to know where you stand on this.' He pulled out a handkerchief from his pocket and sniffed on it. 'I'd imagine you might wish a longer period of time to consider it all, but I thought it important to gauge some commitment from you.'

'I cannot commit to anything at this stage. I hardly know enough information to do that. What else can you offer me? Where does this WSO meet? How long has it been in operation? Who are the members? What are the detailed terms of the financial situation of the WSO? I hardly know anything about this Order. I need more information, hard facts. Can you deliver that?'

'You ask too much before you can commit. This is a secret Order and only members are privy to such information.' He took out his handkerchief again and sniffed it. 'You do not require permission from your Prime Minister, Parliament or anyone else. We will take care of everything. What we need is your personal commitment. Are you in or are you out?'

'So, you want my personal commitment even though you keep me in the dark about your Order and I am to trust you implicitly because ...?'

'Because it will be the better for you to do so.'

'If this is some kind of a veiled threat, Gregory, then I think you had better leave.' She stood behind the desk exuding some controlled agitation.

'My dear Madam, there is no need for anger.' He was on his feet and walked towards the desk. 'Please, Alia. We've been friends for many years. Let us not spoil this. Do not forget our countries are neighbours.' His smile emitted an enchantment that endeavoured to appeal to her sense of loyalty. 'Come, I shall leave you now ... I believe you require more time to consider this.' Alia picked up the phone and asked Parkinson to come into the library. She was surprised with the speed he arrived. 'Parkinson, please see His Majesty out to the front door.' She turned and looked at the king and calmly said, 'Goodbye, Gregory.'

'I am sorry to see that I am leaving on an unfortunate note.' He bowed graciously to her and followed Parkinson out of the room.

Immediately, she rang Jillian. 'I want you to quickly get as close to Parkinson and His Majesty and observe if anything unusual transpires between them.'

'I'm just in the next room. I can see them clearly. I'll go out and hide behind a pillar. I'll come in afterwards, ma'am.'

Alia waited with some apprehension for Jillian's return. A few moments later she was in the library. 'How did it go?'

'Your Highness, Parkinson walked next to His Majesty at all times. He opened the door and His Majesty stood in the doorway for a few seconds and I heard him say, "Thank you Parkinson" and then left.'

'You did well, Jillian. Thank you. You better get the tape for me.' The tape was retrieved from under the desk and her assistant left the room. As she held the tape in her hand, she pondered the whole situation and found it almost surreal. She achieved a sense of calmness and decided that this recording apparatus would go into the personal safe in her bedroom where she kept some of her jewellery. Better to scatter the evidence than keep all the tapes together for some unwanted hand to swipe them in one haul.

Alia sat in her bedroom for a while and tried to comprehend her predicament. It was impossible to make sense of it all. Deflated and dejected, she sat there in the hope that it would vanish into thin air. She stared at the wall quite absentmindedly and there it was – the hairline crack that made its way halfway down the wall. *You look as bad as I feel*, she thought.

Fortunately, her thoughts were disrupted with a knock on the door. 'Come in.'

'There you are, Alia. No one knew where you were.'

'Hello Mother. I feel like a walk. Would you like to come with me?' She placed her forefinger to her lips so nothing important would be spoken in her room. She was not sure if it had been cleared for any spying devices.

Together they walked out into the garden. They both took coats to wear against the chill that was setting in. 'Mother, Gregory came unannounced today and insisted, in an underhanded way, that I should make up my mind very soon about joining this WSO he set up. He even had the audacity to voice a veiled threat. He covered it up with his charm and alluded to our long-standing friendship, both personal and national.' She glanced at her mother who walked quietly beside her. 'He is dead serious. He's not going to let this go until he gets a positive response from me. What shall I do?'

'I think asking Bob to look into this matter to see if our National Secret Services and the one in the United States have anything to offer is where we start. When Alex gets home, we must meet and see how far he's progressed in all of this.' Queen Sylvia placed her arm around her daughter's and together they continued to walk about the garden. It

10

was not until they reached the southern fountain that they realised Nat had followed them every inch of the way.

Alia turned and clearly saw him. 'He's a smooth operator, isn't he?'

'That's what he is trained to do, my dear.'

'I have left instructions that King Gregory is not to pass our gates again, unless he has a clear invitation from me.' She looked askance at her mother. 'Do you think that will irritate him to a point where he might act irrationally?'

'He is irrational already. How much more can he be so?'

'Oh Mother, this concerns me so much.'

'One step at a time, Alia. We will prevail,' the queen reassured her daughter.

11
. . . . .

At the Aerospace Engineering Centre, Alex showed Bob around his precious domain. Every nook and cranny became visible during this inspection. More importantly, the workshop was imminently in their sight and Alex was anxious to find out if any subsequent damages had occurred. Mack, his Chief Engineer, was at hand. 'Alex, I'm glad you've arrived. There is no further damage to report, but I'd like you to see the repair job we did on the spacecraft.'

'Mack, this is Bob. He'll be assisting me with a few things around here and you'll be seeing him a fair bit.' The men exchanged greetings as Alex climbed up to the platform to view, in particular, the engine. 'That's a fine job you've done, Mack. It's almost seamless where the damage occurred. I'll need to inspect it at closer range a little later, but with the naked eye I can't see anything wrong.'

Alex descended from the platform and together with Bob they continued their detailed investigation of the entire centre. 'To begin with, what sort of job do you want me to say you have here? What do you feel comfortable with?'

'Certainly not an engineer. What about a liaison officer? But first, I need to view your CCTV film. I know you said they're installed in the main part of your building and the workshop and not in your offices. Is that right?'

'Yea, Bob. Whatever I need to change, let me know. I want us to work together.

More importantly, I need you to investigate these few names: Ebba Nilsson, my personal assistant, Mack or should I say Malcolm McIntyre the Chief Engineer, the CEO Gustof Fischer, and the foreman Frederik Ferguson. We'll begin with those names. Oh, just one more. Check on Ebba's mother who is in a nursing home – not sure which one. Two more names, Lars Gilmar and Jacob Einheimmer. One other person, Blake is all I know except for a phone number which I'll give you in my office.' He noticed that Bob had recorded everything he said to him without a comment from him.

'I am afraid this is not all. We have troubles in the palace – major trouble. King Gregory of Cumbia is forcing his views about a secret "Order", the WSO, which stands for World Secret Order. Several Heads of State have joined, and they mean business. You either join or they force you to do so – and I'm sure it's not through legal means. At about the same time I was having these sabotage problems here, Alia was experiencing the heavy force of Gregory's insistences. The list of people there are: King Gregory, the WSO, Parkinson our butler ...'

'Parkinson?' Bob interjected, surprised.

'I know. It seems ridiculous — unthinkable, but he has access to the entire palace and grounds and in an eerie way he seems to pop up when you least expect him.'

'Isn't that because he is an experienced and professional butler?'

'Yes, I've thought of that too, Bob. However, the stakes are too high, and I cannot disregard anyone who might have the ability to spy on everyone in the palace. Please check him out. The other one who has recently become chief dog handler is Hans ... I'm not sure of his surname. As a matter of fact, why don't you check on all employees of the palace? Things are really getting serious.'

'You mean, everyone – even your father?'

'I can't be biased about this – I mean everyone.'

'Perhaps a thorough search on everyone at your engineering firm might be useful as well. What do you think?' Bob prompted Alex.

'Do what you consider is best, but search the names I've given you first.'

'How many employees do you have?'

'About one hundred and fifty ... not absolutely sure.' Alex appeared a little puzzled.

'Leave it with me. I'll need an office space of sorts and it will be impenetrable. Just as your centre here and the palace will be, too.' There was a tone of optimism in Bob's voice.

'Very good.' Alex noticed that they had arrived in the administrative building where his office was located.

11

'We'll go into my office and introduce you to my PA.' They entered the waiting room and then Ebba's office just off to the side. She sat behind her computer in a total state of concentration. Her surprise was quite noticeable to see them there in front of her.

'Oh, Dr Glandore, I didn't know you were coming in today.'

'Ebba, this is Bob. He will be working with me here for a while.'

'Please to meet you, Bob.'

'Likewise.' His response was curt, and he sensed an uneasiness about her. The last thing he wanted was for her to suspect anything. 'Have you been working here for a long while, Ebba?' He asked in a softer voice.

'The last four years. It's a good job.'

'Great. I'll see you later.'

They both entered Alex's office and as the door closed, Bob placed his finger to his lips to indicate not to say anything of importance — Alex immediately understood. He was impressed with the speed Bob found the offending recording device, which was in the light stand, next to one of the armchairs in the office. When they were satisfied that everything was cleared, Alex asked in a noticeably agitated manner, 'How the heck did it get there?'

'It's easy enough to install one of these. It must be someone who has access to just about everywhere. Who has this access?' Bob asked.

'Well, those three names I gave you do. Possibly others as

well. The company has grown a little too big for me to keep up with all the staff. I think you're right, Bob. A search of all the staff in the centre is a very good idea. How long will it take to do that?'

'Not as long as you might think and then it depends what sort of investigation we're doing.' He saw Alex's concerned face. 'Don't worry. We'll do a very thorough search on everyone.'

'I know I can rely on you, Bob. Whatever you need is yours. I suppose a list of names of all the employees, to begin with. You name it and I'll produce it,' Alex assured him.

'Thanks, Dr Glandore. That will be a great start. I'll use our National Secret Service's equipment and get as much as I can on everybody here and then I'll double-check with my contacts in the US. If anyone knows anything of this type of sabotage it'll be in America. Fortunately, my initial services within America have kept me in good stead for something like this. But even if that wasn't so, Her Highness left such a great impression when she visited the country that since then, her efforts to keep a workable relationship between Rubinia and the good ol' USA has placed Rubinia well up on their list of allies. Don't worry, they'd be willing to help us out.' He looked Alex squarely in the face with just a ghost of a smile. 'Needless to say, your time spent in the aerospace industry there, on such a high military level, will not hurt our chances of a positive response, either.'

Alex gazed at Bob in utter disbelief. In all those years he had known him, he never once voiced such a loquacious communication of words – in anything! He was lost for words, momentarily, but eventually uttered the first thing that came into his head. 'Right you are, Bob.'

'I'll go into my office you provided, and give me the names in hard copy. I'll process them into my computer.'

'Okay, I'm onto it now.' He sat at his desk chair as Bob headed out to his own office. He clicked the employees list and was surprised to see there were one hundred and sixty-one employees. He clicked the print icon and placed all the printed papers together in a manila envelope. As he entered his personal assistant's office, he said nothing at all but continued towards the waiting room door and he felt her intelligent eyes piercing his back.

He was pleased to reach Bob's office and went in immediately without knocking. Bob simply looked up and casually asked, 'Have you got the list?'

'Here it is.' Alex handed him an envelope and waited until Bob glanced over the pages of names, addresses, marital status, number of children and other personal information which is the usual procedure when employment in such a company is sought.

When the task was completed, it became necessary to make Bob acquainted with Blake's voice recording. 'Everything seems to have happened in the last few days. I received a call and I recorded the conversation. You will note that tomorrow, being Tuesday, I'm expected to meet him in the Cortesta District at Victor's Café, twelve noon. No other explanation given … oh, just one more thing he said, 'come alone.' I'll let you listen to the tape and tell me what you think of it.'

Bob promptly began the process of analysing the voice, the tone, the noises in the background and a metallic sound hidden deeply within the fusion of the digital tape. Alex sat in the armchair opposite Bob's desk and quickly glanced at the door to double-check that it was closed. He observed Bob with much interest; his powers of concentration, patience, and particular attention to detail. He played the taped conversation several times; he rewound it time and time again to gauge the various sounds that were not audible first and second time round. He continued with his notations on the computer as he listened and re-listened until he was satisfied with most of his analysis. 'Dr Glandore, I will need to take this to our National Secret Services where the equipment is highly advanced and intricate. The things that I found difficult to identify will be made clearer then. I'll ask for a private analysis, just in case there has been any kind of infiltration even there. You can't be too careful.'

'I knew you were the right man for this job. When will you go?' Alex queried.

'If I can go straight from here.' Bob had a satchel with him, but the recorded conversation he kept on his person. 'While I'm there, I'll place all these names through the system and see what comes up.

'Bob, will you delay it for a little while. When you are there, I'd like you to scan the names of everyone who works at the palace. There have been strange things happening there also. But one very important person to check out is King Gregory from Cumbia. See what you can find out about him and also the WSO, World Secret Order.' He saw Bob's look of amazement. 'If it's too much to do all in one go, it can be left for later on. I think you're a little overwhelmed by it.'

'No, not overwhelmed by it, just surprised. When I was in the States looking after Princess Alia, one of my friends in the Intelligence Service there mentioned the WSO – all that time ago.'

'What exactly did he say about it?'

'That it existed, but they were not taking it very seriously – at that time ... what is it ... about nineteen years ago?'

'About that.' Alex pondered briefly the situation. 'Bob, how easily would you be able to be given access to such a renowned Intelligence Service, if there was a royal visit to the States and you, or someone you nominate, went along, as well?'

'The access could be more promising ... but, I don't think essential in this case.'

'The results of the tape, will that take very long?' Alex asked uneasily.

'I'll have them here by late afternoon. I guess you'll be here?' Bob asked.

'I will wait for you. But first I'll go to the palace and get the list of employees who work there.'

'It's not necessary. I'll pick up the list of names on my way to the Intelligence Services and work on both.' Bob closely regarded Alex's expression. 'Will you still be in your office when I return? I'm going to be a couple of hours later than I mentioned.'

'I will definitely be here.'

Together they left Bob's office; he conspicuously carried the satchel as Alex walked beside him. 'Okay then. Good luck Bob.' Alex veered towards his own office while Bob left the building. Alex's personal assistant was hard at work word processing the day's letters and documents. She looked up as he entered the office.

'Dr Glandore. Someone rang for you ... wouldn't leave his name ... sounded a bit rough. He said he'd ring your cell number. Then he just hung up.'

'Thanks. If he rings again put him through.' As he finished imparting this information, Alex's cell phone rang. He answered it immediately and went into his office and firmly shut the door.

'Listen and listen good. Make sure tomorra ya come alone. That's all!' The phone went dead thereafter. Alex looked at it and pressed the red button to end the call from his phone. It was a swift reminder that had all the signs of a threat, yet not stated.

He sat in his desk chair and could not stop thinking about the whole situation, both at work and at the palace – there must be some connection, he thought. It occurred to him, sequentially, that Ebba must not be in her office upon Bob's arrival at the centre. He called her over the phone. 'Will you come in, please?'

11

Ebba arrived promptly. 'It appears to me that you have been generally working many long hours. Today, I'm giving you an early mark, so by five you can leave.'

'Oh, it's not necessary, sir. I've got a lot of letters and documents to ...'

'No, Ebba, I insist. You've been working too hard. Leave everything else for tomorrow. I'll remind you at five if you're not ready.' There was nothing more she could do but return to her office desk and work until five. She felt annoyed behind the assured smile she gave Alex.

12

By five o'clock in the afternoon, Alex began to make his way from the workshop to his office. He was pleased that the damage caused to the airplane was rectified. In fact, the extra time it took to repair the engine enabled Alex's team to make minor changes to the missile-like body of the aircraft which would minimise the pressure waves that come off the plane to suppress the sonic boom normally created. It was important to test the airplane and see if it could go the distance of sixty-two thousand feet high by the use of the hybrid gas-turbine technology.

More importantly, Alex wanted to know how the reduction in jet engine emissions would perform – that was the key secret to the design and production of the sonic plane. He had to convince the Department of Commerce and Industry that his sonic plane was thirty percent fuel efficient which overcame the economic and environmental challenges of supersonic flights. With its capability of carrying seventy-five thousand pounds of fuel, or nearly three thousand four hundred kilograms of fuel, it would reach its projected height and passengers would actually be able to see the curvature of the planet earth. After having experienced this blatant sabotage, Alex was more than ever determined to succeed.

When he arrived at his office it was just after five. Ebba was in the process of leaving; the lights were off and only a shaft of soft light from the waiting room lit part of her office. As always, she made her obligatory goodbye with a recognisable smile that spread across her face just long enough to be seen. She swiftly turned her back on Alex and walked firmly and steadily out into the waiting room, looking immaculately dressed and projecting an image of a prim and proper personal assistant. Alex opened his office door and went into the waiting room to switch off the light and lock the door. Just as he was about to shut the door, it quickly swung open and almost hit him full on. It was Ebba. She came crashing into his chest with the pretext that she left a pair of leather gloves in the drawer of her desk. For a moment she appeared at a loss to find Alex in her office. He was taken by surprise but managed to find his voice. 'Would you like me to help you find them?'

Ebba quickly stepped back and quietly said, 'No, I can manage. It's raining outside.' She immediately went to the drawer and produced the forgotten gloves. Slowly and carefully she pulled the glove over her hand and meticulously tugged deeply into each finger as she brought the leather to fit snugly and exactly over her entire hand. Alex stood stunned as he watched the precision and manner that dictated her whole demeanour. Then, without a word, she disappeared from the room as suddenly as she entered it. When Alex gained some measure of distinct focus, he folded his arms on his chest and softly said to himself, 'Now, I wonder what she really wanted.' His eyes roamed towards the drawer and he went over to investigate. He opened the last drawer on the left side of the stainless steel and glass-top desk and rustled around for anything unusual. There was nothing there. He placed his hand directly under the drawer and there he found the offensive item – another spy hearing device.

He was furious with her. All he wanted to do was dismiss her from the job. Yet, he could not prove that she or someone else placed it there. Although his emotional instinct was to dismiss her immediately, his brain was telling him to let reason take its course. He needed her close so he could observe all her movements and decided there and then that he'd jolly well have Bob or someone else monitor her comings and her goings.

When Alex's chest ceased heaving with anger, he set about to sweep the rest of Ebba's office, his own office and the waiting room. If there were any more spy devices hidden anywhere, he was determined to find them. There were no others in his personal assistant's office; he progressed into his office; it was dark enough by this time and as his eyes surveyed the room, he saw the speck of red light high up on the wall directly next to the security alarm system, which could easily be taken as part of the alarm apparatus. He pushed the desk hard against the wall, climbed onto its leather top, raised his feet on tiptoes and stretched his arms as far as they could reach and just managed to touch the device. He plucked at it a couple of times, down it came, and it soon found his pocket. It was certainly not there when Bob searched his office earlier. He scoured the room once more but discovered nothing else. He was emotionally and physically exhausted from the day's work and concerns but pushed on to the waiting room. The intense search produced nothing there.

For the first time he felt relieved to leave his workplace and go home; he was too tired and disconsolate to do anything more. He would wait for the morning to see the situation clearer in the daylight. Then he remembered Bob. He needed to ring him. 'Bob have you finished your search? Not quite? Listen, it might be best to leave our meeting for tomorrow morning, here at work. Okay. I'll see you bright and early tomorrow.' As he was about to switch off the phone, Alex recalled his appointment with Blake at twelve noon tomorrow. 'Bob, are you still there? Tomorrow, I also have the twelve o'clock appointment with Blake. Will you be there, incognito? Good. See you then.' As he pressed the off button of his cell phone, he was relieved that Bob's presence offered some assurance.

He secured his office and checked that the safe in the wall behind a well-hidden panel was locked and, being satisfied with the other two offices, he fortified himself with a warm woollen coat, mohair scarf and leather gloves. His driver waited patiently by the car until Alex finished work to drive him to the palace. Trent could see Alex as he came out of the Engineering Centre, and for the first time in memory he saw his boss coming towards him with something of a laboured gait. Not that anyone else could discern this, but Trent's constant time with Alex helped him to acutely notice it.

Alex was unusually quiet on the trip home to the palace. Trent was always ready to fill him in with what was going on outside of his own engineering world. Tonight was a different matter and Trent respected his silence and private thoughts. It was sufficiently late in the evening and they avoided the bulk of the traffic, so when they reached the entrance of the palace, they were both surprised how little time it took to get there. The gate opened and the car slowly and carefully parked at the front steps. Before Alex could get out of the car, Parkinson was at the opened door, ready to welcome him home. He was the last person he really wanted to see, but he put on a brave front and asked where Alia and the Queen were at present.

'I believe, sir, they are both in the private lounge.'

'Thanks,' was his concise response.

He first went to his own apartment where he desperately wanted to get out of the stifling business suit which was too much of a reminder of the lacklustre day he had had at work. Much to his relief, he found his casual clothes already spread over the king-sized bed. The navy worsted trousers were accompanied with a fine navy-lined striped white shirt, which he wore open necked and it blended well with the navy casual jacket. This was set off with black leather loafers as a comfort to his feet. In no time at all he was ready to meet Alia and the Queen. Alex never dallied about his dress code. He knew exactly what he wanted to wear as did others who assisted him in that. He walked briskly to the private lounge and knocked on the door.

It was the Queen's voice. 'Alex, come in, take a seat.'

'Thank you, Your Majesty.' He quickly scanned the room for Alia and noticed her by the window. He made his way towards her and planted a kiss on each side of her cheeks. She responded in kind and then, much to her surprise, he embraced her and held her tightly for several long seconds. He stood back, looked enquiringly into her face and ushered her to an armchair. Not a word transpired between them. Alex settled himself on a chair next to Alia.

'Would you like some coffee, tea and supper?'

'Yes, I will, Your Majesty. I've not had dinner.'

'We'll ring for some dinner to be sent up.' The queen was prompt to reply.

'No, no, I'm fine with the supper.'

'You must look after yourself. There's a lot ahead of us and you need to be well.'

'Thanks Alia. I'll try.'

'Alex, fill us in with what is happening at work.'

'Well, ma'am, quite a lot. Bob has been inducted ...' He suddenly came to an abrupt halt. 'Has anyone checked for listening devices here?'

'Yes, Trent came in and checked out the whole room,' Alia added quickly. She was keen to hear the news from the plant.

'He's settled in his new office and has taken on the official title of Liaison Officer. He now has the names of all the employees at the Engineering Centre and of the palace, and the checking process has started – on everyone.' He was going to continue, when suddenly Alia stood and began to pace the floor.

'It makes me really mad to think that things have gone on for so long unnoticed.' She stopped and looked squarely at her mother. 'We're the Castelers! Nine hundred years we've held this kingdom together. Our ancestors have seen worse things than this. We must fight and win.'

'You're right Alia. That's what we're trying to do now … short of a full-scale revolution.' Alex tried to allay her agitation.

Instantly, Alia ceased pacing the floor. 'That's it!' She shouted louder than intended.

'What's it?' Alex asked urgently.

'A revolution. We need a revolt. It's not crazy, just listen to what I have to say. We need the people to rebel at the WSO's ideas. But the question is how do we do it?'

'Who do you suggest should revolt, our people? Haven't they gone through enough? Look at all the wars in Europe and then Communism. What are you saying, Alia? I have seen what upheavals do to people. No, there has to be a different way.' The queen was adamant.

'Nothing's going to happen unless we think about it

carefully and see what course to take.' Alex turned to address his views to Alia. 'This country is still a Constitutional Monarchy with a government based on democracy. How are you going to convince Parliament of that?'

'I don't know yet, but I'm sure going to try.'

'Look, the idea is worth considering and needs the influence of those who can make these things happen.' Alex tried to weigh up the idea.

'Yes, Alex. Our secret service.' Something sparked in the queen's mind. 'The Castelers were never ones for shrinking away from a fight and not necessarily a physical one, either.'

'I think we need Bob on this. I was supposed to meet him tomorrow morning at work, but I'll now ring and ask him to meet us here at 7.30am and discuss this idea.' The cell phone was instantly in his hand. 'Bob, instead of meeting me tomorrow morning at work, meet us at the palace at seven thirty. Yes, in the private lounge.' He looked over at the two women and he could see the strain on their faces. 'It's done. He'll be here tomorrow at 7.30.' He then spoke in a quieter voice. 'Let's leave this now, go to bed and we'll see what the morning brings.' He turned to address the queen. 'Ma'am, would you like me to walk you to your room?'

'Thank you, Alex, but I will be fine on my own.'

Alex opened the door for Her Majesty, and he saw her walk down the long hallway, straight backed and regal as always. He admired her tenacity and her staunch regard for tradition and culture. As he turned into the lounge room, he caught Alia carefully studying him with those cinnamon sweet eyes that captured the exotic essence of the East and the fundamental knowledge of a heart's desire which expanded over an eternity. He suddenly brought himself into reality and quickly said, 'There's some credit in your idea, Alia. It just needs some refinement.'

'Yes, I know ... like my life.'

'What do you mean by that?'

'Look at our life. Can't you see anything wrong with it?' She sighed and placed her arms across her chest. 'It's taken a catastrophe to be civil and talk to each other. Not even with all that's going on around us can we stop and take note of our life together ... uhm together? I mean apart.'

'Everything has precedence. This has to be sorted out or no one will have a proper life together or apart.' He walked closer to her. 'Have you stopped considering the impact this problem will have on everyone? It's bigger than just you and me! We have a whole life ahead of us, but we won't if this whacko Order has its way.' All Alia could do was to look at Alex regrettably for all that had happened to them. 'Do you know, Alia? I'm standing right here in front of you and regardless of what I've said, I just want to hug you so hard that you meld in my arms.' Alia's eyes widened and her arms dropped to her sides. For a moment she became so softly pliable that he could visualise her in his arms. Then she spoke and that captured moment was shattered.

'We can't be doing this all the time, Alex. First, we need to sort out our problems for us to be right again. That's the only way. Do you understand?'

12

'Yes, I do. Good night, Alia.' He turned and found the door. He pulled it open and didn't bother to close it.

Alia followed him with her eyes and felt his distance as he walked away from her. A distance that measured a million miles from the top of the staircase directly to her. She saw him disappear down the steps and did not stop to look back. As he vanished from her sight, she involuntarily called out his name. 'Alex.' She ran to the top of the staircase, but he was nowhere to be seen. She felt the depletion of oxygen around her, the shortness of breath, the dizzy light-headedness, and with a tremulous hand she held the banister tightly while her right hand came automatically over the left side of her chest in the proximity of her heart. 'Oh, God! What have I done?' Slowly and sorrowfully, she made her way to her bedroom.

13

In the light of day, Alia felt no better than the night before. Her independent stubborn spirit often overarched everything, as it did last night. She moved slowly from her bed to the bathroom. She could not remember how many times she had brushed her teeth while her thoughts flew back to Alex's words. As she replayed the events of last night, she tried to justify her actions. There was no way she was going to capitulate at his beg and call. 'I'm stronger than that,' she muffled through a mouthful of toothpaste. Then she thought of his tender words and loving face as he poured out his heart to her. No, it wasn't good enough. She was tired of playing this "on-and-off game". They had to finalise their differences. As she continued brushing, she looked absentmindedly in the mirror only to see the top of her nighty covered with dripped toothpaste. She groaned some more and quickly spat out the remaining toothpaste, washed out the sediments in her mouth and wiped her lips with the towel. All at once, she realised the shower had been running the entire time while her mind was preoccupied with other things. She stripped and went under the stream of water. The warmth soaked her skin and a thorough shampoo of her hair was done whether it needed it or not.

Out into her bedroom, she dressed quickly, scrunched her wet hair and allowed it to dry into its natural curls. She placed a couple of combs on the sides of her head to hold back some of the hair and left the rest to drop naturally over part of her forehead and down the sides of her neck. She couldn't remember the last time she wore her hair in that way, but it would have to do. The morning's outfits were already on the made-up bed and after dismissing her chambermaid, she dressed alone. Her aim was to go down to the dining room quickly. It was already seven in the morning.

As she opened the dining room door, Alia saw Alex and her mother speaking quietly and seriously with each other. Her mother was first to look up. 'Good morning Alia. Come and join us.' The queen looked closer at her daughter. 'You look different this morning. I can't quite put my finger on it.'

Alex looked up also and couldn't stop staring at her. 'This is how I remember you as a teenager.'

'Awkward and ugly.'

'No, that's not what I meant. You look lovely.'

'Thank you.' She looked around the room and could not see Stephan. 'Where's Stephan this morning?'

'He had riding lessons, but it's raining outside and too wet for that. He's upstairs with the Martial Arts instructor.' The queen responded in a matter-of-fact voice. 'I must go to the private lounge and see that it's prepared for our meeting with Bob.' She took the napkin from her lap and as she was about to stand, Alex was there to pull out the chair and assist her. 'Tell Alia about our conversation.'

When the queen left the dining room, Alex drew up a chair next to Alia. 'Before I begin, I need to explain something to you about last night.' He looked into her face and once more he saw that irrepressible young teenage girl he fell in love with, such a long time ago. 'You were right. We do need to fix up our problems, but as I see our situation, we have to do it quickly and now. Our other alternative is the silence and the distance between us. You choose and I'll go with your choice. As far as I'm concerned that's the end of the matter. There are too many other serious things we need to consider, one way or another.'

'Don't dictate to me like that. I'll do what I want.' She was quite furious with his attitude towards her.

'I'm tired of this hot-and-cold thing. Either we're husband and wife or it's back to the silence between us. Now you choose ... but do it quickly.' Alex was in a no-nonsense mood that morning.

'Okay! Enough said.' She went to the buffet and poured a cup of coffee for herself.

'Have something to eat. It's going to be a long day.' He spoke softer to her.

'Are you now ordering me about my eating habits?' She sat at the table and tried to swallow the coffee. It was almost impossible to do so.

'Alia, look at me. Do you want a divorce? Is that what you want?'

She was shocked at his suggestion. 'Where did that come from? I never mentioned anything like that!'

'No, but your actions show it.'

'You're just thinking about sex.'

'That's not what I'm thinking about. I can get sex anywhere if I want it. It's about the love that leads to sex – like the love that you and I had. Sex is easy to find, but love, true love is rare. What we had was unique and precious, that's now lost. Without it our life is filled with recriminations and without trust, then sex is useless.' He stopped speaking for a few seconds and in a softer voice added, 'Do you remember our life on the Greek island?' Alia turned instantly and looked at him.

'Of course I do. But we can't be on a honeymoon at all times!'

'I know – but we should try and work towards an approximation of it, with love, trust and faith in each other. When these things are missing, then we might as well call it a day!' She was quiet and appeared there was nothing more for her to say. 'Alia, we have a child and it's always the children who get hurt, no matter how many psychologists they go and see. But even that is useless. We are all so self-centred and when we place these young hearts on the altar of sacrifice and convince ourselves that everything will be fine – it never is! We can take either road and Stephan has to weather it as so many other children do. I want you to think about it and let's, for *heaven's sake*, choose one road or the other.' He sub-consciously raised his voice and quickly came to the realisation of it. He took a deep breath and then spoke a lot softer. 'I am tired and it's hard to cope with this indecisive situation. Tell me once and for all, what is it you want to do?'

For the first time in her married life Alia understood the seriousness of their marital problems. 'I want us to find a solution to our marriage — for both of us. Is that possible for you to do?'

'Yes, it is. Do you agree we should work towards that, but also prioritise this national catastrophe that is threatening us?'

As Alia was about to answer, her phone rang. 'Yes, Mother. We're coming. Is Bob there? Good.' She turned to Alex. 'Bob's ready in the private lounge.'

'Before we go, I need you to answer my question. Do you agree on the importance of this national problem?'

'Yes, of course I do. I'm not indifferent to it. I know the importance of it. I just want you to promise me that you will make time for us to work out our differences. Will you assure me of that? Will you be by my side at important events?' Alia asked pressingly.

'Yes, I will, just as I hope you'll support a few of my endeavours, also.'

'That's fair enough. I'll agree to that.' She looked down into the cold black coffee and pushed the saucer and cup away from her.

13

Alex stretched his arm towards her and held out his hand. 'Come on, let's go or Bob will wonder what's happened to us.'

'What were you and my mother talking about when I entered the dining room?'

'It's best I leave it for her to tell you. I'm sure she will at our meeting.' Hesitantly, Alia took his hand and together they made their way to the private lounge room where she hoped that, at least there, one thing might be resolved in this national disaster.

At the door she took her hand out of Alex's and both entered the room. Bob and the queen were seated around the coffee table in deep conversation. 'Alex, Alia, come and sit down.' Her Majesty indicated the couch at the other end of the square coffee table. She noticed that there was something different about both of them – perhaps a little more relaxed with each other. The way Alex waited for Alia to sit first and the surreptitious semi-smile that slipped past his lips so quickly. It could not be detected by anyone else, but by someone whose powers of observation were only sharpened by the intimate knowledge of both of them. Alia looked up into his eyes and for a split-second they were interlocked with Alex's. A warm flush reached her cheeks and she looked down onto the coffee table with the pretext of giving her iPad a serious check, as if some expectation of information would jump out at her.

The queen began the proceedings. 'Now that we are all here, I would like to make a statement that is well and truly overdue. This monarchy has endured many setbacks.

There was the time when Klaus the Second endeavoured to take the rightful throne from his brother, Timithius, in the fourteenth century. Although Timithius was not the combatant his brother purported to be, he used his intellect to overcome such a menace. He spoke in public arenas, festivals, the steps of local government, the marketplaces, literally anywhere he could be heard by as many people as possible. They heard and they revolted. They bolted the massive iron doors to protect the castle and the people also used ingenuity to hold the enemy at bay. Their archery skills developed to include the new technology of the crossbow, the design and adoption of a plated armour, rather than the chain mail, which protected them from the dangers of spears and arrows. The moat around their stronghold offered the extra defence they needed and gave their warriors time to regroup and the people time to gather and play their part. I don't want to overstate our medieval history, my point being that this WSO must be exposed among the people, they must be aware and allowed to voice their concerns with demonstrations and anything else that will make the whole world stand and take notice.' The queen's passionate talk took Alex and Alia by surprise. 'The rest of the Western world and anyone else who wants to hear must be informed. They cannot have the upper hand in this. We must fortify ourselves and let our people know the evil that's brewing around them.' She suddenly stopped and eyed the three who sat around the coffee table absorbed in every word the queen uttered.

'Your Majesty, if I may interrupt. Who in this scenario is going to play the part of Timithius for the people to listen?' Alex was genuinely interested to see if she actually saw this whole thing through.

'I am looking at two of the most intelligent, talented and vocal people that I know,' she replied in a calm and decisive manner.

'Mother, you mean Alex and me. Don't you?'

'Yes ...'

'But, what about diplomacy? We're not meant to meddle in politics. We're a Constitutional Monarchy. What are you saying Mother?'

'We are not to meddle in our national *internal* politics. This is an external affront and an attack on everything this nation holds dear. It cannot be ignored. We have worked for centuries to have come where we are and no one, absolutely *no one* is going to topple our values, beliefs, democratic politics and our faith. No one!'

Alia was astounded. She had never seen her mother so pointedly driven by passion and decisiveness as she saw her that very moment. Alex sat next to Alia and absorbed the entire speech and scene. As the conversation between mother and daughter receded and a slight silence filled the room, Alex spoke up. 'It seems to me that Her Majesty has made a strong case for the nation and we don't even have to go way back to the medieval times to find examples of such fervour. A quick look at the French Revolution will reveal that ordinary people, who had no sophisticated technological weaponry, used ordinary tools: pitchforks, clubs from tree branches and ripped up cobblestones from the streets of Paris, and they charged the Bastille. This gave them the bold confidence to later assault in the same manner and force their way through into the Palace of Versailles and overthrow the monarchy.' He looked over at the queen whose eyebrows were raised and a smirk appeared around her lips.

'I certainly hope it will not be a sign for *this* monarchy to go.'

'No, ma'am. I give this as an example for the passion and persistence of the people willing to fight and make a change in society.' Alex glanced again at the queen. 'The difference here, Your Majesty, is that the threat comes from without not from within the nation. This WSO is working covertly snaking its way into all areas of life. And here is the importance of what you have said. We fight differently to them. We fight with demonstrations, speeches and shout it out from every hilltop to let people understand what is secretly worming its way into their lives, into their freedoms – we tell them the truth.'

'I'm glad you explained it clearly, Alex. For a moment there I thought I might be beheaded.' The queen gave a broad smile and even Bob gave a shallow chuckle.

Alia joined in the mix and pronounced, 'That's my revolutionist!' and tapped Alex's thigh as he sat next to her.

'Now, Bob, we have not heard from you.' The queen asked, 'How do you see this whole situation?'

'Your Majesty, from everything I know and from what

13

I've just heard I think before we do anything at all, we must consult our allies, especially America and possibly the UK. It's a must. Don't forget the US has vested interests in our hills where they mine uranium. I believe this should be done before it's mentioned to our national government – you just don't know who else is involved in this. First, I'll make some enquiries and I really think that Princess Alia and Dr Glandore should, if they can go, set off for the States. It's different when you are face-to-face talking about important issues such as this one. We have better bargaining power.'

'But surely, we must tell the Prime Minister, at least.'

'No, Your Majesty. At present, the fewer people who know what's going on, the better.' Bob came across confidently and as someone who knew what needed to be done. 'This should be a low-key visit and the prime aim will be to engage the secret service. We'll know better when I've made more enquiries with some top people in that area over there.'

'We can be quiet about it, but in the meantime, they're working full steam ahead, hell-bent for our destruction.' Alex looked over at Bob and continued to explain his thoughts. 'I guess they have their plans and we need to get ours organised as quickly as possible.'

14

As the meeting disbanded, Alex took Bob aside and reminded him of his appointment with Blake at twelve that afternoon. 'That's right, Doc. What's the time now?' Bob looked at his wristwatch. 'Nine forty. I'll have time to check my computer for the reports on the analysis of his voice – at least we'll be armed with something.'

'I'll be in my office. Let me know when you're ready.' The men shook hands, and each departed in different directions. Alex made a call to Mack. 'How are things at your end?'

'Glad to say no other sabotage found. The prototype aircraft is looking almost ready. The tests we've made have proven successful. All we'll need is a pilot.'

'Mack, that's great news.'

'Gotcha and out.' Mack clicked his cell phone off.

Alex began to walk back to his office and came across Alia in the main entrance hall. 'What are you up to for the rest of the day? I'm going to my office if you need me.'

'I think I'll see the whereabouts of Stephen and spend

14

some time with him. He has a way of clearing my mind and calming me down.' She looked at his intent gaze upon her. 'I think you've experienced that, as well.'

'I have. Enjoy his company, Alia,' and with that he continued to walk towards his objective. It was none too soon, he thought, that his wife took a real interest in their son. His days were as precious as hers and as busy as hers, but he made sure to be with Stephan, to hear his stories from school and the friendships that he formed. He was certain if he asked Alia who was Stephan's best friend, she would not know. Perhaps, he thought, *I am too hard on her – she is, at least, trying now.*

As Alia walked towards the playroom, where some muffled playful noises could be heard, she found her mind thinking about Alex, especially his inexplicable stare he gave her. 'No doubt,' she thought, 'I've hardly spent enough time with Stephan and I know that. However, what I find hard to accept is that he made sure he spent time with our son, but never considered the time he should have spent with his wife.' She was outside the playroom door and forced herself to stop thinking of what Alex should or shouldn't have done. She pushed the door open and went in.

'I can hear all this laughter and where there is laughter I want to be there, too.'

'Mum, you're here. We're playing cops and robbers. Do you want to join in?'

'Of course. Who am I?'

'You can be my police partner.' Stephan turned and looked hard at his mother. 'But you must do everything I tell you.'

'Yes, sir!' Alia saluted her son as she came to attention and the game was on.

In the meantime, just as Alex arrived at the office, his cell phone rang. 'Bob, what news?' He focused on each word with some disappointment. 'So there is no record of this male's voice? What's our next step?' Again he listened carefully to what was said, and he agreed that the tape should be made available to the Secret Service in London and Washington DC. 'Bob, we must leave in half an hour and get to the designated café a little earlier than twelve. Where will you be? Okay. I'll see you shortly.'

It intrigued Alex to discover what this was all about, but at the same time he realised that it was no child's play – this was serious. Someone out there had it in for him. As his thoughts swept over a few scenarios, the knock on the door that he was anxiously waiting for arrived. 'Come in, Bob.' As he entered Alex saw the small box he carried with care. 'What's all this?'

'You're going to be wired up, well and proper. Every word you speak and what Blake says will be recorded.'

'Where will that take place?' Alex asked.

'I took the time to go to Cortesta and left a white van near the café so I can do a proper job of it. If you're taken by force or otherwise, I've Plan B to enforce.'

'Really. Why would he do that?' Alex waited for Bob to respond. He didn't.

All he said was, 'Let me wire you up.' He pulled out of the box a minute earpiece which was promptly placed into his ear. 'With this you will hear everything I tell you.' Bob scrummaged through the box and produced a pen. 'And this you will definitely need.'

'I don't need a pen, Bob. I have a perfectly good one in the inside pocket of my jacket.' Alex felt the left pocket of his jacket and confirmed to himself that it was still there. 'In any case, why do I need a pen?'

'This, Doc, acts like any other pen with an important exception. It's a digital voice recording pen with a hidden microphone. Should anything unexpected happen you can record, if possible, without giving the game away, and I'll be able to hear you and anybody else's voice.'

Alex held the pen up into the light with a reverence that was reserved only for heroes. 'Nifty piece of work, Bob.'

'Take the pen out from your jacket and replace it with this one.'

Alex did as he was told. 'You didn't answer, why he would want to do that?'

'Look, Dr Glandore. This is serious. He wants something from you and if I've interpreted the tone of his voice correctly, he'll do it one way or another.'

'Oh, I got that, Bob. I just want to know what exactly does he want?'

'I'm hoping he'll tell you when you meet.' He looked at Alex and saw that he was out of his element. This was not a precise science or mathematical equation. It did not come with a clear-cut recognition of what it was and that disturbed him. 'Ask questions and get as much information as you can.

Don't worry, I've got your back.'

Alex stated, 'It's not my back I'm worried about. This is much bigger than I thought.'

'You're spot-on there! I know just a little bit more than you and the mind boggles.'

'Tell me what you know,' Alex demanded

'I can't right now. One step at a time, sir.' Bob circumnavigated his demand.

'I have no choice but to leave everything in your hands.' Alex noticed the digital clock on his desk. 'We better move along. I don't want to be late.'

Both men left Alex's office and made their way through the softly-padded carpets in the hallways and peaceful ambience that surrounded them within the familiar walls of the palace. The final hallway naturally opened out into the main entrance hall where they found Parkinson standing dutifully and ready to open the grand front door. Bob and Alex glanced at each other and made no comment. As they approached, it was promptly opened and Alex simply said, 'Thank you, Parkinson.'

Down the steps they went and noticed that their car was waiting in anticipation of their arrival to use it. Alex turned to Bob and quietly asked, 'Did you order the car?'

'Yes,' he whispered. The driver opened the back door of the car just as Bob intercepted it. 'It's fine, Trent. I'll be driving today.'

'Right-on.' He looked at Alex. 'Will you be needing me for the rest of the day, Dr Glandore?'

'I might. I want you to be around here in case I do.'

'Yes, sir.'

In the car, Bob took the wheel and Alex sat next to him. He motioned to Alex not to speak and as the palace was lost from view and the car left the boundaries of the estate, he pulled over onto the side of the road and checked to see if the car was bugged. His thorough search inside revealed nothing. He shot forth out of the car and carefully looked under it. There at the rear was an obnoxious tracking device. Bob pulled it off with some careful manoeuvring and it quickly became dysfunctional. Alex was out of the car and witnessed the whole process. 'I guess it is clear for me now to speak.'

'Go for it, Doc.'

'I wonder who did that?' Alex asked incredulously.

'One thing for sure, Dr Glandore. We'll need to put CCT videos in more places around the palace than what's there at present.'

'If we get out of this alive today, I want you to make a list of where we have to replenish with more CCTVs.'

'Sure thing.' Bob gave Alex a quick look and reminded him, 'We've got to go or you'll be late. Now, this is what I'm thinking. I'll drop you off in a side street, about a hundred metres away from the café and I'll make my way to the van. I've timed it so we can get to our destinations at the same time.' The rest of the journey was mainly in silence, each man with his own thoughts. They left the car parked in the small street with the two left tyres on the sidewalk and the other two aligned with the gutter. Most cars were parked in that manner. It gave all vehicles room and safety in which to travel.

Both men left for their designated areas. Bob found the van easily enough and went in to coordinate the radio frequencies for clear reception. The earphones sat comfortably around his head and over his ears. He was ready with the recording device which was to pick up all the conversations from Alex's side.

Alex found Victor's Café right on the main street of Cortesta District. The façade had long windows from ceiling to floor, with outdoor black tables and dark wood-grain tabletops. The chairs reflected the table style with black wooden frames and dark wood-grain seats and backs. In the middle of each table was a small clear glass vase of fresh coloured flowers. As Alex opened the door to enter, he observed that the outside décor neatly reflected the inside room of the café. He found a table by one of the windows and sat there. As he placed his hands on top of the table, he saw the time was eleven fifty-five on his digital wristwatch. A young waitress with a blonde ponytail and a flamboyant bright pink scarf tied around it began to walk towards Alex. She wore a matching ready pink smile and spoke with something of a squeaky voice.

'What can I get you, sir?'

'A cappuccino, please.'

'Soy, almond, coconut, zymil, cow milk, or goat milk?'

'Just cow milk will be fine.'

He looked around to see if he could identify Blake. It was impossible, of course. He had never met him, but that didn't

14

stop him from trying to match the voice on the phone with some of the patrons in the café. Before he could analyse anyone clearly, he heard a squeak beside him. 'Your coffee, sir.' She left just as quickly as she came.

'Thank you,' he managed to respond before she was out of earshot.

He continued to sip slowly on the coffee and still no one had approached him. Again, he looked at his watch – twelve o'clock on the dot. He picked up the menu and softly spoke into it. 'Still no one here.'

'He'll show up, don't worry,' came Bob's voice into his ear.

As Alex continued to look astutely through the menu, he felt a firm tap on his shoulder. 'So you've turned up. Wasn't sure you'd be here.'

Alex swiftly turned his head to the side and there, standing rigidly upright, girdled with a heavy grey coat and red scarf, was a middle-aged man of fifty-six or so holding a walking stick and looking quite stately. He stood to face him fully. 'You're Blake, I presume.'

'You got that right.' He extended his arm for a handshake and Alex obliged him.

It wasn't until he saw past Blake, that Alex realised he was not alone. Two rather tall and burly men stood directly behind Blake, announcing in silence their intention to act according to the direction this meeting was going to take. Alex's glance diverted back to Blake. 'I see *you've* not come alone. I, on the other hand, am alone. I can't see a balance here.'

'There is no need to balance anything. Come with me to my office in the back room.'

He had no alternative but to follow him, while his two guards walked closely behind Alex. As they reached the door, Blake suddenly came to an abrupt halt almost forcing Alex to walk into his back. Quickly, one of his men came around and opened the door and simultaneously switched on the light. As they all entered, Alex was taken aback at the sumptuous office. It was massive in size, with a chandelier at each end of the room and down-lights to direct light in parts of the massive study. The desk was made of thick Corinthian marble legs and a strong glass top sat strategically on those ancient columns. It was difficult for the eye to take in the entire extravagance of the room. Blake sat behind his realm and indicated that Alex take a seat opposite the desk.

As Alex sat, Blake began to talk. 'It has come to my attention that you've become a stumbling block to my progress.' He swivelled in his desk chair so Alex had a clear profile view of him. He continued to speak in that precise position. 'I have to tell you, I'm not happy with that! You have placed me in an awkward situation which has become most unfortunate ...' and there he made a pregnant pause, 'for you.'

'I have to interrupt you here. First and foremost, I have no idea what the heck you're talking about. I have never set eyes on you, until now. Who in the world are you?' Alex's tone was stronger than he wanted it to be.

14

'You had better calm down.' His two guards looked directly at Blake waiting for his instructions. 'You two, get out of here.' He paused impromptu for a couple of seconds and then continued. 'Come back if you hear any unusual noises.'

'Yea, Boss,' was the laconic response as they left the room and closed the door behind them.

'So you want to know who I am. Fair enough. I'm Blake Crowley and this establishment you see here, and many more, are mine.'

'So?'

'You'll have to learn to be more patient, my man.' Alex took a deep breath and exhaled to try and remain calm. What he really wanted to say at that juncture was 'I'm not your man and never will be,' but he kept quiet and looked at him cuttingly in the eyes. 'You did me out of a venture, which I was prepared to purchase and you just out-bid me. I find that greedy. You have so much of it. Why would you want more of this small spacecraft engineering business?'

'Do you mean Einheimmer's business?'

'You catch on quick,' Blake blurted sarcastically.

'Why your big interest for that particular business? Are you in this business yourself?'

'No, I'm not. *But* I'm clever enough to know that this sort of business will be really important in the very near future. Nearer than you'll ever know,' Blake conveyed with contempt.

Alex retorted incredulously, 'And how is this my fault? Why didn't you bid above my price?'

'Because, that old fool Einheimmer, preferred to sell it to you! But then, here we are! *You* have it and *I* want it.'

'Why didn't you use the same tactics as you're using with me now and get it off Einheimmer instead of complicating things with me?'

'This is *not* complicated.' He reached for the top middle drawer of his desk and pulled out a document. 'All you need to do is sign this little weeny paper and we're done.'

'You haven't answered, why didn't you use these tactics to get the business off Einheimmer?' Alex asked with determination.

'I don't have to tell you anything, but I will, just to shut you up. The old fool kept the sale of his business to you so quiet that your transactions with him were finalised and recorded before I knew it. Are you happy with my explanation?' He didn't wait for an answer. 'Let me tell you. Business is all about timing – always about timing. As you can see, not timed so well for me. But I'm sure you will reverse this *disappointing* state of affairs.' He pushed the document towards him with a ready pen for Alex's signature.

'Now, hang on a minute. I can't sign this. Even if I did, my signature would be worth nothing. I borrowed money to buy this business and the person I borrowed money from has a large slice in my engineering firm.'

'My search at Rubinia's Business Registration department showed only one signature. Yours!'

'This deal is a private one – between me and this other person. His signature is not registered.'

14

'I don't care. Take the document and get him to sign it.' Blake picked up the document, folded it up neatly, came away from his desk and stood by Alex's chair. 'Here, stuff it in your pocket.' He pushed the paper hard into his front left-side pocket of his jacket, walked slowly and pointedly back behind his desk. He leaned with his clenched fists on the glass desktop and raised his eyes to stare Alex in the face. 'I want your signature and his,' and there he purposely paused, 'or *hers* by tomorrow at twelve noon, here. Now, get out of here!' His voice raised to a crescendo as he spat out the last few words.

Before Alex could get out of the chair, his two bodyguards came rushing into the office about to pounce on him. 'Let him go,' Blake yelled at them and then in a softer voice and with a grin spread across from ear to ear, he uttered softly, 'He'll be back tomorrow.'

Alex stood up out of his chair and walked towards the door. 'Remember, I know where you live and everything about you.' Blake's menacing voice came blaring in Alex's ears. He paused at the door without turning around, then opened it and went out. The café was quite full by this time and he went over to the counter to pay for the coffee. The man behind the counter looked him up and down and bluntly requested 'Three sixty.'

By the time Alex took out his wallet and the money, the blonde waitress came quickly by his side and said, 'Mr Crowley said it's on the house.'

'And I say it's not. Here take this.' He placed a Rubinian

five-dollar note on the bench top, swerved suddenly around and left.

Outside he breathed in the crisp cold air and swiftly began to walk towards the van. He spoke softly and clearly to Bob. 'Did you get all of that?'

'I sure did. You're lucky he let you out of there. You know where I've got the van?'

'Yes, I'm almost there. See you in a minute.' When he got to the van he found Bob busy packing up all the necessary equipment. 'Do you need any help?'

'No, I'm almost done.' He placed some electronic equipment in zip-up bags and carefully left them safely in the rear of the van.

'I was thinking, Bob, that you might need to drive the van and I the car back to Castelneuf. I think we should go to the engineering plant and talk in my office.'

'Sounds like a good idea.' He searched in his pockets and found the keys. 'Here they are, Doc.' He threw them at him.

'Okay,' he said as he promptly caught the keys and left the van to walk in the direction of the car.

On his way, Alex realised that he still had the recording pen in his pocket and the listening device in his ear. As he was about to remove it he heard the ringing of a phone. 'Yep, he's gone. No, I don't think so. He's too caught up with everything right now. Of course not. I'm here alone. Come to the van.' Then everything went dead. His shoes seemed to be weighed down onto the sidewalk. He couldn't move. He suddenly thought, *What was happening behind his back?*

14

Did he make a mistake? He must force himself to go to the car. *What if the car was bugged, as well?* It was impossible for him to stop the myriad of questions flying through his head.

In a split-second decision he knew he had to go back to the van and see who it was that turned up. Quickly, he picked up his walking pace and was glad to see that the van was still there. As he approached, he walked slower and went around the back and then crouched until he reached the sliding door of the van. He didn't knock. He quickly slid the van door open and there next to Bob was Nat Bolland. Alex was still standing outside the van as his voice rose in sharp tones. 'What's going on in here?' Bob looked surprised to see Alex at the door as was Nat. 'What are you two up to?'

'Doc, you're surprised to see Nat here. I asked him to come in case there was trouble at the café. Nat was my Plan B. We drove up together and I told him to stay here while I went back to the palace in his car and he stayed with the van.' He could see Alex was still not convinced. 'I knew you were worried, and I didn't want to add to that by telling you that Nat was here should things get bad.'

'I just hope that nothing goes "bad" *now*. I want to see you in my office, the minute you get to the palace.'

He slid the van door shut so hard he thought it might've come off its hinges and then began to walk towards his car. He was quite shaken by the whole event and wrestled with the idea of Bob's unexpected and secretive behaviour. The cold air around him helped to gain some perspective. As he looked up he sighted the car and walked briskly towards it.

He sat quite still in the front seat for a few seconds until his composure returned and then suddenly realised he was still wired up. He pulled out the earpiece and left the pen in the inner pocket of his jacket. *This* he wanted to keep. It was imperative that he reached the palace before the bodyguards, so he started up the ignition and sped away. How could he prove that Bob and Nat had ulterior motives other than the explanation they gave him? He forced himself to refrain from thinking about it. Somehow, he needed to clear his mind and think logically.

The outer gates of the palace were quickly opened as the gatekeepers saw who it was. 'Have Bob and Nat driven through these gates as yet?' He asked as normally as he could.

'No sir. Not yet.'

Alex lost no time and quickly drove towards the palace. He parked the car at the rear and entered through a side door as he often did when he was a child and wanted to meet Alia. Instinctively, he had this sudden urge to speak to his wife and quickly walked in the direction of the main building. As he approached the entrance hall, he came upon Parkinson. 'Where is Her Highness?'

'At her office, I believe, sir.'

Alex turned in the direction of the staircase and went up the steps with sheer purpose, emboldened by his anger and immediately found himself at Alia's office. 'Jillian, is Alia in?'

'Yes, go right in.'

He opened her office door and shut it immediately behind

him and leaned against it for a few seconds. 'What's wrong? Are you all right?' Alia looked up from the paperwork in front of her and thought she saw a ghost.

'I don't know. I need to tell you something.' He felt his heart thumping as he sat on a chair and faced Alia behind her desk. 'I will have to be brief because I'm meeting Bob and Nat at my office shortly.'

He began to retell his ordeal of the whole day and in particular his surprised discovery of Bob's secret plan which was very conveniently not relayed to him. The account of the day was told with complete honesty and in detail. It somehow relieved the angst he felt by sharing the day's unusual events. 'There you have it. What do you think?'

'The first thing that comes to mind is you were placed in a very dangerous position and secondly, you have no hard evidence to the contrary of what Bob told you. The third thing is you were right not to take it on face value, but now what do we do with it?'

'Exactly my dilemma.' He looked up at Alia's beautiful face and totally opened his heart. 'I feel utterly spent – emotionally and otherwise, and I have a meeting with both of them, any second now.' He looked down at his wristwatch, closed his eyes and rested his head on the back of the chair. All he wanted was this nightmarish anguish to be dissolved permanently into the ether of infinity, by the time he opened his eyes again. He didn't hear Alia move from the chair, but he did feel her yielding soft lips on his, which he knew so well, and a pair of silky hands cradling his face. He looked up when those lips were removed from his, stood and entwined the love of his life so hard to his body, he never wanted to let her go. He just whispered into her neck, 'What are we to do?'

Alia found the familiarity of comfort in his embrace and allowed those old warm feelings of love permeate her very soul. She whispered into his chest, 'I can hold you like this forever,' and he kissed the top of her head and squeezed her a bit longer.

She looked up into his face and asked, 'Do you want me to come to this meeting with you?'

'This is something I have to sort out myself. I'll tell you the outcome of it.' He kissed the top of her head again, held her at arm's length, leaned forward and softly brushed his lips against hers and just before he left the room gave Alia the pen recorder and the ear piece. 'Put them in the safest place you have – that pen is very important.'

'I'll do it immediately,' she said as she clutched onto the things that Alex gave her.

Bob and Nat were in the waiting room as Alex arrived and told them to go into his office. He informed his personal assistant not to disturb them and hold all calls. Each man took his appropriate position and Alex proceeded in a calm and collected manner. 'What I'd like to know is why you found it so important not to inform me of your plan, Bob? I know you said you didn't want to place any more stress on me than what was already there, but considering we are dealing with *my* life, I felt it was necessary for you to tell me everything. As you can see, this has raised speculation as to whether I have faith in you anymore. So, what else have you not told me? I want the absolute truth.' Alex remained unmoved in his determination to find out everything.

'Sir, you have every right to demand the whole truth and in retrospect, it would have been best for you to know everything.' He looked over in Nat's direction. 'But we are not dealing only with *your* life. As you can see, Nat is a lot younger than me. He's come directly from the Secret Service in America and he told me that the Home Office, the President and the Secret Service are aware of the WSO that has taken hold in central and further west of Europe. It is his belief that the President is going to contact the queen, privately, not the government, and discuss the situation with her. The US has plans, which are under cover at present and when the right time presents itself, they will unleash their plans with overt force and covert identity.'

'Why the queen of Rubinia and not some other state?'

'Because the US is assured that the queen and her family are most definitely against this sinister growth of the WSO and there are long-standing relationships with each other.'

'How can the US be so "definitely" assured of that?' Curiosity got the better of Alex.

'Because of us,' and Bob pointed to himself and Nat.

'Explain yourself, Bob.'

'Even nine years ago when the princess visited America, the WSO was well known to the US. But, nothing was done about it, because there were rumours that Prince Gregory, at that time, wanted a union with the princess and to join

Rubinia to Cumbia. It was not thought the right time to approach Rubinia with such news, not knowing which way its loyalty lay.' He paused there for a moment and looked earnestly at Alex. 'But let me tell you sir, this has been going on for about twenty years – nothing new. But what is new, is that the WSO is ready to take action and has done so already.'

'Hence, Blake's big interest in the aerospace industry. I would not be surprised that he's embroiled with the WSO in some capacity. I'm sure he's thinking that the production of military spacecraft will make him a very, very rich man,' Alex remarked retrospectively.

'That's exactly right, sir.' Bob paused for a second or two and recollected his thoughts. 'That's the other reason I didn't say anything to you. I needed to know where *you* stood and whether you'd break down and sell him Einheimmer's small plant. If he gets his hands on that, there's no stopping him. He'll get your space engineering company in no time after that, by hook or by crook.'

'Assuming that everything you tell me is true, what's the next step?'

'Well, Dr Glandore, my contacts in the US recommend that you and the princess make a quiet trip to America, without raising any suspicions. It's been a while since a royal member has visited.'

'Why both of us?'

'Because your aerospace work is of the utmost importance to the success of this whole operation.'

'Well now, that makes sense.' Alex scrutinised both of

the bodyguards. 'So you are not here only as bodyguards, but spies, as well.'

'Not in the truest sense – it's sometimes done when there's an international crisis. But first, we have to find out who has been bugging your workplace and the palace. We can't tell anybody else, it's only you, me and a couple of others who know ... and Her Majesty and the princess will need to know too.'

'So let me get this straight. You're paid by the monarchy, but you also report to the Secret Service in the US. Right?' Alex stared at the two men.

'It's not so clear-cut – only during emergencies.'

'I think you're being evasive, Bob. I call that being a double agent. What do you call it?'

'Not really that.'

'Okay then, that being said, what are we going to do about tomorrow? Blake Crowley wants me back at his café office tomorrow by twelve. How are we going to avoid that without further consequences and damage?'

'Leave that with us. He's going to be highly occupied tomorrow.'

'How?'

'We are not at liberty to say.'

Alex stared at Bob suspiciously and thought there was no way to extract more out of him. The best action was not to delve too deeply in these smoke-and-mirror intrigues. 'We'll see how it evolves. I think that's about all, unless you have something more to say.'

'No, sir.' Bob looked at Nat who had remained silent for the entire meeting and together they left Alex's office.

When both bodyguards were outside on the palace grounds, Nat turned to Bob and asked, 'Do you think he believed you?'

'Not completely. He still has doubts.'

'Why didn't you tell him the whole truth?'

'I couldn't. I just couldn't!'

15

The next morning at Victor's Café, the sun had pushed through a few cumulous clouds and some rays found the elongated windows and welcomed the early customers heading for work with takeaway cups of hot coffee, tea, and chocolate, accompanied with an obligatory muffin, doughnut or savoury wrap. Soon, the early morning rush slowed down and waited for the brunch and lunch patrons that often left stuffy, heated office cubicles to enjoy the natural light and warmth of the sun while having a short break.

The waiters just started to seat some of the regular customers, when abruptly everyone within the café heard an enormous sharp *BOOM*, which liberally spread a radius of one or so kilometres and shook the elegance of those slim elongated windows. The noise volume radiated so loudly around the café walls and ceilings, that the custom-made furniture tumbled and broke on immediate contact with the floor. A paroxysm of percussion sounds gushed all around the room. Smoke began to billow quickly towards the main area of the café which was seized with sizzling tongues of fire. People started to panic with yells of 'FIRE, FIRE!' The upturned chairs and tables on the floor shook with each explosion that emanated from the back room. The chef came running out of the kitchen screaming, 'GET OUT, GET OUT! The kitchen will explode!' He ran straight into the main café room. He did not stop when he knocked down a young boy. His mother attempted to pick him up off the floor, while holding a crying baby on her hip desperately trying to escape from the burning rage that was quickly engulfing everything around her.

The fire engine sirens were screeching everywhere. Police loudspeakers blared at people to get away from the area. Fire hoses were reeled out and puddles of water lay dangerously on the sidewalks and on the streets as people stumbled and slipped, panic-stricken, to save their lives. Someone wearing dark glasses in a Mercedes limousine drove the car dangerously close to the scene of fire. A fireman yelled out fuming with anger, 'Get your blasted car out of there, NOW.' The man got in the car and backed it out of harm's way, but sat there riveted at the collapsed devastation, as if they were building-blocks in a playroom tumbling down at a child's frenzied tantrum.

The story broke on television news almost immediately. The brightly-dressed reporter in a double-breasted lime-green woollen coat and fire-red lipstick on her lips, animatedly spoke while she moved her hands around as if personally caught up in the seriousness of the situation.

This continued for approximately five minutes, and soon she too was told to remove herself and the cameras from the devastation of the scene.

After two-and-a-half hours, some order appeared to reign. The reporters and cameras disappeared, most people disbursed from the area and only two fire trucks remained to put out any sparks that might rekindle from the debris strewn ad hoc in the café site and on the street. Even the Mercedes limousine had vanished from the point of destruction.

Princess Alia's personal assistant received the newsflash immediately on her cell phone. She clicked onto the local news station and there, in cinematic colour, was the whole story. Immediately, she knocked on the Princess' office door, still holding the phone and looking at the flash pictures as the commentator presented them. 'Your Highness, you must see this.' She handed her phone over the desk and Alia looked on with disbelief.

'When did you get this, Jillian?'

'Just this minute.' She saw the Princess' concerned face as small lines formed across her brow.

'I'd like to borrow your phone for a moment.' Alia didn't wait to receive permission. She quickly got out of her chair and walked briskly to find Alex, not knowing if he were in the palace or at work. Her concern was so great that she ran straight into Nat. 'Have you seen Dr Glandore anywhere?'

'Yes, ma'am. He's just about to leave with Bob.'

'Run and stop them immediately!'

Nat bulleted down the staircase and vanished from the entrance hall with hardly a sound at his feet. Alia had reached halfway down the stairs when Alex and Bob re-entered the palace. As soon as Alex saw Alia, he sprinted towards her and they met midway on the staircase.

'What's wrong? Are you all right?'

'Oh, Alex! You've got to see this.' Alia handed the phone to him and as he scrolled through the news, he was visibly shaken by what he viewed.

When he absorbed the enormity of the situation, he turned sharply towards Bob and Nat who stood silently at the bottom of the staircase. 'In my office, both of you!' He looked quickly at his wife. 'I think you should come, too.'

'Try keeping me away,' and all four climbed the stairs where Jill still stood at the top. 'Just wait at your office and I'll bring back your phone.' She nodded and paused until they all disappeared into Alex's office.

Alex dismissed his personal assistant and asked her to take a long coffee break. He opened his office door and allowed Alia to enter and then Bob took control for the rest to follow.

'Tell me. Am I the last to know about this devastation at the café? Did you know, Bob?'

'Almost simultaneously as Her Highness. I thought it would be better to discuss this in depth at your workplace.'

'Okay, we're here at the palace, so let us discuss.' He could feel the tiny rumble of anger bubbling in his chest. 'Were you responsible for that?'

Bob looked blankly at Alex. 'No, I was not.'

'You mean to tell me you had no idea this was going to happen.'

Bob bided his time before he answered. He placed his hands together on his lap with fingers entwined and sat bolt-upright. 'I knew something was going to happen, but not this.' He drew in a deep breath and then exhaled. 'Dr Glandore, you must realise, whatever needs to be done will be done to overthrow the enemy.'

'What about the people? How many died in the fire?' Alex's voice was in danger of exploding at Bob.

'Accidents will happen. My job is to make sure that no accident happens to you or anyone in the palace. We need to sieve out those who are causing problems to the status quo in the world. As you said, sir, this is much bigger than you thought,' Bob tried to explain.

While the discussion was taking place, Nat scrolled down on his phone. 'Dr Glandore, it says here that no one died in the fire. Ten people were hospitalised with smoke inhalation, cuts, cracked ribs and a child with a broken arm.'

'This is not sitting well with me. It's one thing discussing it and another thing seeing it in action with devastating repercussions.' Alex could not abate his anger.

'Sir, this is more serious than we know.'

'So, what should we do, Bob? Just sit and do nothing while devastation happens around us?' Alia was in sync with Alex.

'Your Highness, you must go to the US as soon as possible. Tomorrow if you can. Things will be clearer by then. It's important for the queen to remain. We don't want a complete abandonment of the palace.' Bob hoped this might offer some compensation to the distressed couple.

'We haven't heard the results of your investigation on all the employees at the palace and at my workplace. Have you got them?' Alex found it hard to respond to Bob's comments.

'Yes. Came in just this morning. I was going to show you at your workplace, but here is just as well.' He then looked in Nat's direction. 'Will you get out the documents from the satchel?' Nat obliged and handed him two manila envelopes and Bob promptly gave one to Alex.

'Here are the results of the palace employees,' and he handed the other envelope to Alia.

Alex examined the list and noticed Ebba Nilsson's name had a red stamped asterisk next to it as did Jacob Einheimmer and Gustof Fischer. Explanatory notes were directly below their names.

Ebba Nilsson: daughter of Jacob Einheimmer and Clarissa Smith. Married to Roger Nilsson who died 2009. Born in Rubinia. Worked for Jacob Einheimmer as Personal Assistant. Attended night Business College and attained Diploma as a Computer Analyst 2010. Member of: League of Property Real Estate; Know Your Politics Club. A search of each of these Memberships revealed the following: League of Property Real Estate – how to invest in property and make a profit – ten members – all residents of Rubinia; Know Your Politics Club – a crash course in the system of politics that prevails in the world

– all residents of Rubinia. No police record or membership of any political party.

Jacob Einheimmer: son of Paolo Einheimmer and Ruby Johanson, now both deceased. Lived in Borovia during his formative years — family emigrated to Rubinia when Jacob was five years of age. Attended University of Zurich and graduated as a Chemical Engineer. Part of a research team at Zurich University in the developmental stages of aerospace travel. Worked as a consultant in this field and often travelled to France and Britain in their combined efforts to dominate the aerospace industry. Created his own aerospace company in 1996. Sold his business Aerospace United to Aerospace Engineering Centre in 2014. No police record or membership of any political party.

Gustof Fischer: son of Tobias Fischer and Hannah Pichler. Father deceased, mother in the Rosemont Nursing Home. Father was citizen of Rubinia and mother also citizen of Rubinia. Both born in Rubinia. Gustof attended Stanford University — Graduated with Honours and Masters in Aeronautics and Astronautics Engineering. Worked at the American Aerospace Federation in the USA. Now employed by Aerospace Engineering Centre in Rubinia, since January 2014. He is not a member or affiliated with any political party. No police record.

As Alex scanned the rest of the names on the list, all it produced was a scowl on his face. 'Bob, each of these inquiries has generic results, except for the revelation that Ebba Nilsson is Einheimmer's daughter. I wonder why he never told me – or she? No one has displayed any evidence to the contrary, other than your typical citizen – from the night watchmen right up to my CEO. So, why are Nilsson, Einheimmer and Fischer's names with a distinct asterisk by the side of their name?'

'We found a slight connection to these three. Each one either studied, worked, or lived overseas for a period of time. Nearly everyone else has remained in Rubinia. Now this may or may not be relevant. These names will be investigated, once more, in depth.' Bob suddenly thought there was a name missing. 'You didn't give us the name Lars Gilmar – he studied and lived overseas extensively.'

'Gilmar is not quite officially yet employed by me. No contracts signed so far. But Bob, I find it hard to believe, out of one hundred and fifty employees, or so, that only three or four lived overseas for a period of time.'

'Yes, sir. Of course, a lot of these guys have travelled around Europe, Britain and even America, but to have actually lived, worked or studied for a period of time in a country, it's these four. Ebba Nilsson, of course, travelled because her parents did and as a child, she went with them. People need time to develop contacts to further their cause.'

'I see a similar case with the list of employees at the palace, Bob. We're almost back to square one and the infiltrators continue to have the upper hand.' Alia looked quite concerned.

'Not for much longer, Your Highness. You can bet on that.'

'That sounds to me that you know more than you're letting on,' Alex challenged Bob.

'It could be, sir.' He then made eye contact with Alex. 'There are things when decisions are made that are beyond us. All I can say is be sure we will catch them.' He sensed Alex's mind ticking over and before he could utter a word Bob pre-empted him. 'And all we need to do right now is to bide our time and be alert as to anything unusual that happens both at the palace and at your workplace, Dr Glandore.' He saw the frustration and vexation that was written on the Princess' and Alex's faces. 'Believe me, it's not all doom.' He then added quite seriously, 'You've got your trip to the States and that should be your priority.'

Alex and Alia looked at each other and felt intensely the desperation of the whole situation. 'What concerns us, Bob, if we go tripping off to America, we leave totally open my workplace and the palace.'

'Yes, to a certain degree. But then, even when you were here sabotage happened and bugging devices were found in the palace and at your workplace. What I'm saying is whether you are here or not, these things will happen. If you both authorise the installation of more CCT videos at the palace and grounds and at your workplace, I'll make sure it's done before you return. We're bound to get lucky.'

'And how long is this trip supposed to be?' Alia sighed as she asked.

'Exactly four days, Your Highness.'

'So, you know the exact time. This is already organised,

isn't it?' Alex asked sharply.

'Yes, sir. I have your tickets for tomorrow.'

'Does the queen know?' There was an urgency in Alia's voice.

'Yes, ma'am. I told her today.'

'Are you going to brief us?'

'No, Dr Glandore. Everything will be done at the other end.'

Then again Alex asked, 'We're not using the royal airplane?'

'Too conspicuous! First Class in the "Airbus" Plane; the whole section to yourselves. Mike and Frank will go with you. I'll remain here at the palace with Nat and Kendal. As for your workplace, there'll be at least six or seven more bodyguards. I'm only sending two with you, but not to worry, you'll be surrounded by them the minute you hit American soil.'

'So much for not being too conspicuous.' Alex looked across at Alia. 'How do you feel about all this?'

'What other choice have we got? There is nothing else offered to us, or for us to offer anything else. We have to make the most of this one supposed solution.' Alia was exasperated.

'Exactly.' Alex turned and addressed Bob directly. 'Is there anything else? What time does the flight leave?'

'Eleven tomorrow morning. It would be a good idea that you tell no one you're leaving the country. I will organise it with your CEO and Chief Engineer. They will accept my story and hope news will not break here about your arrival in the US.'

'Is it going to be that much of a secret?'

'It all depends, Your Highness, on what the crew at the other end will decide.' Bob could sense their plight. 'I'm sorry, ma'am, that I'll not be with you. This will be the first time.'

'I know, Bob. It's fine.' Alia felt emotionally drained and she still needed to pack her own bag. 'I think we'll call it a day. Thank you.' Alia stood from the armchair and everyone else did the same.

The room was half emptied. 'I guess I had better go, too. I have a few loose ends to tie up before tomorrow morning.' Alex began to make his way towards the door in deep thought.

'Alex?' He stopped and turned to face her. 'Will you sleep in my bedroom tonight?'

He took three long strides towards her and encircled her in his arms. 'Yes, Alia. Don't worry. We'll see this through no matter what.' She remained in his reassuring arms for a while and then arm in arm they left the silent office room together.

16

Queen Sylvia was thoroughly briefed about the café disaster and immediately made plans to go and visit the people at the hospital who were hurt in the blast and ensuing fire. Nat and one of his assistants accompanied the queen. She directed her chambermaid to take out a navy suit and a pale-pink blouse which would be suitable for her to wear. Appropriate gifts were organised for each patient that she was to see. Her heart went out to these people, for somewhere in the core of that integral organ the blood was pumped with some drops of sorrow.

The entourage arrived at the hospital and the gifts were carried in baskets with colourful decorations of ribbons and bows. Each adult received a bunch of flowers and a small box of chocolates. She comforted them and asked questions about the blast and the fire. One woman said, 'Your Majesty, there was hardly any time to get out of there.' Another male patient was blunter and more vocal. 'Ma'am, I'd like to know who those "bastards" are. They need to be horse-whipped.'

Suddenly he realised his choice of language and looked up at the queen. 'Begg'n your pardon, ma'am,' he said remorsefully. 'You have every right to be angry. Thank God it wasn't worse.'

'And where was *He* when all this was happening?'

'Protecting your life, I believe.' The queen gave him an extra box of chocolates. 'For a quicker recovery.'

'Thank you, ma'am. Good-of-ya to come and see us,' and touched the side of his forehead with his middle and forefinger as a homage salute to the monarch.

The queen was keen to see the children's ward and the Head Nurse walked next to her having been told that she could not go ahead of Royalty as tradition dictated. Eventually they reached their destination and as they entered, all young eyes in the ward were on the queen. She asked to be taken first to the children who were involved in the fire and there towards the end of the ward were two beds: a young boy in one of them with his arm in a cast and a bandaged head.

The Queen walked directly to him. 'Hello. What is your name?'

'Ben,' whispered the boy.

'Ben, how do you feel? Are you in pain?'

'A little bit.' He spoke with his eyes downcast, focused on the blanket covering his bed.

'Do you like trucks?'

Soon the eyes were diverted and looked straight up at the queen. 'Yes,' was his monosyllabic answer.

Someone handed the queen a colourful covered box and

she handed it to the boy. 'Can you manage to unwrap it, or would you like me to help you?'

'My hand is sore.'

'I'll unstick the tape and you can pull off the wrapping paper with your good hand. Is that all right with you?' The queen asked gently.

'Yes.' They both managed to unwrap the present and pull out the truck from the carton and a trailer attached filled with building blocks. He was so taken up with the gift, he began playing with it immediately.

'What do we say to the queen, Ben?' the Head Nurse reminded him.

'Thank you,' he said with a smile.

The toddler in the next bed had her legs and hands bandaged. Her face and head seemed fine. The queen asked for the soft giraffe toy and gave it to the little girl. She lisped, 'Sank you,' and held the cuddly toy to her chest.

'You're welcome, my dear,' and the queen moved to each bed that was in the ward, spoke to every patient and gave out gifts to one and all.

She left the hospital with mixed emotions. As the queen sat in the back seat of the car, with Nat seated facing her, another assistant was in the front with the driver and she felt glad that the visit was made, but the devastation the blast caused was heart-wrenching. Replaying in her head the whole morning's event, it suddenly came to mind that Alia and Alex would already have left for the US and there too, her heart went out to both of them. They had gone through a lot in the last few years and now external events were challenging them.

As the royal limousine sped towards the palace, people recognised it along its journey and waved to the queen and she reciprocated in kind. It lifted her spirits to see this, but nonetheless, she was pleased to reach the palace. At the entrance gates, the senior gatekeeper came around to the side of the car insisting on speaking with Nat and he got out of the car.

'Look, there was an issue here, while you were away. We had strict instructions not to allow King Gregory into the palace grounds and he turned up demanding to be let in.' He paused there for a while and wiped his forehead with the back of his hand. 'He was hopp'n mad. We just kept on insist'n for him to go. Eventually he left, in a huff and a puff.'

'Was he alone or did he have anyone else with him?'

'There was someone else in the car – I dunno who, but the king got out of the car and ranted and raved.'

'Are you all right? You weren't attacked or anything?' Nat asked cautiously.

'Na, we can take care of ourselves.'

'Where were Bob and Kendal?'

'Bob went and bought the CCT videos and was installing them on the other side.' He raised his eyebrows and continued, 'I wasn't about to call out the Royal Guard.'

'You handled it well. Thanks.'

'What was that all about, Nat?' the queen asked upon his

return to the car.

'Oh, just a bit of a problem with the gate. I'll let someone know to come and look at it.'

This explanation did not sit very well with the queen, but she did not want to discuss it further with the driver there. As the car parked in front of the palace steps, the car doors were opened, and the queen got out. Nat followed her up the steps to where Parkinson stood ready to allow Her Majesty into the palace.

'Parkinson, we can always rely on you.'

'Ma'am,' he said and bowed his head.

'Nat, I want to see you in the private lounge now, please.'

They both went up the staircase and at the very top the queen's personal assistant waited impatiently. 'What is it, Laurence?'

'Your Majesty, you have been inundated with calls and there is a very urgent one.'

'I will be at my office shortly.' She turned to Nat and together they walked in the direction of the private lounge. They settled into armchairs and the queen looked at him for a few seconds without saying a word. Just as she was about to speak, Nat spoke up.

'Your Majesty, I couldn't speak with the driver in earshot, but there was a problem at the gate this morning while we were away. It appears King Gregory arrived with someone else in the car demanding to be let through the gates. This, of course, did not happen and he became very angry and left.'

'I'm glad you told me the truth, I wasn't sure if you would.'

'How do you know, ma'am, that it is the truth?'

The queen gave him an all-knowing look and simply said, 'You're not the only one who has inside information.' She stood indicating that the meeting was over. 'I will be in my office, should you need me.'

Nat quickly went to the door and opened it for her. He observed how she walked down the hallway with that quiet confidence he always admired.

Inside her office, her personal assistant looked concerned. 'Now, Laurence what seems to be the problem?'

'Your Majesty, we have had several calls from King Gregory insisting to see you and he simply wouldn't believe that you were not at the palace. As you probably know, the gatekeeper also informed me that he made a nuisance of himself at the front gates. What do you want to do?'

'We shall write a letter. Are you ready?'

'Yes, ma'am.'

To His Majesty the King,

    Dear Sir,

    It has come to my notice that in the course of this morning you have endeavoured to contact me without much success. Please be assured that I was absent from the palace and it was impossible for me to see you.

    If you still require an audience with me, let us make a time that is mutually acceptable. Perhaps next week, some time. A call to my personal assistant will rectify the situation.

    My best wishes to yourself and Their Majesties, your parents.

Yours faithfully

Her Royal Majesty, Queen Sylvia

'Laurence, make certain that this is posted out today. Now, what other intriguing calls did I receive?' They both settled down to the task at hand and acquitted their labour effectively.

17

About a three hours' drive into the land of Cumbia, King Gregory made a unilateral decision to call an Extraordinary General Meeting of the World Secret Order for that evening. He made the calls himself to retain the secrecy of the order. He rendered his outburst of anger and frustration, which occurred at the Rubinian Palace gates, to his intellect and vowed never to display this form of weakness ever again. Then, with some physical and mental effort, he reached a sense of equilibrium, which returned his perception of power and self-control.

The meeting was called at his country-house retreat about one-and-a-half hours' drive from his palace, some would need to come from a lot further away. It was empty and quiet there and King Gregory left earlier to go and switch on the heating system and warm up the house. It had not been used since summer. The car made its way up the drive and was parked at an angle to cue the other vehicles that were to arrive. Gregory entered the house and switched on the lights at the main electricity switchboard. The place looked a little gloomy with the cover sheets over all the furniture. He cleared the dining table and chairs and also removed the sheets from the rest of the furniture in the room. He brought some drinks and glasses on a silver tray from the sideboard and made certain that the old port was up front and centre. He found the ashtrays and placed some around the table to be used for Cuban cigars and cigarettes. There was no food, but by the time everyone arrived they would have had dinner. He could feel the heat radiating around the house.

The first to arrive was Vassili, sporting a furry hat on his head and earmuffs that cosily covered his ears. 'A lot warmer here than outside, Gregory.' He took off his coat, hat and gloves and proceeded into the dining room as he followed his host. Soon, within a minute of each other, all six were present and seated around the mahogany table. Brandy, whisky, bourbon, rum and port were generously shared between the members. Some took advantage of the cigars and cigarettes and very soon the mood was set.

'The meeting is to come to order,' Gregory called out. Everyone quietened down and focused on the President. 'I did not bring you out here in the cold for no reason at all. This extraordinary meeting is the result of some serious occurrences. It distresses me to think of one in particular. So, to begin with, why don't we discuss this one? I am certain that you all are aware of the blast at Victor's Café in the Cortesta District in Rubinia. I can assure you this was no accident. The enemy has already reared its ugly head. In the last twenty years we have been preparing for an event such as this. It is with deep regret that the café has been a total demolition exercise. Our good friend Blake Crowley has been set back, but not destroyed. He is part of our brotherhood and we shall help him financially and in any other way to recover his costs, whatever the insurance company does not pay. He is our eyes and ears outside this inner sanctum. I strongly stress that the acquisition of Aerospace Engineering Centre has become a priority as of this very minute. As for the royalty, they will pay their dues, shortly. Any comments up to now? Yes, Gunter.'

'I am pleased to report that our Secret Service Military and Reserve have been training strenuously with combined exercises in our forests' most northerly deserted mountains and they confirm that our troops are ready to face the enemy. There is just one thing that we are in dire need of – planes and more aeroplanes.' He looked directly at the President. 'I know, Gregory, that your wish is to be patient and slowly infiltrate his engineering industry.' He paused and pointedly stared at each member around the table. 'I don't think we have much more time to go slowly, slowly. We must act *now*! How many more blasts can we endure? How much longer are we going to give him to strengthen his industry day by day?' A poignant pause ensued and his demeanour instantaneously found its softer side. 'According to my insider at his plant, it's becoming harder and harder to acquire information. Obviously, he and others in his employ have woken up to some of our plans.' There suddenly arose whispers among some members. 'Gentlemen, this does not mean that things are not under control. They are!' He spoke emphatically, and confidence returned to the table. 'What I want to gauge from this meeting is when are we going in for the *kill?*' His voice deflected loudly on the last word and charged the room with a riotous applause and many words of 'hear, hear' echoed well past the dining room door. His speech again was reduced to a quieter tone. 'All we need, gentlemen, is the sanction to action from everyone in this room and we will be ready to go, if only on the ground.' Confidence spread with unstoppable inspiration around the room.

Gregory remained completely unaffected by the euphoria around him. He sat back in his chair and with cagey precision chose the exact moment to speak. He stood and waited till silence reigned around him. 'Gentlemen, it warms the cockles of my heart to hear the enthusiasm with which you received Gunter's suggestions.' As he spoke, he began to walk behind the seated members at the table. His circular pathway was driven with purposeful intention and cynicism. 'There is something in what Gunter says. *But,* at no time whatsoever, should we let our emotions get the better of our head. In one breath we are ready to unleash our military, with which we have taken pains and guarded it in secrecy all these years, and in another we have no air cover to support our ground manoeuvres.' Suddenly, he stopped directly behind Gunter and he lowered his head towards him. 'What do you think of that, Gunter?' Gregory didn't wait for his answer. Round and round he continued. 'I agree wholeheartedly that the aerospace industry in Rubinia has to be ours – there's nothing like it anywhere in Europe or countries in its vicinity. It is important to stick to our original plan. Yes, we've had one setback and we will address this, and as much as I would like to unleash our forces upon them, they will be expecting us to react with vengeance. I say, let us foil them. When we have gained control of the airspace, then I will expect another resounding applause for action.' He returned to his chair but remained standing in front of it and the table. 'And who else has something to say?' He sat as Vassili began to speak.

'You will all be pleased to know that many schools have begun to change their curriculum. Slowly but surely, from young to old, children are becoming indoctrinated with our cultural thinking. They desire to think for themselves, rely on their intellect and support their understanding with physical facts that are the cornerstones of thinking. As I mentioned at our last one hundred and twenty-sixth meeting, we are slowly but surely erasing the notions of religious thoughts, allegiance to national flags and anthems, which confuse the students and their intellect. More importantly, I was determined that one school in particular needed to be infiltrated and begin this process of thinking.' There he paused and looked directly at Gregory. 'The Palace International School.'

Gregory straightened his back from the comfortable position, stood and applauded enthusiastically. 'Well done, well done, Vassili.' Everyone else joined in the chorus with some adulations. 'This is what I call progress.' When the air cleared of the jubilations, Gregory spoke again. 'I know that you are all trying your very best and will continue to do so. I have heard of your successes in all areas and I am pleased. However, there is one prime importance. We must totally capture the aerospace industry in Rubinia. I have been thinking and in a little while, depending on certain outside factors, I believe our objective will be made possible. At present I cannot elaborate any further. In fact, when the news breaks, you will all understand the connection.' He stared down at his wristwatch and saw that it was late. 'Friends, time is of the essence. We have been here for a few hours and must return to our homes. I appreciate your loyalty and support for our cause and this will not go unrewarded. I personally have a lot to accomplish over the next few weeks. Each of you will be kept abreast with developments, not by any technological contact – they are too easily penetrated. You will receive your written code and each of you will know where to meet me. Thank you for attending spontaneously on this cold night.'

Each member left the house with expectations of better things to come and their goodbyes and handshakes were warmly received and exchanged. Gregory was the last to go. He placed the sheets once more over the table and chairs, switched off the heating system and the lights at the switchboard and shone a small torch attached to his key ring to light the path to his car. It was very dark outside. No

17

evidence was to be seen that an urgent meeting had taken place in the house which formed the backdrop as Gregory's shoes crunched the gravel and walked towards his Jaguar vehicle. The clouds above appeared ready for snow as the bleak northern front brought a bitingly chilly wind and he pulled his scarf closer around his neck. He couldn't wait to get back to his warm palace.

18

Queen Sylvia woke to white soft drops of snow and as she looked outside from her window, it never ceased to amaze her how beautiful the blanket of snow appeared all around the palace. A kind of enchantment fell upon the garden with small creatures scurrying quickly to find their winter beds and some deer who boldly dared to approach the palace stared wide-eyed in the hopes of finding food before the snow rapidly covered all their hopes. It was almost six thirty and she needed to shower and dress. The knock on the door announced her chambermaid, and a quick discussion as to the appropriate form of clothing for the morning was effectively done. Soon she presented herself in a smart royal-blue dress and matching jacket and briskly walked towards the staircase.

There at the top of the stairs she met Stephan. 'Are you going for breakfast?'

'Yes grandmamma ... but I don't want to have it up in the nursery. Can I have it with you in the dining room?' he implored her.

'With such a sweet little face, how can I say no? Come along with me.' She turned to Susanna. 'I'll be fine with him. Come in about three-quarters of an hour.' Hand in hand with her grandson, they both went down the winding staircase. The dining room door was suddenly opened as they approached.

'Parkinson, just in time. Thank you.' He did not respond, just bowed his head.

In the dining room, the aroma of freshly brewed coffee, tea, mulberry pancakes, eggs, bacon, sausages, sautéed mushrooms, toast, and marmalade filled the room around them. 'So what would you like?'

'Pancakes and one sausage and chocolate milk.' One of the attendants in the room filled Stephan's plate with what he asked and promptly gave him the hot chocolate milk as well.

The queen asked to move the table setting next to her grandson. There they sat and ate their breakfast and chatted about school, the snow, sport, drawing and reading. Then out of the blue Stephan asked something quite unexpectedly. 'Grandmamma?'

'Yes, Stephan.' The queen reached over and drew a few strands away from his forehead.

'Do you believe in God?'

'That's a very big question for a little boy.' She looked carefully at her grandson and could see he was serious about his question. 'Well, yes I do. I am the Head of the Church, you know.' She placed her cutlery on the plate in front of her and gave him her full attention, but not before she dismissed the attendants from the dining room. 'Do *you* believe in God?'

'I think so.' He left his cutlery half on the plate and the other half on the placemat. 'You know, Papa believes, too.' He turned and fully faced his grandmamma. 'I'm not sure, because my teacher says that there is no God and we should not believe in fairytales. I didn't know God was a fairytale. I thought he was real.'

'And who was the teacher who told you this, Stephan?'

'Ms Barbour ... she's very nice to us. I don't understand if God is real or not.'

'Let me ask you, Stephan, do you love your Papa and Mummy?'

'I do ... '

'Tell me, can you see "love" ... the feeling of love especially when they are with you?'

'Not really ... but I can see it when they hug and kiss me and play with me.'

'And what about the times you do not see them, and they are far away. Do you still think they love you and feel their love in your heart?'

'Yes, I can.'

'Well, that's how God is. Even though we can't see Him, He is there always loving us, protecting us and helping us when we pray to Him.'

'Do you pray, Grandmamma?'

'Of course, I do. All the time. Especially about you, young man.' She observed the serious face that looked up at her own. 'Do you know Stephan, there are some people who do not believe in God. We have to respect their beliefs, but then they also have to respect people who do believe. No one should force the other to believe what *they* want them to believe. I think that's only fair. What do you think?'

'I think so, too.' A frown crossed his brow as he asked, 'Why did Ms Barbour tell everyone that it's wrong to believe in God?'

'I guess she has a very strong belief that there is no God, so she wanted everyone else to believe the same.' Then with a sunny smile and a straightening of her back the queen continued, 'But we are strong in God and no one can make us change that, either.' She soon reached out, ruffled his hair and tickled his sides to squeals of laughter.

Susanna arrived during this display of frivolity and smiled at the whole scene as she stood by his side and waited to take him to his first lesson for the day. 'Do I have to go, Grandmamma?'

'If you want to learn lots of wonderful things and be a clever boy, then you should go.' She leaned over and kissed him on the head. 'I'll see you later in the day.'

As the door shut behind them, the queen sat back in her chair and a sombre, serious mood came over her. She sat there mulling over what transpired between Stephen and herself. *They've already infiltrated our school and who knows what else. How and why did it happen?* Her thoughts were unceremoniously disrupted as she heard the door open and there stood Bob and Kendal.

'Ma'am, we've installed a whole lot more CCT videos here and at the engineering plant. We've viewed all the videos and not one shows any suspicious character. We did, however, find quite a few blind spots with the old camera locations. So, now we hope we've covered everything.' He stopped talking and looked a little closer at the queen: she appeared wan and weary. 'Your Majesty, is there anything I can do for you?'

'Take a seat, Bob.' He came into the room while Kendal remained outside the door. He sat in one of the chairs with the dining table between them. 'Who is the other bodyguard? I've not seen him before.'

'Ma'am, his name is Kendal. He's been here for about six months, but he's young, strong and has a sharp brain to think outside the square ... I think that's important – especially the way things stand now.'

'I leave all these matters to you. I know you choose your men well.' The queen looked directly at Bob and proceeded to explain her conversation with her grandson. 'Let's see if we can think outside the square here as well. I have a copy of our school's curriculum and one subject which is compulsory for all students up to the tenth grade is World Religions. This helps students to understand how religion is an integral part of culture within a country. Knowledge of other people's culture gives us understanding and better communication with each other. It helps to alleviate prejudice and racism. The thing is the WSO has infiltrated our school. How could this happen?'

'Quite easily, Your Majesty. These organised "Orders"

18

have sleek operators. They induce some of the top people from all around the world and pay them well to remain there. So, if they can do that, it's easy to convince a young teacher in a primary school. The best thing is to tail the teacher and see who the other contacts are. If we can gather them up and interrogate them, we might find out a bit more. Does that meet with your approval, ma'am?'

'Of course, it does. You must do what you think is best.' She sighed involuntarily. 'Have you heard from Princess Alia and Dr Glandore?'

'Yes, ma'am. They have had a successful touchdown in the States.'

'Well, at least that's something positive.'

'Your Majesty, I need you to be very careful and very alert. If you think that there is something not quite right, report it to me immediately.' The queen stood and Bob followed suit. 'Ma'am, I'm confident that with the new security installations in the palace, around the grounds and at the engineering plant, we will have some success.'

'Thank you, Bob. Continue the good work,' and with that she left the dining room, not knowing whether she should be alarmed or accept everything at Bob's word.

19

The Airbus plane touched down at Washington Dulles International Airport and the tyres screeched as they almost came to a complete halt. It taxied very slowly towards the designated gate number and Alex and Alia gazed out of the window at the numerous planes already comfortably berthed at each gate. They both took this short space of time not to specifically think of the significant task that was to follow. Their personal flight attendant broke into their peaceful moment as she approached them. 'Ma'am, sir, we'll allow you to disembark first, before the other passengers. If you wish, I will take your luggage to the front of the plane.'

Before either of them could respond, Mike was directly next to her. 'No thank you. I'll deal with that.' He called Frank over and between them organised the luggage.

Alia stood and stretched to soften her shoulder muscles. Alex extended his arms unceremoniously and when he let them drop by his side, he reached for Alia's hand and together they made their way down the aisle. They thanked

19

the flight attendants and soon sighted their two bodyguards and walked calmly towards them. As their eyes met in the expansion of this unique airport space, they became conscious of being surrounded by three secret servicemen who directed their small party of four into a private lounge. How different it all was from the first time Alia landed at this airport: the guard of honour, the bands, the flags, the people and the cheerful colour of voices that filled the air. Not so now, but then the pressure exerted upon them of late was absent at that time.

As they entered the private lounge, they clapped eyes on the Vice President and a small entourage consisting primarily of security staff. The Vice President stood immediately as he saw his guests. He walked confidently and precisely towards the princess and the doctor. 'I welcome you both to my country, ma'am and sir.' He gave a slight bow of his head and extended his arm for a handshake first with Alia and then with Alex. 'An honour to meet you both.' He took one step back and spoke to both of them in a most serious manner. 'I must apologise from the outset. Not everything is going to be done in the customary way you're used to. Your protection and secret arrival are the key things here.' His solemn voice had been chiselled and polished through many years of bureaucratic interplay. He asked them to follow his personnel through some uncharted corridors, twists and turns, very rarely taken by passengers who entered this country.

They were soon ushered into a vehicle without any specific

markings of identification. It could have belonged to anyone. The thickly-tinted glass provided just the cover they needed. The Vice President sat in the back seat with Alia and Alex, which helped him to communicate with one of the security men in the front seat. A stream of words were exchanged between them and then the Vice President proceeded to tell Alia and Alex, 'Tony has just reminded me that the car will park in the back area of the White House so your entrance will be more secure and secretive.' He glanced at the young couple, who had not much to say and he truly felt for them. His duty was to begin this drama with a successful "touchdown", which was also the code name for this secret operation.

'Mr Vice President, were you ever in the secret service or military?' Alex had to break the tense atmosphere in the car.

'Why yes. In the secret service. How did you know?' He stared curiously at Alex.

'Oh, just a lucky guess. I take you for a man of discipline and order.'

'Your deductive powers are very impressive, sir.' He then tapped Tony on the shoulder and looked dead straight ahead of him. 'When we stop, go ahead and make sure everything is clear.'

'Yes, sir,' came the prompt reply from Tony. If he were standing, Alex thought he would have given a snappy smart salute with a resounding acknowledgement from the Vice President.

As the car drew near the electronic front gate, Alia

looked through the hazy dark window only to see the senior gatekeeper was the same man she had encountered on her first visit. She quickly looked away as he endeavoured to see who was in the car. Eventually, Tony jumped out, pulled out some identification papers and soon the small party of people reached the rear entrance of the White House. All five quickly got out and headed towards a semi-opened door leaving Tony and Ben, the driver, to bring in the luggage.

Alia clung tightly onto Alex's arm and together they were ushered towards the elevator to take them upstairs to their bedroom. They were asked if they wished one or two bedrooms and both simultaneously voiced 'one.' Alia pressed her cheek into his upper arm and whispered, 'I can't wait for privacy in our room.' Alex just squeezed her hand to indicate he understood and concurred. The guest bedroom suite was grandly spacious with a lounge area, sofa and armchairs including a four-poster bed sporting posts in oak with a curtained canopy of cream silk and fringes. 'Oh, Alex, what have we got ourselves into? I think it's really getting to me now.'

'You're just tired. We'll get an early night's sleep. Are you hungry? Shall I order something?' They both sat on the edge of the bed and Alex had his arm around Alia's shoulders.

'No. I'll have a drink of water and then go into the shower.' Alia stood and Alex did likewise — he went to open the bags and she went directly to the shower. As he unpacked, the sound of water gushing from the shower head could be heard while he finished hanging up all their clothes. Alia came out from the bathroom with a towel around her body and a shower cap over her hair. 'I didn't take any nightie into the bathroom with me.'

'I've placed a couple on the bed. The rest are in the closet.' He paused at what he was doing and observed her as she moved lithely around the bedroom. Her grace and beauty always affected him. He sighed as she picked up a nightie and retreated into the bathroom to wear it. 'How things have changed,' he thought, 'but then there are more serious things to consider at this point in time'.

20

The morning brought a wake-up call for a meeting with the President and the head of the Secret Service. Alia and Alex were already dressed as their breakfast was brought into their suite. One of the bodyguards who escorted them from the airport came in wheeling a trolley with an array of breakfast food. 'Ma'am, sir. Your appointment with the President is in forty-five minutes. I'll come and take you to the office.' He was thanked and with that he left the room.

'So unemotional and businesslike, isn't he?'

'He has to be, Alia. Emotion gets in the way of straight thinking and quick thinking. Don't forget he's got our lives in his hands.' Alex tried to find a middle ground of understanding.

Breakfast was set up at a round table that was pushed away from the window, with all the finery of a silver service accompanied with crystal. As they sat there, conversation came naturally to them. 'What are you going to do about work, Alex?'

'When we go back, I'll have to make some very hard decisions. I'll be interested to see what Bob comes up with while we've been away. What I can't understand is why Einheimmer didn't tell me about Ebba being his daughter and why he thought Les Gilmar is up to no good. How does he know that and who in the end do you believe?' His fork was suspended in mid-air with a small piece of bacon dangling at the end of it, as he contemplated his situation.

'Try not to think too hard about it. We still have all of this to deal with here.' Alia paused a few seconds as she sipped tea from fine china. 'There's also so much going on at the palace. I wonder how Mother is getting on.'

At that juncture there was a knock on the door and a couple of bodyguards entered. 'We're ready to go, sir, in ten minutes,' they were told with some urgency. Soon, they were both ready to meet the President as they were escorted by two bodyguards. In the hallway, they saw Mike and Frank waiting for them. As they continued along the hall of the White House, it impressed Alia's mind, as if a conduit in the present connected with vivid memories of the past — of the joy in being shown around the Monroe Room all those years ago. It was as if she stepped back in time to relive the pleasure of those images, which now were bittersweet because she could not share them with Alex who walked beside her and held her hand.

They arrived in a part of the White House that Alia did not recognise. The hallway they turned into was narrower, the runner on the floor appeared well trodden and the walls

20

were not adorned with any priceless pieces of art, although there were some attractive copies. Suddenly they stopped in front of one of the many similar doors they had walked past. The sound of 'Come in' was clearly heard. One of the bodyguards went in and a few seconds later came out again and ushered Alia and Alex in the room. It was a makeshift office with a desk, an opened computer prominently displayed, some padded chairs and a satchel by the side of the desk. The two men who stood in the middle of this sparse and small room were the President and the Head of Secret Services. 'Your Highness, Dr Glandore, a pleasure to meet you.' As the President shook hands with both of his guests, he introduced Gus Herbert. Alia and Alex responded appropriately and soon they all sat on the chairs, which were placed in a semi-circle for the meeting to start.

'Let's begin with the WSO. For a long time, we have been aware of this secret Order. At first, it was of no threat and to a certain extent we expected it to fizzle away.' The President looked at his guests and with a wry smile nodded his head. 'As you well know this has not happened. We are here, however, to reverse the situation. Our understanding is that the tactics used are covert and dangerous. We cannot stand by and allow this to happen. Our allies are with us and we want to minimise the damage that will occur. At this point I will let Gus continue.'

The President sat in his chair as Gus stood and began to pace the bare boards in the room. 'I'm not happy with what's going on and we'll have to *crush* some people.' As he voiced the word crush, the pound of his fist in his hand was heard. 'Madam, sir, we are not brutal people, but our choice of action has to be swift to succeed. They are thugs of the worst kind. They are the whisperers of evil in people's ears – of old and young – no age is exempt. Action is near ... there is no more time to waste.' He continued to walk and talk in the same vein as if he were talking to himself. Suddenly he came to a sharp halt. 'Madam, sir, there is no action for *you* to take, leave everything to us.' He was about to continue with his ardent address when the President intervened.

'What Gus means to say is that we have safe and assured plans ready to go to stop this threat that is confronting us. At this stage, Your Highness, sir, we feel it would be best that you sit tight and do nothing that will ...' He paused a couple of seconds to think of the appropriate word, 'endanger any of our plans.'

'Mr President, Mr Herbert, with all due respect, how can we just fold our hands and wait like idle statues while we see *our* nation being infiltrated by such monstrosities.' Alex turned sharply and stood simultaneously, 'You do not live there nor does it appear to affect you here in this country. How can we not do anything? Which, by the way, brings me on to another topic. Were you responsible for that blast in the café in Castelneuf?' By this point Alex was starting to show his impatience.

'Sir, we know *nothing* about that and even if we did, we couldn't tell you. All I can say is that we need your endorsement. I know we are thousands of miles away, but

20

we need your support.' Gus Herbert was a stocky man of medium build which did not attract anything specific about him, but the face separated him from others. While he spoke, his expressions were intensely focused, unblinking pale grey eyes, as their appearance seemed set on future visualisations.

Alia was on her feet by this time and stood next to Alex. 'Do you know that people were hurt in that blast? Blood was spilled and this will incite our enemies to revenge this act. Where is it going to stop?'

Emotions were high and the President stood as well. 'Let us try and use our rationale.' He then closely observed his two guests. 'What happened in that café will draw them out, force their hand openly. We will know who they are and how many there are. I have to agree with Gus, you need to go along with us. The other thing you will need to consider is your positions. You must not be seen to be involved in any of this. Leave it up to the experts. We are allies, after all. You, Dr Glandore, worked in this country for quite a few years.' He then turned and looked at Alia. 'As I have heard, Your Highness, you visited this country with such resounding success that we all felt a special bond by the time you left. I know it's sad that circumstances are not the same, but the bond is still there for us. We hope that it's there for you too.'

Alia drew in a deep breath. 'Mr President, there is no question about our bond with each of our nations – that is not the point. The point is this situation must be handled with as little violence as possible. I am not that naïve as not to know some force may occur. But we don't also want a "gung-ho" attitude on all of this. Surely there must be ways to overcome this secret Order. You have one of the most efficient secret service forces in the world. I'm certain they can infiltrate the WSO systems they've set up and disable them. If we are to support you, a constant contact with each other as to what is happening must exist between us.'

'Perhaps Gus can answer this.'

'Ma'am, we would try as best we can, but we cannot promise continual contact. It is best for you not to know everything. If things get really bad, and they may do, you'll be in a better situation if you don't have inside knowledge of our plans ...'

Alia impatiently interrupted him. 'Mr Herbert, you know more than you are saying, and you will not reveal anything else to us. Isn't that exactly what you mean?'

Gus looked at the President for an answer and he received one with a nod of his head. 'Yes, ma'am, that's exactly what we mean.'

'Well, thank you for an honest answer, at long last.' Alia was well on the way of irritation.

'Alia, we have no other option. It is clear to me.' Alex tried a conciliatory approach.

'Dr Glandore, your aerospace industry is of the utmost importance in this whole scenario. It is imperative that the WSO does not get their hands on your engineering company.' The President spoke urgently and passionately to Alex. 'We know the problems you have had there, and

20

we are prepared to reverse this situation. Are you willing for us to do this?'

'You are asking *me*, Mr President, when you very well know I have no other option but to say yes.'

'Well, that's good. We have made long strides towards finding some solutions and greater understanding of where we're all at.' The President looked at Alex and Alia and in a kindly manner suggested that the meeting come to an end. 'We shall meet again tomorrow and bring more definition to our plans without giving anything away.' He walked up to his two guests who stood closely to each other and gave each a warm handshake. 'Will you join me for dinner tonight in our second dining room – it's more private.' He bowed his head slightly and walked out of the room followed by two of his bodyguards. Alex and Alia watched as they all disappeared from sight.

'Ma'am, sir, are you ready to return to your bedroom?' One bodyguard came and stood in front of them, the other stood behind them. They all left the room and marched down the hallway.

21
· · · · ·

In the privacy of their room, Alia and Alex sat facing each other in comfortable armchairs. It was natural for them to examine and analyse the meeting they had attended. 'Did you realise, Alex, that much of what they were telling us was, more or less, similar to what Bob had to say. I don't like being left in the dark as to what goes on.'

'I agree ... in a way. I understand what they were both trying to say and perhaps the less we know the safer we may be – I think? I'm not sure.' Alex leaned forward with his elbows on his knees and buried half of his face in his hands.

'No matter which way we look, there are difficulties.' Alia sat there quietly for a full half a minute, then suddenly jumped out of her armchair and clapped her hands together. 'Right, we're not going to sit here and brood. Let's go out in the garden and breathe fresh air and check out what grows in the cold here. I don't suppose they'll let us go out and have lunch somewhere.' Alia stood next to Alex's armchair and extended her arm to take his hand. 'Come on – up you get.'

21

Lazily, he lifted his hand towards hers and as she clasped it, he surprisingly pulled her onto his lap. He stared down at the familiar face he knew nearly all his life and traced the contours of her mouth and eyes with his forefinger. 'You're just an angel,' and with that he leaned down and brushed his lips with hers as if a feather had touched them. He noticed Alia had closed her eyes and was unwilling to open them until she felt the sensation of his lips once more on her eyelids. 'Are you now ready to get up?' he whispered in her ear.

'Yes, I am,' she said just as softly as his whisper.

'Come on, then,' Alex responded in a louder voice, which had the effect of causing Alia to open her eyes and blink them into focus.

'And I was just getting comfortable.' Alia stood and playfully endeavoured to pull him off the armchair, as well. 'Do you think we can escape from them and go out without their knowledge?'

'You're a better person than I, if you can pull that off.'

Both walked slowly to the door and Alia carefully opened it a tad, just enough to catch a glimpse of Mike and Frank astutely patrolling the hallway. Still holding onto the door handle, she turned to Alex and mouthed that there were two out there. In the process of trying to accomplish her furtive communication with her husband, a loud knock was heard from the other side of the door. 'Madam, sir, is everything all right in there?'

Alex smiled at Alia as he shook his head and instantaneously the door was swung wide open. 'Oh, there you are, Mike, Frank. We were just wondering if we can get out from here and go for a walk in the garden?' Alia asked sweetly.

'Well, not without us two. I'll need first to let the Yankee team know before we go anywhere.' Immediately he contacted the appropriate person with as little dialogue as possible. 'It seems we can – but cover up, camouflage yourselves with hats or beanies.' To soften the tone and reality of the situation he added, 'Besides, it's freezing out there.'

Alex and Alia looked at each other and knew exactly how the other felt. Alex rummaged in the closet in an effort to look for beanie hats, knowing fully well that they did not bring any with them. Mike came to the rescue. 'I think, sir you will find them in the third drawer, right.' Mike informed him.

'You think of everything, don't you?' Alex blurted while trying to help Alia wear her purple knitted hat on her head. 'Not exactly made by the Royal Milliner, is it?'

'We aim to please, sir.'

'Hmm,' Alex grunted and pulled the navy beanie hard over his head.

'Come on, let's go, or it'll soon get too dark to walk outside.' Alia gave a light giggle as she saw Alex all trussed up for the outdoors. He reacted by taking her hand and pulling her close by his side.

Mike and Frank gave them a little bit of space for some privacy. 'There's always a first time for everything. Never wore a beanie hat before,' she announced.

21

'You look enchanting, madam.' Alex glanced towards Alia and brought her leather-gloved hand to his lips.

'Oh, you're such a charmer!' She then brought his bare hand to her lips and kissed it. 'You must be freezing without gloves.'

'There are a couple of mittens in this jacket, but I'll be darned if I'm going to wear them. They remind me of my school days when I worked in Mr Hollenbrook's café and had to wear them to ride my bike home.'

'I remember those days with so much joy. Do you remember when we gave you a lift in our car on your way home from Hollenbrook's during a blizzard? Yet you kept peddling on.' She was silent for a moment and then added thoughtfully, as if she were reliving the scene right there, right now. 'I loved you so much.'

'And now?'

Alia turned and glanced at Alex's profile. 'Now? I can never erase those years and the love I felt.' She looked down at the scant snow that covered the ground. 'Now? I wish I could feel those exact feelings I had back then – with the same purity and intensity.' Her voice was almost reduced to a whisper and suddenly she felt his strong hand take her other arm and forced her to a halt.

'It can still be like that ... do you want it to be like that between us? As you said, that feeling can never be erased. It's still there in both of us.'

'We're older now. Responsibilities and life's everyday pressures come between us. I don't know if we can relive what we had.' Alia's doubts boomed in Alex's head.

Just as Alex was about to respond, he heard the crunching sound of boots coming towards them. Mike and Frank quickly swung around in the direction of the noise and realised it was one of the National Marine Servicemen. He approached them speedily and as he spoke, small billows of warm mist escaped his mouth. 'You're all getting too close to the border of the garden. I think it's best to come in.' They soon began to walk back on the same path and the Marine approached Alex and Alia, somewhat hesitantly. 'Ma'am, sir, we've set up movies for you both to see in the cinematic theatre room. You have a lot of movies to choose from.'

'Thank you. I'm sure we'll find one that we like.' Alex took Alia's hand and moved quickly towards the back entrance of the White House, while the three men kept pace with both of them. It seemed colder all of a sudden, but they continued with their trek.

Inside they were both pleased to remove their thick bulky padded jackets and especially the beanies. Alia shook her head of hair and ran her fingers through the chestnut locks that graced her face. 'Alex and I need to go to our room before the movie viewing. What time is dinner?'

The Marine answered, 'Six-thirty for cocktails and seven for dinner.'

'Well, we've got plenty of time,' and without waiting for a response she took Alex's hand and together began their way to their bedroom with Mike and Frank promptly following

21

them. 'This is really getting to me. I feel like a prisoner in a five-star luxury establishment. How do you feel?' She spoke softly so not to be heard by their keepers.

'Not the best. I'm starting to resent this total control they have over us. But Alia, a lot of it is for our protection, if you stop and think about it carefully.'

'I'm getting sick and tired with the whole thing, carefully or otherwise.' She placed her head on Alex's upper arm and her arm went around his waist as Alia spoke into his thick jacket in a muffled voice so she could not be heard. 'We're supposed to be here for four days. How about we cut this visit short and go back home tomorrow.'

'Let's wait and see what the President has to say to us tonight and whether it's necessary to stay for the duration of our visit.' Alex had the mitten out in his hand with the pretext that he coughed intermittently into it to cover his real intention of the conversation.

Glad to come face to face with their door, they opened it quickly before Mike or Frank had a chance to close it for them and they went in without a word to anyone. 'What a relief! Thank God we're alone!'

'It's affected you badly, Alia. Do you want to sit here and talk or watch a DVD? There's a bunch of them over there.' Alex pointed to the drawer.

'I would love nothing better, but it'll be construed as very rude of us and we can't do that to our host.'

He looked at her flushed cheeks from the cold crisp air they had encountered outside, and he might as well have been looking at a renaissance painting. 'I, uhm, guess you're right.' Alex looked at his watch and realised it was a quarter to five. 'I have an idea. In an hour and a half, we need to be ready for cocktails with the President. Why don't we say that it doesn't give you enough time to rest before dinner, so we can't go to the cinema room.'

'Why just *me*? I think we should use the plural *us*.'

'Okay, okay. I'll be in good company.' He ruffled her hair as he walked by and opened the door to inform the bodyguards of their decision. He then closed the door and approached the bed, threw himself on it and stretched out with a yawn only to find that his fingers touched some buttons on the side of the bed. He fiddled about with the push buttons and discovered that one of them was for heating the bed. He pressed it and waited for the heat to spread over the entire bed as if a warm wave of water had flooded the mattress and penetrated its warmth up to the top bedspread. Alia came and laid down beside him. 'It's warmer under the bedspread and blanket,' he said half sheepishly.

She suddenly jumped off the bed, threw the bedspread onto the chaise lounge at the foot of the bed, took off her shoes and quickly ducked in between the sheets. 'Well, come on. It was *your* suggestion.'

By the time he took off his shoes and thick sweater, he noticed Alia's eyes were half closed. He slipped into the bed beside her and gently held her hand as he too drowsed off to a sweet release from their problems.

22

They woke to the sound of a strong knock. Alex answered as Mike poked his head around into the room. 'Sir, it's six o'clock and cocktails are at six-thirty.'

'Thanks, Mike. We'll get up and be ready on time.' He turned over to where Alia was on her side trying to gain a few more moments of rest. 'Come on, sleepy head. Up and away.' A quick kiss on the cheek brought some intelligence to the sleeper.

'Do I really have to?'

'I'm having a quick shower and you can get in after me,' and with that he disappeared into the bathroom.

Eventually, they were both ready when the knock on the door came again. They soon found themselves in the company of Mike and Frank who diligently escorted them towards the second dining room. There they found the President standing by the fireplace with champagne in his hand. He left the glass on the mantlepiece and graciously walked towards the couple. 'Your Highness, Dr Glandore.

A pleasure to see you again. Come in.' He turned and faced what appeared to be a waiter. 'Dex, a drink for our guests.' Another turn and he came back face to face with his guests. 'I had to use some of my secret servicemen to serve so we can retain our anonymity.'

Alex responded, 'They appear to be doing a good job.'

The three of them stood next to each other, all immaculately dressed and chatted about everything else except what was foremost on their minds. However, they bided their time to be sure that when it was right, each would have something worthwhile to say. Soon one of the waiting staff came next to the President. 'Mr President, dinner is ready to be served.' The President gave his arm to Alia to escort her to the chair and Alex walked behind until they reached the exquisitely set table. Its oblong shape was covered by a cream-coloured softly embroidered tablecloth with table settings of polished silver, shining crystal and a rush of coloured flowers arranged in an oblong shape in the middle of the table. The chairs were padded in pale-gold damask fabric of silk and cotton. The menu next to each setting informed the guest of the repast:

First Course: Alaskan Halibut Casseroles with Crêpes, Asparagus, Chanterelles, Baby Onions and Lardon and Herbed Butter.

Second Course: Salad on Daikon Sheets, Masago Rice Pearl Crispies, Rice Wine Vinaigrette.

Main Course: Baby Lamb Chops with Yukon Potato Dauphinoise and Fricassee of Winter Vegetables.

22

Dessert: Chocolate Malt Food Layers with Pear and Almond Brittle.

An American wine will be paired with each course.

Polite conversation ensued at the dinner table while stories of favourite holidays were disseminated and how the children enjoyed or not each one of them. The pets that kept them busy and happy and in the case of the President the latest College that was reviewed for his two children to attend. Every so often a low bubble of laughter wafted softly around the room while wine was sipped and appropriate comments about the food from each course were made. 'I see, Your Highness, you're a sweets-aholic.'

'Hmm, the combination of the fruit and almond brittle was the pièce de résistance. Absolutely wonderful.'

'What about you, Dr Glandore? Have you a sweet tooth?'

'Not really. I'm a cheese and crackers guy.'

'I'll make sure we have some when coffee is served.' The President turned and engaged the attention of one of the men who served. 'Will you make sure that an array of cheese and crackers are served with coffee as well?'

As dinner came to an end, the President motioned for someone to come and pull out the chairs for his guests and asked if coffee was ready to be served in the adjoining small lounge. To all of these requests there was a positive answer and soon the small company of diners were ushered to the lounge where the aroma of coffee freely floated about them and tantalised the taste buds to savour its brewed perfection.

The President waited till after his guests had settled

themselves on a couch and he sat opposite them in an armchair. The rectangular coffee table was spread with a platter of assorted cheeses, crackers, and a sprinkle of thinly sliced apple, pears and tiny bunches of red and green grapes. A small silver tray of chocolates was at the other end of the table, and cups and saucers were laid out ready to be filled with coffee or tea.

'I guess now is the time for us to have our discussion.' The President turned to the makeshift staff and asked them all to leave the room. 'I am sure you are overwhelmed by everything that is going on and especially as it's at your very doorstep. In these couple of days, it has given me the opportunity to think and look into this situation a bit closer. It is important that we act upon it quickly. As to what action will be taken is still in discussion with some of our allies that are also feeling the effects of the WSO. What I am asking you to do is to go home and continue your normal life until things begin to happen. If we feel that you or your family are in danger of any kind, we will swoop in and take you to a safe place. We believe that the fewer people know of our actions the better ... uhm, particularly for their safety.'

'Mr President, apologies for disrupting your speech. This is not acceptable. It is important that you keep us informed of everything that has been decided with regard to *our* nation. We cannot be left in the dark.' Alia leaned forward with her hands on her knees and continued. 'How can we go back and live a "normal life" when in truth nothing is normal. We are left with a cloud of doubt over our heads. We must insist that you inform us every inch of the way.'

'Alia is absolutely right, Mr President. The importance, as you previously said, of my engineering company in these circumstances, surely needs me to be informed of all that's happening so we know where we are heading. I cannot place my staff and the plant in any kind of danger due to secret actions unknown to me. If this allied joint action you speak of meets with our approval, then you can go for it. I'll stress it again – it's paramount that I know what's going to happen.'

'What I can say with certainty is that you are all in good hands.'

'With all due respect, Mr President, we will be in better hands if we know what's to occur around us.' Alex's response was swift and to the point.

'There is something in what you say, Dr Glandore. We will take everything under advisement.'

Alia saw the ideal opportunity to bring these roundabout talks to an end. 'Thank you for the dinner tonight, Mr President. It's been a long day and I'm certain that we're all ready to bring proceedings to a close.' She stood, then Alex and the President did likewise.

The President remained calm and charming as ever and came around to Alia's side as she proffered her hand and he gave her a warm handshake by placing his other hand on top of hers. Alex and he gave a firm handshake and the President walked with them to the door where Mike and Frank waited for their return. The President bowed his head and smiled as they began to walk down the hallway. He then retreated to the lounge, sat in the armchair, nibbled on some cheese and grapes and thought about their conversation as someone who was pressed for action.

In the privacy of their bedroom, Alex and Alia sat together on the couch at the other end of the room as two people who have just gone through a talking marathon. Alia kicked off her high heels, Alex removed his jacket and stretched his long legs out in front of him. The silence between them helped to regroup their thoughts, then suddenly Alia jumped up off her seat and looked down on Alex with a resignation he'd not seen before. He wound his legs back up as he sat upright. 'What's up?'

'I just can't think about it tonight – information overload. I'm going to bed.'

'Good idea, Alia. Best we discuss this tomorrow morning.' He stood facing her as he placed his arm around her shoulders. 'Come on, you go to the bathroom first.' Alex sat back on the couch as he mulled over the whole dinner's conversation. So deep were his thoughts, he hadn't noticed Alia return and slip into bed.

'Hey, what are you dreaming about?'

'Oh, nothing much,' and with that he made his way to the bathroom.

Alia was too tired to question him further. She turned over on her side, curled up her legs and sometime later she faintly felt Alex's arm over her waist.

23

Alex and Alia could hardly believe how long they had slept. It was already eight-thirty according to the digital clock at Alex's bedside table. 'How long have you been awake? Why didn't you wake me up earlier?'

'It's fine, Alia. It's not a crime to sleep in once in a while. In any case, I don't know what's the agenda for the day, do you? So, enjoy the rest.'

'You're right, of course you're right. I'll just lie in bed for the rest of the day.'

'Yea, right! As if that's going to happen.' He leaned over and touched her cheek with the back of his hand. 'I'm going to the shower first,' and he slipped out of bed and trudged in the direction of the bathroom.

By the time Alia got out of bed, Alex was dressed in warm casual clothes. 'So, what do you think, appropriate or not?'

'You're always appropriate. What am I to wear is more the question.'

'Step by step. Go and have your shower first.'

'You see, always appropriate.' She walked by and with the side of her body bumped into him and quickly dashed to the bathroom, while Alex made initial steps as if he was in pursuit of her, to squeals of laughter from Alia.

Soon they were both ready and as they were about to head for the door, Mike's knock and voice sounded. 'Ma'am, sir, are you ready?'

Alex and Alia looked at each other and Alia's hand came automatically over her mouth and stifled a laugh. 'Come on, let's move it!' She pulled him by the hand towards the door and Alex opened it quickly.

'Good, you're ready. Let's go.'

'Where exactly? We're not moving until you tell us.' Alia stopped suddenly and that forced Alex to do likewise.

'I'm not supposed to tell you. The President will.'

'We don't even know if we're appropriately dressed. Now, where are we going?' Alia dug her heels in and would not budge.

'Okay, but don't tell the President.' Then he leaned a little towards Alia and whispered, 'I'm only doing it for you, Your Highness. Camp David.'

'Really? Thank you, Mike.' She turned to Alex and asked, 'You heard that?'

'I sure did! Let's go.'

'We're going first to the dining room for breakfast if that suits you both. The President's there.'

'Then we had better go, Mike. Can't keep the President waiting.' There was a lighter tone in Alia's voice.

As they entered, the President greeted them both warmly and again escorted Alia to the chair. There were two secret servicemen attending to their needs. 'I thought I would surprise you today with a helicopter ride to Camp David. I think you've been in your room far too long.'

'You read our mind, Mr President.' Alex responded.

Alia remained silent and focused on what she would eat for breakfast and avoided eye contact with the President. He, being a highly perceptive man, recognised the slight rebuff. 'Your Highness, I've specifically requested chocolate croissants for you, I hope they are to your liking.'

'Thank you, Mr President, I shall have one with my coffee,' and she continued to eat her breakfast.

Alex, who sat next to his wife, poked her with his shoe sufficiently hard to shake her out of the inexplicable mood she was in. It worked. She turned sharply to look at Alex and he raised his eyebrows as if to say, *What are you doing?* Fortunately, the President was speaking with one of the servicemen helping out in the dining room and just in case she didn't interpret his facial expression, Alex squeezed her hand on her lap and as he looked down at his breakfast food, whispered, 'Talk.'

She gazed at him indignantly but turned her face just as the President completed his instructions to the serviceman. 'Mr President, you will forgive me for this forward question, but why is it your aim to keep us in the dark constantly. Couldn't you have told us last night what we were to do today?'

'Your Highness, my honest answer to your question is that

I didn't think about Camp David until well after you left the dining room and as you were both so comfortably asleep at length this morning, I didn't consider it right to disturb a well-earned rest since your arrival.'

'Oh, I see. In that case, I thank you for your highly considered resolution to visit Camp David.' Alia's lips formed a slight upturn as if to smile, but never went the distance.

'I am pleased it meets with your approval.' The President looked around the room and sighted Dex. He indicated for him to approach and asked, 'Where are the chocolate croissants? We could die from hunger here.'

'Yes, sir. Straight away.' He dashed out quickly and within a couple of minutes he returned with a basket filled to the brim with warm chocolate croissants.

After a couple cups of coffee and croissants, it had the effect of warming the body and heart for further conversation, which related to Camp David. 'Before we go, I'll give you a few historical facts about Camp David. For instance, it was not always called Camp David. It was initially established in nineteen forty-two and President Roosevelt named it Shangri-La after James Hilton's novel *Lost Horizon*. It wasn't until nineteen fifty-three when President Eisenhower renamed it Camp David after his grandson.'

Alia interjected before the President could continue. 'Lucky boy. He's now immortalised ... unless, of course, another President decides to change the name.'

'Good point, but highly unlikely to occur now. What

23

I think you'll really appreciate is its natural beauty. The retreat is called Aspen Lodge and it's situated in Catoctin Mountain Park and on a spur of the Blue Ridge Mountain in Frederick county northern Maryland. It's about sixty-four miles northwest of Washington DC.'

'What type of trees are there in that region? I ask because my father is a horticulturalist and I think he may be interested to know,' and as an afterthought he continued, 'as well as myself.'

'I am definitely interested in the natural environment. What sort of trees are there?' Alia's enthusiasm was quite evident to the President.

'Well, here we have something in common, Your Highness. Let me think ... definitely oaks, poplars, ash, hickory, and maple trees. For me to try and describe them would do them injustice. They need to be seen to be appreciated.' The President smiled at his two guests, placed two hands together with a low thud in the form of a clap and asked, 'Are we all finished with breakfast? If so, the helicopter awaits us.'

'Now here's something I am very interested in. What type of helicopter will be taking us to Camp David?'

'We either go in the newer, but smaller VH-6ON White Hawk or the larger Sikorsky VH-3D Sea King. When a President travels in a helicopter the call sign is Marine One. You may hear that on our flight.'

'Of course, Igor Sikorsky invented the first workable American helicopter in nineteen thirty-nine. But then there was also the French engineer Paul Cornu, way back in nineteen hundred and seven, who created his helicopter which was the first mechanical machine to have uplift from the ground. I can imagine the excitement in those days.'

'Well, Dr Glandore, you certainly know your engineering history – not that I'm surprised. Your engineering skills precede you. I wasn't aware of Paul Cornu's achievements, but now I am.' He noticed that his guests appeared to be cold as they came outside and began to walk towards the helicopter. 'There are jackets in the helicopter for both of you.'

The whirring sound of the helicopter blades were deafening as all three climbed into the Sikorsky Sea King and settled down in their seats. They were more than pleased to wear the headphones which protected their ears from the loud noise and allowed the passengers and the pilot to communicate. 'All passengers must wear a seatbelt before take-off. When we disembark, crouch and move away from the helicopter from the middle. Do not go towards the back or front. Thank you.' The pilot keyed the mike. 'Washington Tower, helicopter VH-3D Sea King requests take-off.' The reply was prompt, 'Roger that,' and before the passengers realised, the whirly-bird was airborne and began its flight north to north-west of Washington DC.

The more north-west they travelled the thicker the green vegetation below them grew. 'Are they the Appalachian Mountains?' Alex asked while his view was transfixed at the vision below him.

The pilot's voice came over the headphones. 'They sure

are. In a moment you'll see the Blue Ridge Mountain and then Catoctin Mountain Park and down there you'll see Aspen Lodge and ... here's the Ridge to your right ... do you see how it forms a spur ... there it is ... that's Catoctin ... here's Aspen from above ... okay, everyone get ready for our landing.'

As the helicopter came to a halt and its passengers began to make their way out, each crouched, once they were sure-footed on the ground, and directly from the middle of the craft headed towards a small contingent of secret servicemen, among them Mike and Frank, who quickly surrounded the three and escorted them to the Lodge.

Inside, they were directed to the living room where an open fireplace was burning from logs collected around its very environment. 'This is perfect, Mr President. I couldn't think of anything more pleasant right now.'

'I'm glad it meets with your approval, Your Highness. This has been an unusual trip for you ... for both of you. It's the least we can do to make it more pleasant ... so for lunch, we'll be in the Flagstone Patio, outside here,' and he pointed the direction to go. 'Leave your woollies and thick jackets on ... although we'll be around a blazing fire, it's still very cold, but definitely worth it. I won't say any more, I'll just let you experience it.' It then suddenly occurred to him that his guests might be concerned with privacy. 'Needless to say, your security and privacy are of our utmost importance. There are Navy personnel and troops from the Marine barracks and although they don't know who they are specifically protecting, they will protect all three of us if the need arises.' The President looked around for a familiar face and there, just outside the door, he saw Dex. 'Will you show my two guests to their room?' He left the door open and then addressed Alia and Alex. 'I'll see you both for lunch. Dex will show you to your room.'

The room was comfortably casual with both bedroom and bathroom's requirements all in place and in abundance. 'Look outside this window, Alex. The size of the place is inconceivably large. I know we have beautiful national parks, but nowhere the size of this. What did the pilot tell us … 200 acres?' She suddenly swerved to face Alex. 'Do you think they'll let us go for a walk just before lunch?'

Alex looked at his wristwatch. 'I think, but not right now. In thirty-five minutes, we'll be out there for lunch. Maybe after lunch. Why don't we relax? I noticed a couple of brochures here about the park. It may be interesting to read them before we go out.'

'You're probably right. Let me see that.' She went to where Alex stood, and he reached in one of the drawers of the dresser and pulled out the information Alia wanted. Each went to an armchair which was in opposite ends of the bedroom and sat to begin their read about the park. Alia looked up and felt the distance between herself and Alex. 'What do you say we bring these two armchairs closer together?'

'Leave yours where it is, I'll bring mine to you.' He lifted the armchair, placed it right next to Alia's and sat back into it. 'There, that feels better.'

'Are you at that part that mentions the type of bird life in the park?'

'No, but I've just read about the animal life. Brown bears, no less, lurk around these parklands. Oooooh.' Alex gesticulated with his fingers as if some horrific monster were to appear.

'Are you determined to frighten me?'

'Why, is it working?'

'Yes!' Alia looked up from the brochure and saw Alex's broad grin.

'Don't worry. They'd be hibernating by now — for the winter. Did you forget?'

She nodded her head and stood and went to the window to look out again. Likewise, Alex followed and came to stand beside her with his arm around her waist. 'You've always been passionate about nature. I loved that about you.' Alia didn't respond, she appeared mesmerised with the view. 'We should freshen up a little and walk to the Flagstone Patio.'

This had the effect of bringing her back to reality and as she looked at Alex, her eyes welled up with tears, dangerously close to spilling over and down her cheeks. He drew her close to him and whispered in her hair. 'What's wrong, Alia? What were you thinking about looking out that window?'

'I remembered that cold winter's day we climbed our small mountain and how completely happy we were.' Then the waterfalls truly fell and spotted his warm woollen sweater as she pressed her face into his chest.

He just held her close to him and brushed his hand against her hair, interspersed with an occasional, 'It's okay.'

When she stopped crying and the breathing became normal, Alex spoke softly. 'Do you want to go to lunch or shall we stay here? It's nearly twelve-thirty.'

'Oh, no! I better go and wash my face.' Reluctantly, she moved out of his arms and quickly walked to the bathroom. Five minutes later she was back in the bedroom. 'Do I look as if I was crying?'

'No, you don't. You look lovely.'

They were both dressed in padded jackets that they wore in the helicopter and by the time they found the Flagstone Patio, they saw the President already there with a glass of wine in his hand and casually left it on a sturdy stone table as he began to walk towards them. He, too, was dressed warmly in a parka and woollen scarf around his neck.

'Our apologies for our tardiness,' Alia immediately responded when she saw the President.

He reached Alia first and shook her hand and then Alex's. 'It's okay. This place has a way of winding us down and forgetting the time of day. Are you rested?'

'Yes, for sure, Mr President,' Alex said as he chose a glass of red wine, while Alia already had a glass of champagne in her hand. 'Something smells good, coming from that direction.'

'A barbecue for us all. Steak, chops, and sausages. That's all I know, but there'll be a few other things served up as well.' The President stood by Alex and Alia while the process of preparing the lunch was in progress. The conversation flowed easily, primarily about the Park and Aspen Lodge. On each placemat set out on the stone table, there was a picture of a cabin dotted around the parkland. Alia read the name on each mat: Birch Cabin, Dogwood Cabin and Cedar Cabin beautifully portrayed with matching coasters as well.

'Mr President, lunch is served.'

'Thank you. Let's all sit here.' Someone was there to pull out chairs and serve the wine. Platters of food were taken directly to the diners which allowed each individual to choose what he or she wanted. Alia was pleased to select the amount of meat, salads and condiments offered to her. The steaks were huge and she asked if one could be cut in half, which was promptly done, so she could manage to taste a little from all the temptations in sight. She glanced across the table at the President and Alex who were a little to her right as they both ate heartily everything that was provided.

'Mr President, we read in our room the brochure with a description of some of the wildlife, animals and birds. It's a pity that it is late November and the Broad-winged Hawk has migrated towards South America. I would have liked to see it in flight. In September, I believe it leaves,' Alia explained.

'Yes, it does. It's wonderful to see its huge wings as it catches the air current and allows it to go on its journey.'

'I've never seen a Box Turtle. How big does it grow? I guess by its name they must be small – small enough to fit inside a box.' Alia smiled a little at the thought of it.

'You're quite right. They're small and I ... uhm, think they grow about four to six inches, if I'm not mistaken.'

Alex jumped into the conversation before the President went on with his explanation. 'Well, all I want to see is a big brown bear, which I probably can't because they're hibernating.'

'That's true, very interesting animal. I've heard a story where once one of them had the gumption to walk right up to Aspen Lodge. The rangers came quickly enough and made sure he went the other way. Now, I believe, there's an electrified steel cyclone fence that's topped with concertina wire surrounding the whole area of Camp David. I don't think we'll be having any unexpected visitors.' The President was a mine of information.

'It never ceases to amaze me how quickly animals get used to something they deem unsafe.' Alia looked at the two men who had just finished their dessert of sticky date pudding and were fast talking about fishing. What Alia wanted to do was to go for a short walk and breathe in the pristine air and get her joints moving. 'Gentlemen, would you mind if I left you here and went for a short walk. Perhaps Mike and Frank can come with me.'

Before Alex had a chance to respond, the President answered swiftly. 'We'll all go. It's a great idea to digest and take in the surroundings.' The minute the President stood, three bodyguards were on hand at his command. 'Men, you can come along, too.'

The three looked at each other and knew what the other was thinking. There was no way they were going to allow the President to go for a walk with two guests and have only

Mike and Frank act as bodyguards. Mike came close to the three and whispered, 'Glad you're here, guys.' One of them stuck his thumb up to concur with his words.

The trees on both sides of the walking track displayed bare branches, and the only evidence that it was clothed with leaves at any stage lay crunched under their shoes. The soft moss underfoot cushioned their steps as the group continued their exploration of the area. Alia identified a few birds that she had read about earlier in the morning. The Scarlet Tanager was not difficult to identify as it beamed in red and flitted away just as quickly as she saw it and the Blue Jay also behaved in a similar manner at their unexpected noisy footsteps. She thought she saw a Downy Woodpecker, but she couldn't be sure, as it, too, fled away instantly at their approach.

The Appalachian Mountains provided the backdrop scenery as a border of protection. Soon, the adventurers came across a creek with full rippling water as it frothed on every rock it struck along its journey through glen and dale. The grass and moss formed a vista of expansive beauty, and a few times, Alia leaned over and cut a long stem of grass and examined it. 'What have you there, ma'am?' The President's curiosity was evident.

'When I was a little girl growing up, it was my joy to run and walk throughout the estate. I used to cut a broad piece of grass, cut a narrow line in the middle and try to blow through it until it whistled.'

'You mean like this?' The President pulled out a Swiss knife from his back pocket, chose one of the blades, made an incision in the grass leaf with surgical precision and then blew into it to create the whistle effect that everyone waited for with expectation. It was such a clear sound that, surprisingly, birds immediately fluttered from the trees and flew away. Alia's delight was most evident and she spontaneously began to clap. Everyone else followed suit and the President, being caught up in the moment, allowed himself to aggrandise his achievement with a deep bow. In the spirit of the walk, the small party began to make tracks back to the Lodge.

They were all pleased to remove their thick garments and approach the fireplace inside the Lodge that flickered with warmth. The President had his arms stretched in an endeavour to warm them and Alex had his back turned to the fire while Alia stood comfortably next to him. As the President straightened up, he addressed both of them. 'I have made arrangements for afternoon tea in one of the smaller living rooms for us to talk further about the situation that is looming before us. I am certain that a positive solution will result. Shall we say at three? After that we'll return to the White House. How does that sound?'

'That sounds fine, Mr President.' Alex also concurred with Alia.

They were left to their own resources and quickly realised the three o'clock mark was only twenty minutes away. In the privacy of their own room, they refreshed themselves and sat comfortably in their own armchairs. 'What do you think the President will say to us?'

23

'I imagine a similar theme to what he's been saying, undoubtedly with a twist.' Alex looked at Alia who appeared to ponder something in her mind. 'What are you thinking about?'

'How easily everything can slip through our fingers. The bottom line is our power is very limited.'

'We knew that from the outset. That's why we came to America – for their help. We have limited resources to overcome this international order. My understanding is that they have millions of members all over Europe. What can little Rubinia do on its own? Our biggest threat is our neighbour, Cumbia. Do you think Gregory will stop to consider us before he sends in his troops? I don't think so! We need every bit of help we can get, and we need to convey this to the President and assure him we will support and play our part according to *his* plans. I don't want to go from here leaving any doubts in his mind. We must assure him.' Alex gently took Alia's hand in his as it rested on the armchair and continued, 'We will prevail!'

'As always, appropriate. Everything you say is quite right. Deep down in my heart I know I have no choice. I am bleeding for my country to see it reduced to these circumstances. We are pawns in the hands of others. God knows how hard it will be to tell Mother.'

'I think she'll receive it well.' He turned towards Alia and placed her hand to his chest. 'Don't forget this is *my* country, too. We're in it together.' He paused for a moment and kissed her fingertips. 'We are not anyone's pawns. You *must* believe we will have checkmate.' He continued to hold her hand and each remained in his and her own thoughts.

They stayed in this position for quite a few minutes until Alia broke the silence. 'We better get to the living room on time. Come on let's go.' As she finished her words to Alex there was a knock on the door. 'Come in,' came the answer.

'Ma'am, sir, I'll escort you to the living room.'

'Thanks, Mike.' As Alex advanced in front of him, he stopped and shook his hand as an acknowledgement of work well done. 'We couldn't have done it without you.' He then noticed Frank and did likewise.'

Mike's response was a nod of the head and a ghost of a smile as he directed them both towards their afternoon tea.

The tea was a scrumptious affair and they quickly saw the array of offerings that were visibly pleasing. Alia particularly liked the chocolate brownies and asked for the recipe, which was produced very soon after its request. The teas were sipped, the coffees were savoured, and the sandwiches were filled with delectable usual and unusual fillings, particularly in the liberal use of chilli. For Alex it was not so much of a surprise as it all brought back memories of his life in America, but for Alia, try as she might, it was all too spicy and in the end, the President asked for a glass of milk which he requested to be given to his guest. It certainly soothed the palate as she drank it with gusto.

'Are you okay, ma'am?' The President showed concern for her.

'All I can say it was quite an experience.' She looked directly at the President and stated, 'That's certainly something to retell at the dinner table, back home.'

'I think that calls for another chocolate brownie. Will that make you feel better?' A cheeky grin spread across Alex's face as he teased his wife.

'I think so,' was Alia's predictive response.

Soon the President suggested they begin their final talk before they return to the White House. He asked for everyone to leave the room and all three settled down for some serious conversation. The President opened the discussion. 'I know this has been a very difficult period especially as it concerns, mostly, your nation. I have stressed before the importance of trust between us, as individuals and as two nations. All I can assure you is that we are working on this day and night and for security reasons and, more importantly, for your safety not all of our plans can be revealed to you.' He paused and observed both of his guests. 'I need to be reassured that you will accept this procedure, so we can continue this discussion.'

Before the President proceeded with his address, Alia intervened. 'Mr President, as we are putting all of our cards on the table, I must do the same at this juncture.' She took in a short swift breath and exhaled promptly. 'It was *I* who primarily had doubts about the scheme. It was my opinion that we, as a nation, were disempowered in all of this. As a wise man said to me, just a short couple of hours ago, 'it is not a disempowerment but an empowerment of allies.' It's true that we as a nation may not be able to steer the course of action, but it is also true that our first choice would be your nation to captain the whole situation. So, from the outset we, Alex and I, Her Majesty and our whole country will support your decisions and accept as much or as little information as you can impart to us and if we can start our small conference from this positive point of view, it will save us a lot of time.'

'This is one of the things I've heard about you, ma'am, which I like, and that is, you say exactly what you mean and you act upon it – immediately. So be it! We will start from the precise premise as you suggest.' The President ran his hand over his chin and down his right cheek. 'Okay ... I now want to tell you some information which may put both of you at ease. This is not the first time that a secret "Order" has been born from malice and mania. The *Thule Society* which began in nineteen eighteen is said to have inspired Nazism. They believed in The New World Order by decreasing the population. This was done as a matter of course – simply by killing people off. Another one called *Club Bilderberg*, founded and formalised in nineteen fifty-four, attracted the world's preeminent people of business, finance, media, even academics and politicians. Their overarching objective is to control the natural resources of the world, thus creating an impregnable new Order. In our own backyard, the Ku Klux Klan, the KKK, are extremists, want all-white supremacy and they are considered as subversive and terrorists. Although they existed as far back as eighteen sixty-five,

23

they gained real force after nineteen forty-six where their membership was up to six million. Now they're five to eight thousand. I give you those examples, which you may or may not believe, so you know we've been fighting secret societies, such as the WSO, for a very long time. We are not without experience.'

'You must admit, though, Mr President, that these societies can cause a lot of calamitous trouble: The Great Depression, Nazism, with the result of hardships and deaths of millions of people, when all is considered. We don't want this to happen with the WSO,' Alex stated with concern.

'And that's exactly why, Dr Glandore, we want to act swiftly and immediately, before any real trouble begins. So, do I have your complete and undivided support?'

'You do, sir. I will endeavour to co-operate with whatever measures you seem fit to implement in my engineering industry. I expect you'll let me know with whom and when I begin my communications.' Alex's confirmations reassured the President.

'I will give you Her Majesty's and my undivided attention until this whole thing is cleared up.' Alia faulted for a moment and then asked, 'What about our Prime Minister? Shouldn't we get him involved?'

'He must be left out. He's under suspicion. But I am pleased with your positive responses. Good.' The President stood and walked towards his two guests. 'That leaves just one thing to do before the formalities begin and this is to shake hands on our verbal agreement.' He gave his hand to Alia first and then to Alex and the deal was sealed.

'We will need to leave for the White House within the hour. There'll be papers to be signed and taken with you for Her Majesty's signature and for your engineering firm also, Dr Glandore.'

'Of course, Mr President. We will take all documentations home with us. You already have our verbal agreement, and when the documents are scanned by our legal eye, then they will be returned to you promptly.' Suddenly, something sparked in his mind. 'If we give you the names of our lawyers, will you be able to run some investigations on them. Just to be sure they are not members of any such societies or the WSO?'

'Give them to me and we'll get a result — immediately tonight.' The President again rubbed his chin and followed through with the same procedure to the right side of his face. He drew in a deep breath and exhaled immediately. 'I can safely say that our discourse tonight has been successful. May it continue to be so throughout these difficult times.'

'We are both in full agreement on that statement,' Alia assured him.

'We will work with you to our fullest capability,' was Alex's confirmation.

24

The helicopter ride back to the White House was swift and precise. There was no conversation with the pilot or with the President. It landed within the predictable thirty minutes travel time. The second they entered the White House, the President made his goodbyes and thanked his guests for their visit. Lastly, he added, 'The paperwork will be given to you by one of my servicemen, where some documents will need signatures tonight.' He looked closely at the two and then as a final salutation said, 'Safe travels,' and with that he turned away and vanished through one of the many doors that manned the main entrance hall.

It left Alex and Alia feeling stranded on some unknown shore. 'Well that was smartly executed. I wonder where he's off to in such a hurry.' Alia continued to stare into the void from where the President left. 'Do you know what I was thinking Alex?' She didn't wait for him to answer. 'How do we know if he's not a member of one of the societies he mentioned? Perhaps one of those top politicians who is rich and powerful.' Suddenly she turned and faced Alex. 'Tell me, how do we know?'

'We don't! We mentioned this earlier and decided somewhere along the line we have to believe *someone*. I don't know of another alternative. Do You?'

'No, I don't.'

'Do you want to eat anything for dinner? I can ask for it to be brought to our room.'

'No, Alex, not for me. A pot of tea would be nice.'

They wandered towards their bedroom as they held hands without the need for conversation. Within a few seconds of their decision to move towards their room, two secret servicemen, who appeared from nowhere, were suddenly by their side, silent and sullen. It was a relief to open their door and vanish inside. 'Why are we feeling so dreary and so down?' Alia threw herself onto the armchair and regarded Alex as he continued to stand nearby. 'I'm done in!'

'It's been an intense few days ... I think our visit was necessary. Hopefully, it brings a productive result.' He glanced in Alia's direction and he could see a sense of resignation and he knew he must be more positive, if only for his wife's sake. He too moved to his armchair and slumped into it. He took Alia's hand in his and held it warmly for a short moment. 'Come on. I think we're both exhausted from everything. Let's perk up.'

At that very moment, a knock on the door diverted their thoughts. The call was made to enter, and Mike came in carrying a tray with a pot of tea, beautiful bone-china cups and saucers, a bowl of chocolates and a small platter of cheeses and crackers. They were all placed on the coffee table in front of them. Alex gazed on the food with some temptation and simply said, 'Ah, they remembered.' He leaned over and cut a piece of brie and placed it on a poppy seed cracker and while it was suspended in mid-air close to his mouth, he thanked Mike who promptly went back outside the door and took up his post as protector. Alex munched on the cheese and crackers.

'Who's going to eat all of that?'

'I don't know about you, but I'm feeling a bit peckish,' and with that Alex cut into a blue vein cheese, spread it liberally on a thinly sliced piece of dark rye bread and heartily ate it. Before he could take a second gulp of his tea, another knock was heard. 'Come in,' Alex boomed.

Again, Mike approached with a manila envelope in his hand, which he gave to Alex and left the room once more. Alex broke the seal and took out an A4 sheet of paper with the Presidential letter head. It read:

Your Highness, Princess Alia, and Dr Glandore,

These are the findings from our search on your Prime Minister, Mr. Max Wessler.

It appears he was approached to join the WSO two years ago to which he refused. However, there was pressure brought to bear on him a year later and Mr Wessler relented and joined.

His activities in the WSO seem to be silent, at present, evidenced by at least a couple of letters wishing to withdraw from such an Order. To date, he has not been successful in this mission, with the "unfortunate" result of a motor car accident six months ago. It left him in hospital for quite some time with broken ribs and tibia.

We will make it our goal to assist Mr Wessler with his mission. We cannot allow him to be a participating member, which makes it easier for us, as he is also not inclined in that direction. Twenty percent of Rubinia's Gross Domestic Product is a great deal of money to dispense with.

As for the two lawyers' names you gave me, our search came up clear. At this point, it is important to mention that they, being your lawyers, may sooner rather than later be approached to join the Order. We will be monitoring this as well.

These particular situations will be resolved as a matter of priority. There will be further communications in this regard, and we will advise you of your participation regarding this. Please be assured that it will be dealt with swiftly.

Kind regards and safe travels,
Yours faithfully,
The President of the
United States of America

'Well, that was quick. I didn't expect a result until much later.' Alex continued to browse over the letter and then added. 'No wonder he was in a hurry to leave us.'

'It could be that, but it does make one wonder, when they

want things to happen quickly it happens, when they don't, it could take forever.' Alia's words were frostily stated.

'But it is a reasonable explanation. You've got to give him that. By the way, before we call it a night, we have to look over the documents he wants us to sign.' Alex looked in Alia's direction. 'Are you up to it?'

'I've no choice. Where are they?'

'In this envelope we've just received.' Alex spilled on the coffee table all the paperwork within the manila envelope and began sorting them out. There were two that needed their immediate attention. 'Here they are. You take one and I'll take the other and then we reverse the procedure, just to make sure we read everything correctly.' Alex appeared to be looking for something.

'They're over here.' Alia reached over towards his armchair and wedged between the seat and cushion were his glasses.

'What would I do without you?' Alex asked laughingly.

'You can say that again.' Alex began to repeat his question, but Alia promptly stopped him, which had the effect of a chuckle and a smile between them. Both settled down and began to read the documents.

Sometime later an exchange of papers was made, but Alia's attention was focused on a short passage in the documentation. 'What do you think of this part? *and I give permission and authority for the United States of America with its allied nation, the United Kingdom, to search and make any and all enquiries through their facilities available to them on any individual and/or company that may be suspiciously involved with the World Secret Order or any other society of criminal or subversive intentions towards any nation of democratic government that espouses the freedoms of that said nation.*' Alia placed the document on the coffee table and looked up at Alex for an answer.

'I noticed that, too. We're giving them a wide berth to do whatever is necessary to act on any such Order or Society as the WSO. In a way, as a small nation we're being disempowered ... for a good reason ... I think.'

'Let's leave it at that and take the rest of the documents back home and see what happens.' Alia stretched on the armchair and yawned in the process. 'I think I'm ready for bed. We've got an early start tomorrow. As she glanced down onto the coffee table she added, 'You polished off those cheeses well and good.'

'What can I say, I was getting hungry.' Alex stood as well and took her hand. 'Come on, let's go. I'll place this envelope in my case and lock it.'

25

Alex and Alia woke to the semi-twilight dawn and as they looked out from their window the dreary greyness that surrounded them confirmed a chilly winter's day. Most of the packing had been done the night before, but everything that they endeavoured to complete seemed meaningless to what waited for them on their return to Rubinia.

'Alex, it might be a good idea to give Mike the envelope with the signed documents for him to give to the President. I don't trust it in anyone else's hands.'

'I agree.' He went to his locked suitcase and keyed the appropriate numbers on the lock so it would open. There on top of the pile was the envelope. He took out the other documents which were to be transported to Rubinia, and after checking the signatures of the two papers, Alex placed the documents back in the same envelope and stuck it down with glue and he wrote across it: "To be Opened by the President" should anyone put it in their head to open and examine the paperwork within it. He walked to the door and there waiting in the opened doorway was Mike and Frank. 'Mike, take this to the President, himself, immediately and then return asap so we can head home.'

'Yes, sir.' Mike walked in long strides as fast as he could, but without appearing in a rush. Alex could see he communicated with someone through his earpiece and then lost sight of him as he swerved to the right in another hallway.

By the time he and Alia completed packing the few items that were loose in the room and securely locked their suitcases and briefcase, they heard Mike's voice and Alex opened the door. 'All done, sir.'

'Directly to the President?'

'Yes, sir.'

'Good. Then we are done here. Let's go.' Alex carried his own briefcase in one hand, while holding Alia's hand with the other and their bodyguards took control of their suitcases.

Abruptly, Mike stopped in his tracks. He looked around him urgently. 'There should be another bodyguard here! Just a moment, ma'am, sir.' He suddenly began to talk to someone on his cell phone. 'What do you mean, he's missing? Out with it.' He listened again carefully. 'You should've told me.' He swerved around, grabbed Alia's arm and Alex's. 'Come with me and don't make a sound.' He found a rather small room along the hallway and swiftly placed both of them in there. 'Lock the door and don't open up except for me. Not a sound.' Mike slammed the door and disappeared with Frank beside him.

25

They ran fast and were grateful that the usual staff in the White House was not up yet, or they might have knocked them over. Out through the back way they went where the car was parked. There were a couple of servicemen waiting patiently next to it. 'Get away from that car.' Mike yelled at them.

'What's up?' One of them asked.

'The car's wired. Can you see anything under the car from here?'

He crouched carefully. 'Yep. There it is.'

'Let's get behind those hedges. I'm going to lie flat on my stomach and shoot it to explode.' Mike was hoping it might work.

'You're too close. You won't have time to get behind the hedge.' Frank made his concerns loud and clear.

'I haven't a telescopic gun.' Just as Mike was trying to size up the situation, he heard another's voice.

'I have one.'

Mike stood and stared at one of the secret servicemen. 'Who are you?'

'I'm Cody. We need to stand right back.'

All four went behind the hedge while Cody crouched down, took aim through a space in the hedge and precisely hit the offending bomb under the car – then, "BOOM", the whole thing blew up. Flames engulfed it, debris arched in the air and fell all around them. Some of the windows of the building were blown in millions of tiny fragments and the car was quickly consumed with flames turning everything it burned to black charcoal of fetid smells and putrid gases. A fire engine came rushing to the scene and urgently put out the blaze, using foam to prevent the billowing smoke that persisted.

Frank's curiosity was aroused, 'Mike, how did you know about the car?'

'One of the servicemen who was supposed to be with us went missing. It's always a clear sign that he was up to no good. Tampering with a car is often first on the agenda.'

During the confusion in the fray, Mike's senses woke to the fact that Alia and Alex were still in the locked room. He took Frank by the arm and spoke urgently but softly. 'Leave it to them to work it out. Come with me. Now.' As speedily as possible, they made their way through another door on the side of the building. Both went in and ran as fast as they could to the hallway where Mike had left his precious cargo. As he knocked on the door, he got no response. He tried the handle and the door opened. Mike's eyes swiftly scanned the room, but nowhere could Alia or Alex be seen. 'Darn!' he exclaimed. 'Where are they? Let's check every room down the hallway.' Together with Frank, they proceeded urgently with their search. Suddenly, as they reached the end of the hallway, they saw the President and two bodyguards escorting Alex and Alia away from the smoke and smell that was slowly pervading that area. 'Ma'am, sir, stop,' yelled Mike. The intensity of his voice had the required effect of halting everyone ahead of Mike and Frank.

25

'I'm sorry sir, but my two people need to be with me – no one else.' Mike spoke forcibly.

The President was quite shocked at his demand and in the seconds it took for him to recover, he diplomatically responded. 'I understand completely. They're yours.'

'What happened, Mike?' Alex asked. We heard a massive explosion and a few minutes later smoke wafted all over the place. We decided to walk downstairs, but we met the President on our way, and we were all going to find you and see what's going on. Can you tell us?' Alex asked as a matter of importance.

'Yea ... just a little bomb under the car to explode on ignition. That's all. It's not good enough, Mr President. This could've been fatal.' Mike stared at the President, unflinchingly.

'A bomb, you say. It has leaked that you're here!' The President appeared distressed at the thought of what could have been. 'I'm going to get to the bottom of this, I can promise you.'

'We need a new car and we're determined to catch our flight out today. If we rush, we can hold up the plane for half an hour or so and still get on the same flight.'

'Consider it done.' The President was on his cell phone immediately and the order for a new car was relayed instantly.

'Where are your bags? Ma'am, sir,' Mike asked urgently.

'We left them in the room ... in our rush to get out of there. I only managed to grab my briefcase.' Alex replied as he tried to overcome the confusion around him.

'I've got that,' said Frank and dashed away to retrieve the suitcases.

He was back wheeling a suitcase in each hand before the rest got to the top of the back staircase. 'I'll take one, Frank.' Mike waited till all goodbyes were said between the President and his two guests and Alex and Alia walked between their two bodyguards till they reached the new car on the side of the building. Before anyone went near it, both men checked the car all over, including under the hood and only got in when they were both satisfied that it was perfectly safe.

The car came with a driver, but Mike asked him to step out and that Frank was to drive, after all he had spent two years as a secret agent in Washington DC. 'He knows the way. We'll leave the car at the airport and you can pick it up afterwards.'

Their trip to the airport was uneventful and the plane was delayed for just over half an hour before take-off, much to everyone's relief.

26

The plane's touch-down on Rubinian soil made Alia's heart flutter and she didn't hold back in expressing it. 'Alex, I'm so excited to be back home. Right now, I wish I was more like some people who kneel down and kiss their country's ground when they return, like the Pope or some sportsmen who do this.' She clung tightly around Alex's arm and her excitement was quite palpable to her husband.

'I know how you feel. I got a bit excited seeing the alps, our woods and rivers. So, Alia, we have to work hard to retain what we have as a legacy to our children and especially our values.'

'Children? We only have one.'

'Well ... he makes up for two.' Both chuckled at the thought of it.

Mike approached and interrupted their conversation. 'Sir, ma'am, I've organised a car and it's already there waiting for us.' Alex and Alia glanced at each other knowing they were not surprised at Mike's efficiency and forethought.

As they walked outside the airport, there parked on the kerbside was their car and the driver none other than Bob. 'Welcome home, ma'am, sir.' After their greetings they all piled into the car and began their journey home.

'So, Bob, how's everything here at home? At the palace, engineering firm?'

'Dr Glandore, you'll find a lot more CCTVs everywhere, but so far no unusual happenings. As for the palace, we've tightened security and the principal of the palace school is monitoring a teacher, Ms Barbour, who was planted there by the WSO. We're tailing her to check where she goes and who she meets – her comrades. So far, no concrete evidence, but we have a lead for tonight … I think it might be worthwhile.'

'Perhaps then, first thing tomorrow morning you can brief us on everything. I think tonight you'll be busy enough.'

'Yes, sir.'

'Thanks, Bob. We'll see you tomorrow morning.' As the car parked at the rear of the palace, they entered that way and went up the back staircase and walked directly to their apartment. No one was more relieved than Alia. 'What a trip!' She flung herself on the couch and closed her eyes with her hands behind her head.

'Who could say we lead boring lives? Depending on what Bob tells us tomorrow, we'll have to factor in much of what happened and what we learned in the US.' Alex wasn't sure if he were talking to himself or if Alia was listening – she was still in the same posture. 'Hello, is anyone here?'

26

'I heard what you said, stop making me laugh — that's the last thing I want to do.'

'Laughter, my dear Alia, is the saviour of all things. Love and laugh – that's my motto these days.'

'How well is it working?' Alia asked.

Alex responded with resignation. 'Not as well as I want it to.'

'I know what you mean,' and with that, Alia got off the couch and began to unpack her bag. 'I never knew how time-consuming packing and unpacking can be. I think I'll have more empathy for those who do it all the time for me.'

'Well, if nothing else, this alone is a worthwhile lesson to learn.'

'You might be right, there.' Alia then gave a short shallow laugh and added, 'But honestly, I'm glad I'll probably not have to do it anymore – I don't have the time. Starting tomorrow, it's going to be full on.'

'When you're right, you're right. Come on, I'm jet-lagged, I need to rest.' He was not surprised that sleep found him easily.

27

Understandably, they both slept in until nine and they were pleased it wasn't any later. On their way down to the dining room for brunch, they met the queen coming up the staircase. 'Alia, Alex, I was told that you had both returned.'

'Mother, I'm so pleased to see you.' They both embraced and kissed each other on both cheeks and Alex did likewise. 'There's so much we have to tell you.'

'Well, when can we speak? I'm going to my office. Shall we say in an hour?'

'We'll see you then. Where's Stephan?'

'He's back at school. He will be very excited to see you both.'

As they continued towards the dining room, Alex spontaneously said, almost half to himself and straight from the heart, 'I missed that boy so much.'

Something in the way he said it, as if a part of himself was missing without his son, brought an unknown pang to Alia's heart. She simply responded, 'I missed him, too.'

27

Their time in the dining room was unusually silent, each in his and her own thoughts, which prompted Alex to ask, 'Is everything okay? You're very quiet.'

'I could say the same thing about you. I guess there's a lot to process with what happened in the last four days and I'm wondering what news Mother has to tell us.' It was the only response she could make because any analysis of her heart and emotions would have been incomprehensible to her at that moment.

'If you're finished why don't we go up now?'

'I'm not really hungry – it must be this jet lag.'

'You can hold my hand if it'll make you feel any better,' and with that he scooped her hand into his and together they walked towards the queen's office.

The queen's personal assistant, Laurence, was there to greet both of them. 'Her Majesty won't be too long. Please take a seat.' He then rang through, 'Ma'am, they're here.' He looked at the two seated and said, 'You may go in, now,' and stood to open the door for them.

'Alia, Alex, come in. I'm so pleased to see you. Sit down. Laurence will you bring coffee and tea in shortly.' The queen came around from behind her desk and sat in one of the armchairs around a small coffee table. 'So, tell me everything. What news from the US?'

'Where do we begin? It's been quite a whirlwind four days.' Alia glanced at Alex and coaxed him to cut in anytime he wished to contribute. 'The trip was as hush, hush as it could be, but evidently not entirely secret. The President – what can I say about the President? For me it was difficult to work him out. He retained that diplomatic stance, which annoyed me severely, and said as little as he could.'

'But, Alia, you must agree he said as much as was possible and as things stood, word still got out about our presence in the White House. How could that have happened?' Alex asked emphatically. 'I've been pondering on the events in the States, and I agree with Mike. It must've been the missing bodyguard. He played an active part in the explosion of the bomb under the car ...'

'What was that? An explosion? Explain!' The queen became quite perturbed with what she heard, and her anxious concern demanded quick and honest answers.

'Don't worry, Mother, we're okay. Nothing happened.'

'Something must have happened if you're "okay" now. What happened?'

Alex answered the queen's pressing question. 'Ma'am, someone planted a bomb under the car we were to travel in and take us to the airport. Fortunately for us, Mike detected that there was something seriously wrong and warned us, so all harm was avoided. The thing is that there was a lot of information that the President would not tell us due to security. The main thing though, is that they are fully aware of the WSO and have had them in their sights for a long period of time. Now that the WSO has started to act on its plans, it's time for the US and UK to put some plans of their own into place. What those plans are we do not know, nor when or how they'll be implemented. We had to sign two documents giving the US and its allies permission to act in the interest of democracy and the rights of the people under such a government.'

Alia continued from Alex's explanation. 'We've brought home more documents for you to sign. We asked about our Prime Minister and the President said he was under investigation, so it was not worthwhile including him in our plans. He had an updated search on Mr Wessler which showed he was forced to join.' She peered at her mother closely and asked, 'Do you remember when you visited our Prime Minister in hospital after that nasty car accident?' The queen was too engrossed in everything that was relayed to her to speak, she just nodded her head and waited apprehensively for Alia to continue. 'Well, that was no accident. It was the WSO's way of telling him what further things could happen to him should he not join them.' The queen placed her hands onto her face so from the nose down it was covered, she inhaled deeply and exhaled with a sigh into her hands.

Alex could see the queen's distress. 'Ma'am, the President assured us they will very soon reverse this situation and our Prime Minister will be freed from their clutches. We gave him our verbal assurance and written documentation that we will support all their endeavours, whether they choose to inform us of everything they decide to act on, or not. Do you think we did the right thing?'

'If we cannot rely on our allies, then there is no hope for us or anyone else. There have always been people whose minds dwell in darkness, but let's not forget that the light shines even brighter in the dark and eliminates it. So, in answer to your question, yes, you did the right thing.'

'Ma'am, we have these documents for your signature which will need to be returned to the President as soon as possible.' Alex handed Her Majesty the manila envelope that they carried with all the important papers nestled inside there for her to read and sign. 'Alia and I have also read these documents, so if there is anything you would like to ask us about them, we will try and put things in perspective.'

'Thank you, Alex. It appears you have both discharged your responsibilities with much success.'

'To tell the truth, Mother, I couldn't have done it on my own. Alex stood by me when I needed him the most and made me see things in different ways, which were relevant and right.'

'I have no doubt, my dear, that it was so. I always hoped you would both come to realise that there is no Alia without Alex and no Alex without Alia.' She glanced down onto the manila envelope and continued. 'Now, if you leave me on my own, I will lock my office door and sit here and go through these important documents.'

Alex gave a bow of his head and Alia a short curtsy and they left Her Majesty's Office. As they made their way down the staircase, they were contemplatively silent until they reached the floor of the main entrance. 'I have to go to work and take Bob with me, if he's not already there. Are you going to be okay here? I think Kendal will have quite

27

a few things to fill you in with and Nat will be here also. I might ask Mike to come to the plant.' Suddenly he gave her a huge hug and whispered into her ear. 'Be alert and careful at all times. I love you,' and with that he turned and walked out the door while talking on his cell phone.

28

It was not difficult for Alia to find Kendal and Nat. Then she noticed that Nat was quietly observing while he followed all of her movements. 'Kendal, there you are. What can you report to me?'

'Ma'am, I've made a written report of all the work we did around the palace. Bob has signed off on the report and I've emailed it to you. Everything is there.'

'What can you tell me about things that are not in the report? Come to my office and we can discuss everything. Nat, you too.'

Nat chose to stay guard outside the office door in full view of Jillian in her personal assistant's office. He gave her a nod to let her know that he would remain in that position for the duration of the conference inside the Princess' office. 'Your Highness, this is what we know about Ms Barbour. We have her under constant surveillance and hope she will lead us to other members of the WSO. In one part of her usual journey she always turns into a lane and just simply disappears, so whoever follows her cannot work out exactly where she went. The same lane all the time – as it happened last night.'

'What's the name of the lane?' Alia asked

'Rhinestone Lane.'

'Now that's interesting. This particular lane was named for King Samuel's daughter, Princess Rosemund, in honour of her marriage, when he gave her a most beautiful rhinestone as a gift. That was back in the fifteenth century when these crystals were found on rocks on the banks of the river Rhine. They look like diamonds but project the most electrifying colours from each stone.'

'Do you think there is some connection?'

'Not the rhinestone, as such, but *Rhinestone House*, which was also a gift from the king to his daughter on her wedding day, may be relevant.'

'We've not checked behind the thickly grown ivy on the wall, but tonight we're going to use the spy fly drone which has a very sensitive microphone, a high-resolution camera, a one mile range and a one week battery which is camouflaged in appearance. You can hardly tell it from the real fly.' Kendal was so caught up in his explanation of the drone he appeared to be reliving some personal escapade. 'Amazing what nanotechnology can do.'

'I've no doubt, but I believe the house behind the wall is in great disrepair. It's a National Trust home, but as usual there are never enough funds to do anything and bring it to its former glory.' Alia looked over at Kendal who was still in his own little world and asked, 'How did she get in? I know there is a gate there somewhere, but it's been bolted shut for decades. I'd like to know how she got in.'

'We hope that we'll find out tonight.' Kendal continued with his report. 'Now, ma'am, about the palace and the grounds. As for the CCTV installations, it's now possible to monitor a greater part inside and outside of the palace and detect any suspicious activity. So far there is no one to incriminate. But we're vigilant at all times.'

'Was there anything to the contrary discovered about Parkinson? He, after all, has access to every room in the palace.' Even as Alia asked, she found it hard to believe any implication on his part.

'Ma'am, we could not find a thing on him. At present, everyone is monitored a lot closer than before, and the extra equipment has helped us to view each person's direction everywhere in the palace and outside.' Kendal could see the princess was not reassured. She listened, yet her facial expressions told a different story than one of conviction. 'All I can say is that these things take time to be solved and I'm sure this will happen, hopefully sooner than later.'

'I'm sure you are all doing the best you can. Keep me up to date as things begin to happen. I'll speak to Bob as well,' and with that he was dismissed. However, when Alia opened her office door, she found Nat standing guard in front of it, looking quite solemn. 'Is this necessary Nat. I'm quite fine in my own office.'

'No, ma'am, you're not. Everywhere you go, I go.'

28

Alia gave him a smile that signalled a heartfelt appreciation. 'Well then, I shall be in good safe company all the time.' She looked across at Jillian and motioned her to come into her office. 'So, tell me, what has happened in this office for the last four days?'

Jillian carried a briefcase and she gently placed it on Alia's desk. 'Ma'am, in here you'll find all the letters and those I could respond to. You'll need to go over all of them and let me know what changes you require.' Alia opened the satchel and retrieved several letters which had piled up in the course of her absence. 'There are also emails you need to see.'

'I think you should stay here with me and we'll go through everything together. That's faster and more expedient.' They remained in the office for a good few hours and the only disruption was the phone when it rang. When their heads looked up from the totally organised mail in front of them, they divided it in sections, some which Jillian took and the others Alia attended to the task. Emails were next in line. When she managed to clear her mind from the pile-up of mail and emails, she looked around the office and liked what she saw. *It's good to be home*, she thought. Her eyes were diverted towards her office door and there, Nat's defined upper body shape was outlined through the thick frosted glass on the top half of the door. Oddly enough, she felt safe.

When Alia eventually surfaced from her office, she decided to seek her mother and see how she was getting along with the documentation she gave her. The queen was still in her office, but the door was now open. Laurence nodded his head when she arrived, and Alia tapped softly on the door. The queen glanced up and saw her daughter.

'Come in, Alia, and close the door behind you. Take a seat.' She waited till Alia was comfortably settled and retrieved the papers from the locked drawer in her desk. The queen's office door was made from solid wood and Alia could not see Nat, but she knew he would be outside standing guard.

'I've read all of them and they all appear to be reasonable. I could make objections to one or two points, but it would only delay the process and in the long run it would matter very little, as things stand.' She stared down at the documents and nodded her head. 'I know what you meant about feeling vulnerable and disempowered in our own country's problems, but that's what happens when a nation is threatened by forces so evil. That's the time when you need your allies to come to your aid.' Again, she looked straight into her daughter's eyes. 'Alia, I have always been proud of you and never more so than during these crises. Now, tell me, what are we going to do with these signed documents?'

'We will give the documents to Stromson, our lawyer, who will sign a confidentiality document, let him read through them and see what he says. If it's okay, it has been arranged for Mike to travel to America with the help of one bodyguard of his choice, and personally deliver the documentation into the President's hands. No good going electronically. It can be easily detected. To dispel any suspicion, he will go in a private jet and complete this assignment – the sooner the better.'

28

'Who is the pilot?'

'Hand-chosen, Mother.' Alia could sense her mother's deep concerns for the whole operation. 'Don't worry, it will succeed.' She thought to change the conversation a little. 'I wonder how Alex is doing at the plant. I've been thinking about him all day.'

'We will soon find out tonight.' The queen was still not satisfied with the general knowledge of things. 'Is the plane on standby for departure at a moment's notice?'

'It is, but we'll have to check with Alex in case he has something more to convey to the President. I'll ring him and find out. In the meantime, don't worry. We're all trying our best,' Alia reassured her mother.

'Of course, my dear.'

29

Bob took Alex all around the engineering firm and in particular the plant to show him the new installations of CCTVs which Alex confirmed with his approval. The plant was fortified not only with electronic devices as security, but with added security staff. In the hallways of the company there were no more blind spots anywhere; in fact, no one could hide anywhere without being seen. In all the offices, the tight use of surveillance equipment made each working space impenetrable. What remained to be defined was the human element, and that at times was just as impenetrable as a boulder of granite.

'Dr Glandore, before we go to your office, I have some updated news about Ebba's mother. As you know she was born in England as Clarissa Smith and met Einheimmer through her father who worked in a similar field as him. Divorced Jacob Einheimmer ten years ago. For the last three years she has had intensive therapy for multiple sclerosis and undergoes some very expensive procedures. She has used a friend's name, Fiona Ohlson, who died some years ago, so she can remain as anonymous as possible. Doesn't want Einheimmer to know where she is or what's happening to her. To keep that a secret, Ebba's mother was admitted as a private patient without any state health benefits. I guess, sir, your PA is trying to help her mother, especially with the financial problem of her mother's condition, and trying to keep her father happy without raising his suspicions.' He glanced sideways at Alex. 'I discovered an email Einheimmer sent to his daughter. What it said was basically to get as much information from you as she could. I'll quote part of what he said, 'You work there – find out everything you can – especially about the shares.'

'But why the big secrecy? Maybe he can help her financially.'

'No, he was a philanderer and gambler. At present he's steadily losing money at the casino and cards organised by private parties. Ebba's mother doesn't want to have anything to do with him.' He paused there and quietly stated, 'Ebba's been at her father's beck and call trying to do his every wish, especially keeping an eye on your business, because of Einheimmer's investment in your company. I'd say that's why he kept secret that Ebba's his daughter.' It was the empathy of his words that gave rise to a much larger meaning than the actual utterance of his latest report on Fiona Ohlson.

It did not escape Alex's understanding. 'Well, we'll see what we can do.' He peered over at Bob who walked beside him as a stalwart supporter with hands behind his straight back and noticed a hint of a smile on his lips, undetectable in general circumstances, but Alex knew him particularly well.

'What have you heard from Blake Crowley?'

'I was about to get to him. He rang once to speak with you but hung up when he heard my voice. I think he's out to get revenge for the destruction of his café. I felt he is brewing something – I just wish I knew what.'

'He's a devious man and I'm sure he'll not stop until he gets what he wants.' Alex's bull'seye assessment of Crowley left no room for error. 'Those minders of his surround him like vipers. Did you ever find out if he's a member of the WSO?'

'No, he's not. But that doesn't mean that he's not there as a "mole", secretly penetrating his objective. I just can't prove it.' Bob stopped walking to face Alex, and he continued, 'I think the café incident will wreak with revenge.'

'I wish I knew what that was.' Alex exhaled in an exasperated manner.

'Me too. They're experts in their field and hold their cards close to their chest. But don't worry. We're doing everything we can.' Together they walked the rest of the way silently. Bob went to his temporary office and Alex made his way to his own.

Alex's staff had worked with him for several years, especially those in the offices and the plant. External staff, such as security guards, gardeners, and cleaners were also stringently screened, however Bob's investigations were more thorough, and Alex needed to know what the results amounted to. He phoned Bob immediately. 'Have you got the latest reports on all the staff? Perhaps you can bring me up to date with some that are important.'

'Yes sir, I do. This time round it's a bit more interesting than the first investigation. Have you time for me to come to your office now?'

'If you can make it now, Bob, I've got just under an hour before an executive meeting ... Good, see you then.'

Bob collected the printed reports and placed them securely in the briefcase. He avoided emailing them where the chances of a security breach were much higher. Ebba's office door was open, and he entered. 'Is the Doc in?'

'Yes, he's expecting you.' She smiled up at him and then followed him with her eyes as he knocked and went into Alex's office.

'Good. Let's see what you have there.' Bob approached his desk and withdrew from his briefcase a bull-clipped small stack of papers and he handed it over to Alex. 'Take a seat, Bob. So, which are some of these interesting cases?'

'I've highlighted the ones I think you should look at.'

Alex checked every page and in particular those names that were highlighted. 'Who is this journalist ... Nick Matthews? I see he lives in Britain ... he's been in Rubinia for the last three weeks. Explain, why is he of interest?'

'He came snooping around the engineering plant wanting to interview you. I told him you were not here, and I then showed him the door. He's got guts – doesn't take no for an answer. He was back the next day and again I told him to leave. I noticed the CCT videos showed him trying to get entrance through the side door only to be pushed out by security. By this time, I knew he was up to something. I rang security and told them to bring him to me.'

Bob looked over at Alex and saw the intense concentration he projected. 'I detained and grilled him for a whole hour. His story is that while holidaying in Rubinia, the paper he works for, *The Southern Tribune*, told him to cover the fire at the café, for a big extra bonus.' He paused there for a moment in his recollection, then continued with his explanation. 'When he tried to interview Blake, he sensed there was more to this explosion and fire than he was being told by everyone. Blake promised him an exclusive interview, if he came to our plant and extracted information from you who, evidently, knows the reason why the café blew up in flames.' Bob continued with his explanation. 'I told him there was no way that you knew the reason for the explosion, but when I see Dr Glandore, I'll tell him you called.' Bob gave a chuckle before he continued. 'As I said before, he's an insistent little beggar. He told me he won't stop coming to the plant until he sees you. He's about to come any day now. What do you want me to do about him?'

'Next time he comes here, I'll see him. I'm interested to know what he's all about.'

'You realise, sir, that he may be getting paid by Blake just to rattle you up a bit and see what escapes from your mouth,' Bob cautioned Alex.

'Okay. Let's take this as it comes. Anything else?'

'For now, nothing at all. Life should be as normal as possible. I will be heading off a little earlier tonight to try and catch Ms Barbour in action.' Before Bob left Alex's office, he turned to him and suggested, 'I would recommend, sir, that you lock the papers I gave you in a vault.'

'I'll place them, for now, in the briefcase that is locked at all times and take them with me, until I've finished reading them all.'

'Yes, sir,' and with that Bob quietly left Alex's office.

Outside it was beginning to get dark and Bob quickened his step to reach his car. Instinct always told him to err on the side of caution and instantly he checked under the car, opened the hood and thoroughly inspected the engine and as he looked down on the ground next to the front tyre, he thought he saw a couple of small pieces of cut wire.

Immediately, he knew the brakes were tampered in his car. He got out the large torch, a jack which he placed under the car to raise the axle off the ground, rolled out a mat under the car and slid onto it and pulled himself at the right spot to inspect the underside. There he found the cut brakes. As part of his job, his nimble fingers knew exactly what they were doing and in a short time found the parts and fixed the brakes. As a matter of course, he urgently went and checked Alex's car, but all seemed in order. Not satisfied with his results, he rang Mike and asked him to double-check Alex's car again before he got in it for that evening. If this contrived scenario was to delay Bob from getting to the T-junction of Rhinestone Lane and Main Street, then they did not know Bob's tenacity.

He eventually got in the car and drove off while speaking to Nat and Kendal to make sure that the other agents were in their positions. Good fortune followed him with green lights at most intersections and he reached the site after leaving the car a hundred metres away from the junction. He set up the fly drone and from his iPad controlled its flight and enabled it to settle on a soft branch of ivy lying perfectly on the ledge of the wall. The darkness was not a hindrance to take high-definition film of any activity over the wall. The possibility that the teacher simply disappeared along the wall was for certain, so with patience and experience, Bob waited.

Suddenly he heard Nat's voice in his ears. 'Suspect on her way.' Ms Barbour was followed from her house, the bus trip, and the walk for the last two hundred metres. She wore black tights and a black trench coat that covered her body just past the knees. The matching black gloves and beret on her head blended inscrutably into the night. 'Check suspect – wearing dark glasses. Strange at night.'

'Copy that.' Bob lay low with his eyes peeled on the monitor. Not so strange, thought Bob. She was wearing the latest nanocrystal glasses, which turned infrared radiation into visible light and they looked exactly like sunglasses. As Ms Barbour approached the Lane, she stealthily looked around her. Assured that no one was about to see her, she swiftly turned left into the Lane. Bob had full view of her on his monitor. He spoke softly to Nat. 'She's walked a quarter of the way along the wall. She's stopped. Get to the T-section of the Lane – now!' Bob could see that she felt with her hands in among the ivy. Suddenly, she peered closely at what she found. He manoeuvred the camera for a close up. She took off her left glove and punched in the password: S569606. 'Do not approach her. Repeat – Do not approach her.' He saw her walk along the pathway that led to the dilapidated stately old house. She knocked on the door: one, two, waited three seconds and knocked once more. The door was opened and a half-lit entrance hall was visible on the monitor. Ms Barbour went in and closed the door behind her.

'Nat, get the squad team here – right away. Everybody here — where I am!'

Within seconds a squad of five men, Nat and Kendal included, arrived by Bob's side. 'I have the secret password and the way to knock on the door. We need to be so silent in our moves and quiet that no one should know we're here.' He looked squarely at the men. 'Okay, balaclavas on!' Bob led the way and everyone else followed. He reached the part of the wall where he thought the teacher had stopped. As his fingers and hands poked in a few places along the wall, he promptly discovered the gate behind the thick ivy, which became clear as he separated the ivy to gauge a closer view of the electronic lock. Bob shone a tiny torch on the small keyboard and punched S569606, and within seconds the gate began to open. Everyone hurried in and Bob checked to see if there was another keyboard to get out again, which there wasn't, however, to be safe, he left the gate slightly ajar and knew it would not be noticeable from the outside as the ivy made a natural protective cover.

The men crouched and swiftly reached the wall of the house. Bob indicated that they split into two teams – half waited on the left side of the wall and the others on the right. He took off the balaclava and stood in front of the door and knocked in the same rhythm as the teacher. Soon the door was open and there stood a man with a red scarf around his neck. Without sounding a word, Bob pushed the door so hard that the man lost his balance. Before he knew it, he was on the floor with his hands behind his back and duck-tape across his mouth. The rest of the men came in and got him to stand.

Bob stared hard at the man and softly but cuttingly said, 'Just nod where everyone is meeting.' The man would not budge. He just stood there helplessly. Bob went right up to him took him by the lapels of his jacket, leaned over and spoke to him in a soft yet severe tone. 'By the count of five there will be blood spilt – it won't be mine! Tell me where they are!!' Still the man stood motionless. Bob looked over at Nat and nodded his head. He pulled out a gun and placed a silencer as a muzzle device to suppress the sound from the gun. 'On the count of five,' and at that point he placed his hand in front of the man's face, so he'd know exactly how many seconds he had before the firearm was discharged. 'One,' and up went one finger. 'Two, Three, Four,' and at that point Nat took aim. Shaking with fear for his life, the man began to nod his head furiously to indicate he'd tell where the meeting was held. 'Walk in that direction.' The man shuffled with some hesitation and needed to be prompted to continue. At the end of the entry hall was a long hallway and as the squad of men crouched in a panther stance, the man suddenly stopped in front of a door and nodded towards it.

Two of the men took the WSO member and bound him up to a column in the entry hall and then joined their team. Instantly, on went the oxygen masks and Bob opened the door. A steep wooden staircase disappeared into the semi-darkness below them and as noiselessly as a cat on a stairwell they began to descend. They heard someone call out, 'Gunter, is that you? Who was at the door?' Their answer was delivered with an abrupt pounce into the basement. The squad team began to yell. 'Flat down on your bellies ... Flat down ... Flat down.' The surprise attack received its reward. Their shock in seeing the squad wearing oxygen masks and speaking through them in husky, deep, loud voices, thunder bolted everyone in the room with the swiftness of the squad's movements, which left the members no time to think of a reprisal. There were red scarfs strewn all over the floor. Two men stood guard with guns and rifles on the ready. The others bound members' hands behind their backs so speedily that when everyone stood, ready to march them into three vans, a couple of women fainted from the trauma of the night.

30

The paperwork that Alex read kept him engrossed for much of the night. When he did look up, he realised it was well past ten. He could not help but think about each person that made such an important team for his company and found it hard to come to grips that anyone would want to be a traitor, but then some temptations are far too great to resist. He opened the safe in the wall and placed the paperwork where they would remain until he needed any clearer information from the report.

Once more, he realised he'd be home late – again! Will he ever be able to change his habits, he thought, especially now when danger was so close to home. He hurried the process of locking up and as he secured the office door, he was surprised to see Mike standing guard outside of it. 'We're late tonight, Mike. We better get a move on.'

'Yes, sir. I've checked out the car and everything is fine.'

'Good man. Let's go,' and with that they left the building and the quietness of the streets helped them to arrive at the palace sooner than they expected.

Alex found Alia in the private lounge reading some papers. She looked up the minute he entered. 'Are you all right? It's very late.'

'Yes, I am. I was reading the report Bob gave me on the staff. I thought it best to read it in the office and put it away in the safe where it's more secure.' He leaned over and pecked her cheek.

'Do you want dinner? I've got some supper here ... uhm, cheese, crackers, cold meats, tea, coffee, and biscuits.'

'That'll do.' He sat in the opposite armchair and looked straight across at his wife. She had not lost the girlish look that he loved so well when she was a young teenager. Alia poured the coffee with milk, one sugar and gave him a plate with a fork. 'What's happened today, for you?' Alex asked her thoughtfully.

'The best thing was a skype from Isi and Christy. Those two little children of theirs are so wonderful, they've grown so much.'

'So has our Stephan. How was he today?'

'He is so attached to that dog of his. As soon as he came home from school ... I believe he did do his homework, he was out there playing and running around with Basco.' Alia paused for a moment and in an absent-minded way commented, 'And it snowed quite a bit up here. Any down your way?'

'Yes, but, uhm, not as much as I see here.' He gazed at Alia again. 'I worry that I have such little time to give to you and

Stephan.' He sighed and placed his fork on the plate, covered his face with his hands and closed his eyes.

'At least you're aware of it. Perhaps things will get better. It's so important to sort through the problems we've got right now.' Alia tried to convey a sense of understanding.

'You're right.' He pushed the plate away from him and added, 'Well, I've had enough to eat. I'm going to bed. Are you coming?'

'As soon as I've finished these couple of pages.'

By the time Alia went to bed, she found Alex fast asleep. She curled up next to him and placed her hand onto his chest. His measured breathing, which caused his chest to rise and fall, had also the required effect of putting her to sleep.

The crisp morning light shone so clearly that it made the newly downpour of snow sparkle. Bright in its reflective rays it promised of unexpected delights in the day. Alex was up early and a desire to see his father was foremost on his mind. He hadn't been to see him for far too long. He leaned over and kissed Alia on the cheek. She opened her eyes and a long yawn ensued in which she forgot to cover her mouth with her hand. 'Lovely tonsils down there,' Alex teased.

'I'm getting up.'

'No need. I just wanted to tell you, I'm going over to visit my dad. Perhaps have breakfast with him.'

'Okay. I'll lie in a bit longer,' and with that she turned over on her side and closed her eyes.

There was no movement within the palace at five-thirty in

the morning. As he opened the front door, he gasped at the expanse of clean white snow that covered everything in the garden area. He was amazed by the depth of snow that had fallen. It was impossible to walk in his office shoes across to his father's house. Back he went into the closet where the snow boots were kept. He took off his shoes and clambered into the appropriate shoe wear. He held his shoes in one hand and the briefcase in the other. As he reached the bottom of the staircase, he heard a familiar voice. 'Papa, where are you going?'

'Stephan, you're up and dressed. This is a bit early for you.'

Nothing could deter Stephan. He ran down the stairs and from the second to last step jumped into his father's arms. 'Come here, you. I missed you so much.'

'I missed you more.'

'I missed you even more, more, more.' They both laughed and holding his father's hand they went to the front door. 'Now, listen here, sport, I'm going to visit Grandpa,' and before he could finish his sentence, Stephan cut in.

'Can I come with you?'

'*May* I come with you?' Alex corrected him

'May I, please?'

'Okay, but I must let Susanna know where you are.'

'Pa, do you think I can bring Basco with us? You can hear him barking. He knows I'm up already.'

'All right. Wear your snow boots.'

Stephan ran to the closet, threw his shoes off and got into his snow boots in record time. He was beside his father as he opened the front door. 'Will you wait till I get Basco, Pa?'

'I'll be right here.' Alex could see Stephan was struggling to walk in the deep snow and shouted out, 'Go to your right!' He listened and soon the trudge in the snow became easier. Basco kept barking all the while, and as Stephan opened his pen he jumped on his master and down they both went. 'Stephan, are you okay?' Shouted his father.

Both dog and boy stood as one barked and the other laughed while they tried to run in the snow towards Grandpa's house. Alex placed his briefcase and shoes in the car, locked it, and made his way towards the yelping dog and giggly boy. As he approached them the dog came up to him and rubbed his body against his boots. Alex leaned over and patted him. 'You're a good dog, Basco,' and after being gratified with the compliment, Basco went to his master's side.

There was smoke coming out of the chimney and as Alex stood for a few seconds to admire his father's cottage, he took out his cell phone and took a picture. 'Hey, you two. Get over there so I can take a picture of you and Basco in it.' They both obliged and having accomplished that they knocked on the door and were properly surprised to see Jillian there.

'Good morning, Jillian. Is my dad in?'

'Yes, he's in the kitchen making breakfast. Come and join us.' She looked at Stephan and his companion and greeted them warmly. 'You've grown so much, Stephan. Want to have breakfast?'

'I'm really starving ... so is Basco.'

'Well you better both come along.' Jillian encouraged them.

As they all walked into the kitchen, there was Robert Glandore listening to the radio and cooking breakfast. 'Hey you lot. What a great surprise. Come here into Grandpa's arms, young man.'

Stephan dashed to those open arms and Basco followed him. 'Hi, Grandpa. I missed you.'

'I missed you too, my boy.' He squeezed his grandson tightly and then looked down at him and added, 'I bet you're just one hungry young man.'

'I'm starving,' repeated Stephan. 'So's Basco.'

'Well, we'll have to fix this. Come sit here at the table. We've got scrambled eggs, sausages and bacon and wait for it ... pancakes.'

Robert noticed his son. 'Alex, how are you? I haven't seen you in a long while, too.'

Alex came to his father and hugged him, and each man patted the other on the back. 'Good to see you, Dad.'

They all sat around the table talking and laughing at the same time and Basco thought he'd join in every time someone laughed and gave his version of it with a strange deep yelp, which made everybody else laugh even more. As the plates were emptied and hot chocolate, coffee and tea were handed around, Robert Glandore stood and addressed everyone at the table. 'Alex, Stephen, I have some wonderful news.' He turned to Jillian next to him and requested her to stand also. He placed his arm around her waist and drew her close to his side. 'We've decided to get married and you're the first to know.'

'Dad, that's great news.' Alex stood and went over to Jillian and gave her a kiss on the cheek and heartily shook his father's hand.

'Grandpa, does that mean you're going to have a big party? Can I come, too?'

'You most certainly can. You're going to be in it. You're going to be the ring bearer.'

'What does that mean?'

'You're going to carry on a cushion the two wedding rings we will exchange at the altar.'

'Wow, that's important, isn't it?'

'It sure is.' Robert looked at his son and continued. 'We haven't set a date yet – soon, we hope.'

'Right you are, Dad. I'm really happy for both of you. You've made me happier than I've been in a long time.'

Robert Glandore's smile disappeared from his face, momentarily. He came close up to his son and asked, 'Are things any better between you and Alia?'

'Oh, don't worry Dad. Things are slowly being sorted out. Everything's fine.' He quickly changed the subject. 'Christmas is nearly upon us. Will you be here?'

'We'll both be here.'

'That sounds fine.' He drew in a deep breath, which did not escape his father's notice. 'Okay, Dad, I must leave now. Work calls.' He looked over to where Jillian was talking with Stephan and patting Basco at the same time. 'Excuse me,

30

Jillian. Will you walk with Stephan over to the palace?'

'Of course. We should be going, too.'

Alex made his goodbyes and congratulated them once more and then gave his son a hug and kissed him on the head. As he walked towards his car, Mike stood beside it and Trent, his driver, was ready to go. 'Mike, take care of everyone here. I think Bob is coming to the plant in a little while.'

'I think, sir, you'll find that he's already there.'

'Good, I need to speak with him.' He got in the car and Trent drove off.

True to form, Bob was in the office allocated to him. As Alex knocked and entered, Bob looked up and swivelled his chair to face him. 'Dr Glandore, I've been going through some statements that have come to hand and I believe Lars Gilmar was approached and tried to be coerced into joining the WSO. He absolutely refused, but they don't give up easily. They wanted him to wreck your computer system.'

'I asked him to start on the computer system a few days ago. Do you think that's a safe decision?' Alex asked.

'Let him continue on the system and we'll soon find out if he's wrecking the whole works or not. So far as I can see, things are working a lot better.' Bob suddenly stopped and redirected his thoughts. 'Sir, I think you should make it official that Ms Barbour no longer works at the school. She's under interrogation. Just thought you might like to know.'

'You're a fountain of information, today. Should I ask how you know this?'

'Sir, do not ask me anymore because I cannot reply. Be assured of this!'

'You know that's hard for me to do ... not being in the know of what's happening.'

'All I can say is you are better off not knowing.' Bob continued to scroll through some files on his computer and then opened one. 'My only concern right now is Einheimmer. He's obsessed that he does well with his investment in your company and to make matters worse he's starting to show signs of being short of money. Among other things, he's a gambler too.'

Alex, swiftly interposed. 'I have to look up how many shares he's bought. I think I want to buy him out. He sounds like a danger to me.'

'I've got this information here ... right here, uhm, nine hundred thousand euros worth. That's a tidy sum.'

'If he is in debt and running short of cash, perhaps he'll be pleased to find a buyer quickly for the shares. I'd want to buy them off him, but not to know it comes directly from me.'

'He sold his house and racing horse. Don't worry, something can be arranged. Leave it with me.'

Alex stared at Bob incredulously, then gave a shallow chuckle and left for his office, where he knew a mountain of work was waiting for him.

31
.....

Meanwhile, in Cumbia, King Gregory arose from his bed to a thunderous dilemma. The phone call he received so early in the morning played a great part in the direction the day would take.

He replayed the information over and over in his head. There was no more time left in being patient. No one was going to stop his plan and it now became evident that its full force needed to be felt. He could think of nothing else than delivering the impact of his life's work. So preoccupied was his mind that completion of his dress and breakfast was performed with utmost perfunctory actions and lack of thought. Whether anyone was in his presence or not made little difference – he heard no one, spoke to no one and addressed no one when he marched out of his palace door.

The drive would take him to his summer house. Already, he had contacted his leaders for this urgent meeting and in his haste, he did not stop to think of providing food for everyone. Bad luck, he thought. Whatever he had there he'd use, which would be only drinks. After an hour's drive or so, he arrived at his destination, parked the car, and slammed the weighty door as he got out, still mumbling to himself.

With the heavy snowfall, there was no one there to clean a pathway to the house. He trudged in the snow knee-deep, cursing and swearing to himself, and just as he thought he reached the end of it, his next step was so deep, he lost his footing and fell smack on his backside, then struggled up and hastily shook off some of the snow from his two thousand euro coat. A couple more stumbles, but he still retained his stance and he reached the steps of the house. Up he went, relieved to take out the key and open up. As he entered the entrance hall, he felt as if he stepped into an igloo. 'Well, at least there's some wood in here. I'll get it started. If it's not enough, someone else can go out and chop some more.' He continued to grumble and speak aloud that he didn't notice the front door was left open, and standing in the entrance hall were three of his leaders.

'Cold out there, Gregory. Not enough wood, you think? We'll just have to make it a quick meeting,' came his Vice President's voice.

Surprised at the sound of voices from the hallway, he went to investigate. 'Oh, you're here. I've just got the fire going. Come and make yourselves at home.' His voice and demeanour were perfection in the making. 'Come, come,' he said, 'it's too cold out here.' He ushered them in and offered them a brandy each.

Soon, the entire group of leaders arrived, and they all sat

around the dining table while Gregory formally opened the meeting. 'I would never have brought you out here in this weather if it were not of the greatest urgency. Gunter and the majority of his members in Castelneuf city have been captured by the police or the Secret Intelligence Services. Since I've heard about it this morning, it has not ceased to play on my mind every moment of the day. Why did this happen? What went wrong? I've thought and thought. Carelessness! It's obvious someone was followed to the meeting place. Instead of taking a different route each time, they probably took the same way all the time, which eventually built up suspicion on those involved. Now, I'm not going to stand here and bemoan what has already happened, but I'm damned angry about it. Let's look forward. Can anyone suggest ways where we can get Gunter released?' He waited for a few seconds. 'Anyone?' Again he waited without results. 'Very well, it seems that the thinking is left up to me. I will organise something with my team and all I can say to each one of you, start thinking.' Gregory's discomposure was beginning to show.

'By the way Vassili, why were you not at that meeting? You're in charge of education and similar institutions.'

'I was unavoidably detained at one of the biggest universities in my country. I couldn't get to the meeting on time. Gunter was happy to take the meeting himself.'

'Hmm, instead he was taken, not you.' He stared at Vassili fixedly whose face was lowered with intense concentration on his iPad. 'You had better come up with a plan to get Gunter out of detention. He's our military expert. We can't afford to lose him. I want you to resolve this, very, very fast,' he added, pointing his forefinger at Vassili.

Eventually he looked up. 'It won't be difficult to get him out. I have people on the inside.'

'Do you know where he is exactly?' Gregory asked.

'Yes. Leave it with me.'

'I will. I want immediate results.' He sensed his anger raging inside of him and he ceased his talk for a minute or two. 'This was my main reason for this meeting. Does anyone else have anything more to report?'

'We're all ready to go. All we want is for you to say so and it all begins. So, what's it going to be, Gregory? Now or never?'

'Your enthusiasm impresses me, Heinrich, but your timing does not. It will be soon, I can assure you of that, so be patient and be ready at all times.' He scanned the faces around the table. 'Does anyone have anything else to say?'

Antony, his Vice President, spoke up. 'I think everything that needs to be said has been said, Gregory. I see the fire is lowering and there is no more wood, so I think that brings our meeting to an end.'

'Very well. I now close this extraordinary urgent meeting.'

Everyone stood, shook hands, and made their way through the snow to their cars. Gregory locked his summer house and followed suit, still annoyed at what the snow was doing to his precious clothes, yet he continued uttering expletives that should never be heard. More snow began to fall, and he couldn't wait to be on his way to his warm palace in the capital city.

32

Ms Barbour was replaced with Mrs Smithson who was a teacher of many years' experience and soon brought the classroom to its required status quo and high expectations. More important for Alia and Alex was that Stephan really liked her, especially as she particularly enjoyed teaching maths and science. He revelled in the small experiments they did in class and within a week, she was able to assess that some students were capable to be challenged in an advanced class of maths and science.

Often, Stephan would find Basco waiting for him outside the school so they could walk home together with a couple of bodyguards as well. On this particular day, when the class was dismissed and Stephan found Basco waiting patiently for him outside the school, he and a few of his friends ran towards Basco to pat and stroke his thick coat of hair and the dog's indulgence was perfection in patience. The children placed their heads on his back as if it were a pillow, kissed his head and tickled his chin, but no matter what they did, he remained motionless as a statue.

The two bodyguards ceased the jovial play and the children ran off waving goodbye to Stephan and the dog. As Basco stood, he stubbornly refused to budge. 'Come on, Basco. We got to go home.'

It was to no avail. He stood unmovable and in a low growl looked up at one of the bodyguards and continued to sound menacing. The bodyguard looked disturbingly down at the dog. 'What's wrong with your dog? Get the beast off me.'

'He's not a beast, he's my friend!' Stephan shouted loudly at him.

Morris, the other bodyguard, gently suggested to Stephan to take Basco and walk ahead while they followed behind them. 'That's Vanda. He's new here, that's probably why Basco is growling.'

Stephan did as he was told, but every so often Basco stopped, looked behind him, and growled. 'What's wrong, Basco? Don't you like Vanda? We'll be home soon.' Stephan continued to talk to his dog and pat him to reassure him. When they sighted the palace, they ran as fast as they could towards it and fortunately, Parkinson was at the front door and both boy and dog leapt up the steps and disappeared inside the palace.

As they both walked towards the staircase, Stephan heard his mother's familiar voice. 'Hello, handsome. How was school today?'

Up they dashed, Basco well ahead of his master and both fell upon her. Alia crouched and encircled her son with her arms with a firm squeeze and a big kiss. 'You know, soon you'll be as tall as me. What are you eating, anyhow?'

'Lots and lots. Have we got anything to eat? I'm *really* hungry.'

Susanna suddenly appeared and stood beside Alia. 'Susanna, how about ordering some baby cucumbers, cherry tomatoes and carrots, plus cheese and crackers. That should see him through to dinner.' Then she turned to her son and asked, 'How does that sound?'

'Great Mum, but you forgot Basco.'

'Oh, a couple of sausages for Basco, too.' Alia waited by the staircase as Susanna returned and the three of them went into the nursery room and she departed for her office.

Having finished the afternoon snacks and his homework, Stephan wanted to go outside and play with Basco. So, all three traipsed down the staircase and when they reached the grand entrance hall, Stephan ran to the closet for the thick parka and snow boots to wear and dashed outside with Basco, leaving Susanna a little behind. 'Hey guys, wait for me,' she called out.

The snow was still thick in areas of the garden, but a lot of shovelling had cleared the main pathways. Stephan and Basco romped around in the snow falling over, getting up, throwing snowballs at Susanna and she in turn at Stephan. In the midst of this merry play, Hans turned up and insisted that Basco had to return to his pen to be given his dinner. Stephan asked if he could go with his dog while he ate, but the request was denied because he was too busy with a lot of dogs that night. All Stephan could do was to stand next to Susanna and watch Basco being taken away.

Both spectators were so caught up viewing an unwilling Basco forcibly removed from them that they did not hear the footsteps in the snow. It was dusk by this time and rather quiet around the palace. Suddenly, Stephan felt a strong hand around his arm and a thick croaky voice addressed him. 'Come on you little brat – you're coming with me.' Morris, who was nearby, suddenly sprang into action and was on top of him, but Vanda managed to grab the truncheon in his holster belt and whacked him on the head unconscious.

Immediately, Susanna became aware of what was happening. She jumped the man, and he pushed her hard onto the snow. She grabbed his leg down in the position she was at and bit it as hard as she could. He gave a painfully loud cry, and then swung around and hit her across the face as hard as he could. She, too, lay motionless on the cold icy snow. While this was going on, Stephan managed to escape from Vanda's hold. He attempted to run towards the palace and fear kept him without voice. All he could do was inhale oxygen.

Instantly, the fire alarm was heard screeching in the open air. Vanda raced after Stephan, abruptly picked him up and threw him over his shoulder. He ran as fast as he could to a nearby four-wheel drive. Urgently, Mike appeared and gave chase as if his life depended on it. All he could do was to reach the car as it sped off into the distance. Nat had the foresight to drive one of the cars out from the garage and pick up Mike and take chase. Vanda did not use the front gate. He had another old gate already open two hundred metres along the estate border. They drove over half an hour, but the car was nowhere to be seen. During their chase they contacted Bob and he immediately set forth the search with the secret service and police.

By the time they returned to the palace the whole place was in an uproar. Susanna was taken to hospital with severe concussion. Alia was beside herself and kept pacing the floor in the entrance hall. 'I cannot believe this has happened. Where were the bodyguards? Tell me, where were they?' she yelled at some of them who rallied after the fire siren went off. There was nothing anyone could say to allay her fears. The tears flowed freely, and she didn't care who saw her.

The only one who remained in a measure of calmness was the queen. She had her arm around her daughter's shoulder and just simply stroked her hair while she cried. Every so often, Alia removed herself from that position and asked futile questions in the hope of receiving some positive answers – none were forthcoming.

'Morris was among the bodyguards, Your Majesty. Bob and the police have been notified according to Mike and they're on their way back here.' Kendal looked at Alia with all the pity that was in his heart but showed none of it. 'As to where all the bodyguards were at that time, most were doing the rounds of the palace grounds, not knowing that Stephan was outside with his dog. Morris and Vanda were outside in the front of the palace guarding the boy. Unfortunately, we didn't know Vanda's motives. He hit Morris on the back of the neck, and he was unconscious when all of this was happening. Susanna was also hit across the face and she too fell on the snow unconscious. I found it strange that the dog was not with Stephan and when I went in search of Hans, he'd disappeared.'

The Queen felt sympathy for both of them and asked, 'How are Morris and Susanna?'

'He's come to, but Susanna is still under doctor's care, Your Majesty. I think they'll eventually be okay. It was a good thing that Parkinson alerted everyone with the fire siren. Otherwise, we'd be totally in the dark.' Kendal endeavoured to raise Princess Alia's spirits and added, 'At least the CCT's showed us the type of car that was used, and the authorities were alerted immediately.'

Alia sat next to her mother and tried to bring a sense of peace in her fearful state. She thought she was doing quite well, and then Alex appeared with Bob. She turned and ran to her husband as he sprinted to her and they clung to each other as if bound by twine. She cried and he tried hard to give her courage and every so often he'd cup her face with his hands and kiss her forehead and they continued to hold each other tightly, afraid to let go.

They remained as such for a few moments and then they heard Robert Glandore's voice. Both parted and together embraced him.

'Dad, I'm so glad you're here.'

'Where else would I be, son, but by your side.' Robert

32

found it hard to find words that could really comfort them. He noticed Jillian at the other side of the room with some of the staff huddled together and each looked forlorn. He left his son and the princess and walked over to Jillian who immediately fell into his arms with more tears.

Bob knew it was time to take control of the situation. 'Your Majesty, Your Highness, Dr Glandore, I must inform you all that the abduction has taken priority over everything else. The police and the National Secret Service are devoting themselves to finding the kidnappers. This is going to be made known nationally and internationally to show our enemy that we are not afraid to come out with the truth. The whole world needs to know what kind of scum we're dealing with. We will find Stephan if I have anything to do with it.' He paused and looked at all the distraught faces and especially Alia and Alex's. 'The news will break tonight. Television, radio, internet – the whole works. Don't lose hope. We will find him.'

Alia had recovered in a small way as she clung onto Alex's arm next to her. She asked, 'Bob, how could this Vanda creep come into our service? Why weren't his true credentials exposed?'

'There are professionals out there that make their living from faking identities so well, you'd never know the difference,' Bob explained and repeated, 'Ma'am, we will find Stephan.'

'I want him alive, Bob, *alive!*' Alia's heart was shattered. Her body shivered and trembled at the thought of Stephan.

Jillian asked her chambermaid to bring a cardigan or a shawl for Alia to throw over her shoulders.

'Yes, ma'am. That's how I want him, too,' Bob tried to reassure her.

'Oh, Alex. Where have they taken our son? Where will he sleep in this cold?' Alia began to weep again and out from the depths of her heart she called out, 'God help him.' And a little softer, 'Help my son.'

Alex signalled to the queen to come over and as she approached, he nodded to sit next to Alia and comfort her. 'Oh, Mum, what shall we do?'

The queen was slightly taken aback. She could never recall a time that her daughter referred to her as Mum. It was always the formal, Mother. 'Well, my darling. The best thing is to have faith and believe with all our heart and soul that Stephan will return to us, unharmed ... believe it, my girl.' Alia closed her eyes and placed her head on her mother's shoulder for quite some time.

Alex took Bob aside and earnestly asked what could he, personally, do to help. 'I can't stay here waiting for something to happen.'

'I know, Doc. But right now, things are so sensitive that I'd be concerned you too might be abducted. It's not unforeseeable. So, please, stay here, and if anything turns up that we need your help with, you'll be the first to know.'

'I need a doctor for Alia. I think she needs a sedative tonight.' He paused and took a deep breath.

'Consider it done.'

32

Later, he saw Bob talking with Parkinson and writing down a number which he immediately dialled. Within half an hour, the royal family doctor arrived. Alia rejected the idea of a sedative and refused all suggestions of it. However, as the evening grew, she knew her strength was weakening and she couldn't relax or sleep, so when Alex presented her with a sedative and a glass of water, she took it.

'Ma'am, would you like a sedative as well?' he asked the queen.

'No thank you, Alex. I'll be in my bedroom to rest a while.' She stood and without a word left the grieving group of people and went upstairs as quietly as possible to her room. Alone with her private thoughts, she opened the drawer of her side table on the right of her bed and took out a Bible. It appeared well-read as there were sticky strips in various places to indicate certain passages of interest.

Sylvia Amsler Gilland knelt by the side of her bed as she held the Bible closely to her chest and with bowed head prayed for her grandson's safe return. Slowly, the tears trickled on her cheeks and left a few stains on the Holy Book. She didn't know how long she had remained as such, only when she endeavoured to stand she found it difficult to do so from the stiffness in her knees, but she left the Bible on the bed and with some effort tried to pull herself upright. She rubbed her knees to allow some circulation of blood to return and then calmly got herself ready for bed.

33

There appeared to be some semblance of normality in the palace the next morning. Parkinson made certain that all the staff under his care went about their duties with a measure of diligence after the calamitous events of yesterday. Queen Sylvia, upon having a light breakfast, asked to see Bob in her office. He arrived as quickly as possible with some anticipation of the queen's urgent questions. 'What has happened since last night? I want to know everything.'

'We were fortunate enough to be able to track this Vanda character through his cell phone up to a certain point. It seems they were heading north-west towards Saint Anna's Pass, but he must've realised it and ditched the phone. We've got a Child Abduction Emergency alert as well as an AMBER alert which involves all kinds of broadcasting emergency responses. This means, Your Majesty, every electronic, digital newspaper and social media has been alerted to look out for your grandson. It also includes a lookout for Hans and Vanda.' He stopped there and glanced at this grand lady whom he respected during all those years in her service. She looked a little pale, the eyes a little sunken, the lips tighter together and her brow lines carved a little deeper. 'The response so far has been amazing – from all sectors. If you look towards the front gate and follow the fence line, you'll see already the number of flowers that have been left there. I think, ma'am, the whole nation and the whole world is willing and wishing for Stephan's safe return.'

Queen Sylvia stood and went to the window, and although the fence was some distance away, she could see the beginnings of a sea of colours along the palace's border. 'I have always relied on the goodness of people,' she spoke softly and then returned to her desk. 'Have you spoken with Her Highness and Alex?'

'Yes, ma'am. I told them exactly what I've told you.'

'Thank you, Bob, for everything. Keep me constantly informed.'

'Yes, ma'am.'

As Bob began his descend of the staircase, he noticed Alex and Alia coming along the hallway. He waited for them to reach him. 'Ma'am, sir, I'm going to check all the mail, emails and internet, but most importantly check in with the detectives at the police station. Who's in charge of the mail here?'

'You should see Parkinson for that.' Alia informed him.

Bob allowed the couple to go down before him and as he observed them holding hands and speaking softly to each other, he realised that they drew strength from each other's relationship. It put a light smile on his lips to see them display a revelation of something of their former selves, their former love. He could not help but contrast the queen's solitary state at a time of such heightened sadness and yet he sensed a strength within her so silent that anything else would be superfluous.

At the bottom of the staircase, Bob ran into Parkinson carrying a basket filled with mail. 'Parkinson, I'm afraid I've got to go through all of the mail myself. Where do you sort it out?'

'Come to my little office down this hallway towards the main kitchen area.' They walked together and soon Parkinson pulled out a key from his pocket and opened the door which led into a confined area where a desk, a cabinet and three chairs made up the bulk of the room. A rug of burgundy and blue hues gave warmth to the place. Bob was surprised to see a computer on the desk.

'I'm impressed, Parkinson. You've learned to use the computer.'

'Necessity makes us masters of the most improbable things.' He sat behind his desk and Bob found a chair opposite him, which he thought looked the most comfortable, for he knew this task was going to take quite some time to sort out.

'I think this will be the best system. I'll look at each letter and the obvious ones which are formal with official stamps and seals, I'll hand them to you. The rest, I'm going to have to open them. Dangerous times call for drastic measures.'

Bob scanned several pieces of mail and handed them to Parkinson and as he continued to put into practise his system, he eventually found an envelope which had all the ear markings of suspicion written all over it. The manila envelope was badly addressed, it was postmarked from the centre of the city and heavily sealed with sticky tape. 'Bingo, Parkinson. I think we might have it.'

Parkinson looked on astutely as Bob began to unravel the sticky tape and carefully opened the envelope. Having executed that with great attention, he pulled out a white sheet of paper with letters cut out from a newspaper which read: If You Want To See Your Son Again – You Know What You Have To Do!

Bob finished going through the rest of the mail and being satisfied that there were no others indicative of foul play, he left Parkinson to his own resources and quickly went to find Alex and Alia. They were both in the library. 'Dr Glandore, ma'am, I have something to show you. I think I understand the meaning behind it, but I want you to confirm it.' He gave them the sheet of paper and as Alia finished reading, she gasped and placed her hand over her mouth.

'It's the WSO. They did it! They took our son. Alex, *they* took our son.' She clung to Alex's arm tightly as he brought his other hand around and touched her face gently.

'I'm sorry, ma'am, to distress you, but I had to be a hundred percent sure. Dr Glandore, do you agree? Do you think it could be anyone else?'

'Blake is another definite possibility, but we can't rule out the WSO, either. They've been after us to join them for quite a while. These are the tactics they use to force people to join. Once you're in it's hard to get out.'

'Yes, sir, I know. I just had to clear that with you first. I'll need to go to the police headquarters. I think they've found the four-wheel drive.'

'Do what you must do, Bob. Just let us know everything you find out.'

'Yes, sir.' Bob left directly for the police headquarters.

'I just can't go to the dining room. Shall we go to the private lounge and order coffee and tea there?' Alia halted her walking pace and glanced up at Alex as she spoke.

'Right you are. I'll ring and order. What do you want to eat?'

'Just toast and cheese.' She continued to hold him by the arm as they began to go upstairs. 'I was thinking, we should ring Isi and Christy and Dave. What do you think?' Her voice was low and husky.

'We'll do that when we settle in the lounge.'

As if on cue, Alex's cell phone rang. 'Isi, I'm glad you rang. I was about to ring you.' He listened to his friend. 'I'm so torn-up inside, I don't know what to do. I feel so helpless. Yes, she's here. Isi and Christy want to speak with you.'

Alia took the phone and simultaneously drew in a deep breath. 'Thank you for ringing, Isi. I just can't believe it. I'm beside myself. Yes, thank you ... Yes, I would like to speak with her. Hello. Oh Christy, I'm so devastated ... I can't believe such a thing has happened.' She tried hard to hold her emotions in check, but the whole situation was overwhelming. Soft tears rolled continuously on her face and a box of tissues was at hand as she intermittently wiped her puffy eyes and dabbed at her nose. 'I know, I know. Can you do that? I'd love to see you. What about the children? Your mum can ... that's good of her. Thank you, Christy, thank you. I can't wait to see you tonight. Text me your flight information and I'll send someone to pick you up. Yes. Bye, bye.'

'Christy's coming tonight and Isi tomorrow. They're such good friends.'

'While you were talking to Christy, I got a call from Dave. He's somewhere in Peru and catching the first flight tomorrow morning for here. He's a good one, that Dave!' Alex took Alia's hand and squeezed it. As they reached the lounge and settled down for their morning tea, another call came through from Charlie. She wanted very much to be with them, but with the expectation of her baby being born any day soon, the doctors would not allow her to travel.

Alia was on her cell phone speaking with Princess Carlotta and Prince Edvard; their outpour of sympathy touched Alia's heart. 'Anything we could do – anything, please let us know.' There were similar sentiments from Prince Albert and Princess Rosalind.

A few moments later Josh Landers called, who promptly offered a private helicopter not too far off from Rubinia which could be used for the search. Anything that they required would be at their disposal. 'Josh, you have always been a true friend. Thank you for your generosity. If there is anything you can help us with, I'll be first on the phone to you. I've just spoken to your sister Rosalind as well.' Alia felt humbled and grateful by the many enquiries and offers of help.

Last, but not least, Jonathan Levinson did not ring, he just turned up at the palace. He was staggered at the number of trucks, cameras, and journalists that appeared camped outside the palace. A contingent of police was there, also. They stopped him as he began to approach the gate, and when he was asked if he had an appointment with the princess, he replied, 'Ask the gatekeeper, he knows me well.' The policeman motioned to one of the gatekeepers to approach him.

'This man says you know him well. He wants to go to the palace.'

Jonathan stared at the gatekeeper and in an urgent voice uttered, 'Look, you know me. I don't want to be bothering the princess with phone calls. I just want to see Her Highness and Alex. I've been in and out of these gates hundreds of times. I was one of the groomsmen at the Princess' wedding! Now open up this gate before I do call her and she gets mad at you. Now!'

The policeman asked again, 'Do you know this man?'

'Yep, I do. What he says is true.'

Jonathan looked at the policeman and stated, 'You see, it's true.'

'Okay, Mr Levinson.' The gatekeeper opened the gate

and Jonathan drove through as he fleetingly watched the gatekeeper, in the rear-view mirror, staring at his car as it made its way towards the palace.

Jonathan parked his car on the side of the palace and as he walked towards the front, he noticed that Parkinson had opened the door and stood patiently waiting for him to arrive. 'Parkinson, true as ever. How did you know I was coming? No, don't answer that. The gatekeeper.' Parkinson nodded his head a couple of times and simultaneously closed his eyelids as he did so. 'Where are they?'

'Upstairs – the private lounge, Mr Levinson.'

Jonathan Levinson strode across the entrance hall and climbed the staircase three by three as if he were a twenty-year-old. During his years of marriage and with the number of children he'd accumulated, the pounds simply fell off him. His new athletic body was a testament to his commitment to basketball and/or jogging every morning with the staff from his company. He expected everyone who worked for him to be at their optimal ability. What else could he do but be the prime example to them all.

As he reached the top, he found Alex waiting for him. 'Jono, thanks for coming.' They shook hands and embraced as they had always done.

'Listen, my friend. I've known you all my life. We will find Stephan. Anything I can do – I'm here for you.' He looked at Alex as they walked together along the hallway and noticed the obvious drawn pallid face and the sadness in his eyes as they hid behind the glasses. As if he had read Jonathan's mind, he took a hold of the left side of the glasses and pulled them tighter towards his forehead.

As Jonathon entered the lounge, he was quietly taken aback by how frail Alia looked, not that she would ever admit to it. A brave front was always her motto, but he'd known her all his life and she could not hide the ache that penetrated her heart and soul. As soon as Alia saw him, she stood, walked towards him and hugged him as hard as she could. 'Jono, your being here means the world to me.'

They all sat around the coffee table and tried to understand this senseless act of terror. Their talk was punctuated with gaps of silence, each in his or her own thoughts. The quietness lay around them like death. There was a void and that was being filled with the distant faint sound of a dog's whimper. Jonathon looked up abruptly and sliced the silence like a forced reminder of the present. 'What's that sound?' He got up and went to the window. 'Alex can you hear it?'

Alex was soon beside him. He listened quietly. 'I think that's Basco. I've forgotten all about him. That poor animal, he must be missing Stephan.'

'Maybe we should bring him up here for a while. I can't bear to hear him like that. Who's looking after the dogs, now?' Alia sounded concerned and she too joined the men at the window.

'I'll find out from Parkinson, he'll know.' Alex placed his arm around Alia's shoulders and drew her to him.

All three stood there staring out of the window as if an

answer would be presented to them by some miracle, but nothing of the sort happened. After a while they all sat again in their armchairs and conversation became mundane as the background awkward whining of a dog was forefront in their mind. What could anyone say, who had not gone through anything like this, to soften the blow? All that was left was for Jonathan to make his earnest farewells, being careful as to what he could and could not say to two of the most precious friends he ever had.

Alex escorted him to the front door and was surprised how quickly the day had darkened. Upon his return, he found Alia looking forlorn as she gazed out through the window. Alex went next to her and took her hand in his. 'It's still snowing,' Alia said softly.

Fortunately, the phone rang in the room and Alex stood to answer it. 'Good, escort her to the private lounge.' He turned and faced Alia. 'Christy has arrived. Parkinson is bringing her here.' Alia took a deep breath. Her fingers ran nervously through her hair and waited anxiously until Christy entered the room. She felt a knot in her chest that naturally travelled to her throat and silently thought she had lost her voice.

The door of the lounge opened and Christy entered the room. As soon as she saw Alia, she walked quickly, and Alia did likewise. They met halfway, embraced, and the heartfelt tears fell freely as they comforted each other. Eventually, Christy held her at arm's length, 'I'm so pleased to be here with you – really I am.'

'I could hardly wait for you to get here. Thank you,

Christy. Your visit means everything to me.'

Christy then noticed Alex who reservedly observed how naturally his wife opened up to Christy and allowed all those pent-up emotions to spill over and be shared with her long-standing friend. It did not matter that being together was intermittent, the important thing was that their friendship picked up where it left off. She calmly walked up to Alex and they hugged one another. 'Alex, how are you holding up?'

'Everything that can be done is being done. I wish I knew what else I can do. I can't bear just sitting around.'

'You're a tower of strength for Alia and that's important, too. We all need to be patient and pray.' She noticed Alex withdrew into himself and kept company with his own thoughts.

Ultimately, he said, 'It's easier said than done, Christy.'

'You're quite right, Alex – hour by hour and day by day.' Christy paused and then asked quietly, 'What do the police say?'

'Well, that's the thing. They've found no trace of where Stephan was taken. All they've found was the four-wheel drive they threw him in.' He looked down at his clenched fists and uttered as if to himself, 'It's not good, not good at all.'

34

Bob was not seen or heard from until the next morning. His arrival was early and unannounced. He deliberately did not contact Alex or Alia or Her Majesty. What could he say to them? There was nothing to tell. It was as if Stephan had disappeared from the face of the earth without a trace. The stolen four-wheel drive was taken in and forensics checked for fingerprints – they found none – except the original owner's. The snow overnight did not help either, also the group of members they captured had no idea of the plan, not even Gunter.

He took courage and after breakfast sought to find Her Highness and Alex. They were in the Blue Lounge. As he knocked and opened the door, he was surprised to see Christy and felt the sense of desperation in the room, although they stood and fronted him with a measure of optimism. 'Bob, we were worried you did not contact us yesterday. What's the news?' Alex was quick to ask.

'Ma'am, sir, not very much, I'm afraid. We did find hair in

the back seat of the car, which was identified as Stephan's, so we know he was in there for sure. Vanda and Hans were also identified as being in the car, through two bottles of water we found on each side of the front seat. Their saliva identified them easily.' He knew he was coming to the crunch and he wished there was a way of avoiding it. 'However, as to where they took him, we can't say. The car was left at the bottom of St Anna's Pass, but helicopter after helicopter has scouted the area and there is no sign of life or anything there.'

Alia spoke up decisively, 'There has to be Bob — there has to be.'

'Ma'am, we're not done yet. There's one piece of good news. We know who sent the extortion note. Forensics carefully unstuck the postage stamp on the envelope and ran it through their system, only to find it was Blake Crowley's saliva. I guess these guys are so set not to show fingerprints, they don't consider the obvious — saliva.'

'Where is Crowley now?' Alex asked and knew the answer before it was given.

'He's in hiding, but he'll be easier to find ...'

Before Bob could continue, Alia interrupted him with a renewed sense of energy. 'I don't care about *him*. I want my son found.' Christy quietly went to Alia's side and encouraged her friend to sit with her on the sofa.

'Yes, ma'am. I understand.' Bob glanced at both of them and felt helpless. He turned to Alex and quietly said, 'Dr Glandore, I've got an appointment to see Her Majesty.'

'Okay. Thank you,' and Bob left the room.

34

Alex crouched next to his wife and held her hand to his lips. 'He's trying his best, Alia.' Deep down she knew it, but she could not make an appropriate response. Alex stood and found an armchair to sit while silence was all around them.

At that moment Parkinson entered the room and broke the sullen atmosphere. 'Sir, a call just came through to say that Mr Dave Malloy will be arriving tomorrow morning at ten. I have all the details of the flight and an organised car to meet him at the airport.' He regarded Alex who appeared to become a little animated at the news. 'Also, sir, Mr Isaiah Cumberbatch will arrive tomorrow at midday. All details are at hand and I've organised transport.'

'Parkinson, that's very good news. Thank you.' He turned to face Christy. 'Has Isi sent you a text of his flight particulars?'

'I've not looked at my mobile since I've come. I think it's still on flight mode.' As she spoke, she picked up her bag beside her and scrummaged through to find her cell phone. There were two text messages, both from Isi. 'Ah, here it is. Tomorrow morning at twelve noon.'

'That's good. I'm pleased.' Alex thought for a moment and then said, 'I might go with Trent to the airport and pick him up – if it doesn't cause a commotion.' And then he remembered. 'Dave will be here ... maybe he'll want to come along, also.'

'You might want to pass that by Bob. I don't know if he'll think it's a good idea, considering the way things are,' Alia reminded him.

'Yes, of course. I'll consult first with Bob.' He then turned to both of the ladies and said, 'If you'll excuse me, I need to make a call to work.' Alex left the room, glad to be on his own for a while. He had not heard from the plant in two days now.

He reached his office, sat in his chair, leaned back and closed his eyes. This is a nightmare, he thought. All he wanted was to have his son returned to him. Suddenly, the only way he knew to see this through was to immerse himself in work. That was how he managed his heartache when he was torn away from Alia for eleven years. Then he opened his eyes, leaned forward, wrapped the lower part of his face in his hands and thought again. 'No, this is not the same – this is an imminent matter of life and death.' He slowly got out his cell phone and rang his workplace. He wanted to speak to Malcolm McIntyre, his Chief Engineer. 'Mack, is there anything I should know from the plant?'

'Alex, how are holding out? Any positive news about Stephan?'

'No, nothing as yet. By the way, thanks for the flowers and card. It's so much appreciated to know others are thinking of Stephan.' He drew in a deep breath and as he released it asked again. 'So, what's happening at work?'

'You'll be pleased to know there has been no more sabotage. One more week and our prototype will be ready to show it off.'

'Thanks, Mack. I'll be in whenever I can.' He hung up the phone and sat there staring into empty space and was glad for the interruption from Bob.

'Dr Glandore, some good news – at least I call it that. We scouted again the start of the snowed-in pathway that leads up through St Anna's Pass and found this green plastic dinosaur. Would that be Stephan's?' It was in a clear plastic bag and held it up to show Alex.

'Have a look under its belly. Has it got a red mark?'

Bob turned the dinosaur over and examined it carefully, while protected in its clear bag. 'Yea, just near the back part of the belly.'

In his excitement, Alex stretched his arm and asked to see the dinosaur. 'Before I give it to you, wear these plastic gloves. This could be vital evidence.' Bob produced a pair of disposable gloves and gave them to Alex.

'I won't need them. I can see the red mark through the plastic bag. It's definitely Stephan's. He marked it with permanent red pen where some other dinosaur injured it during their fight.' He could hardly contain his racing heart. 'What does all this mean, then?'

'It means it's highly probable that he was taken somewhere along the Pass. But we've searched and searched this area without any success. Apart from the Monastery where we've gone in and searched high and low, there was nothing else there. In any case, the monks would have told us if they knew anything and they didn't know of any other place along the Pass. Mind you, they did say they haven't moved past the Monastery in years. All their food stuff has been brought to them by helicopter – especially in winter.'

In a rather dejected voice Alex said, 'Oh, so we're back to

square one again.'

'We're still trying sir. Don't give up hope.'

'Don't give up hope?' Alex's voice rose to a pitch which he never imagined possible. 'My son is somewhere out there, in the coldest winter ever recorded, freezing to death, if not already dead, and you're telling me to have hope. I've put on a brave front for Alia's sake, but it's not good enough – do you hear me? It's not good enough!' With a tremor in his voice he lunged forward, elbows on the desk, hands holding his forehead as his head hung down in front of him.

'Yes, sir. I understand.' Bob spoke as gently as he could, empathising with a wretch of a man he's known ever since childhood. He left his office quietly.

The queen's office was not that far away from Alex's and when she heard that desperate cry and the words that followed, she froze in the doorway and with fingers to her lips she knew that right then, he would be inconsolable. She chose to use one of the back staircases to find Alia and her guest. As she stepped into the entrance hall, Parkinson appeared and directed her to the Blue Lounge.

As Her Majesty entered the room, both Alia and Christy promptly stood and made a quick curtsey. 'Christy, so good of you to come in our hour of need. How is Isaiah?'

'Very well, Your Majesty. He'll be here tomorrow at noon.'

'I am pleased to hear that.' She then glanced at her daughter. 'How are you Alia? Have you had anything to eat or have you been starving yourself all day?'

'I'm fine Mother. We've had some cheese, crackers, biscuits,

34

and other tidbits. Shall I pour you a cup of tea?'

'No, my dear. I must move on. There are a few more things I need to do.'

'By the way, Mother, do you know who's looking after the dogs, now that Hans has disappeared?' Alia asked as a matter of priority.

'According to Parkinson, one of the stablehands. Why do you ask?'

'I've been hearing Basco whimpering and I think he misses Stephan. I might bring him inside here and see if he can calm down a little.'

'A very good idea, Alia. Now if you will excuse me?' Both Alia and Christy curtsied again, and the queen left the lounge.

Christy could not help but see through the veneer of words that passed between mother and daughter, each nursing her pain with an invisible protective guard around her. She knew that there was no other way for both of them to survive the trauma of this magnitude.

The rest of the day was spent in a semblance of harmony and Alia was more than grateful for Christy's presence. 'Alia, how much work have you got to do?'

'I can't face any work right now.' Alia shook her head as she spoke.

'I understand. Show me the way to the kitchen and I'll follow you.'

'And what are we going to do in the kitchen?' Alia asked curiously.

'What we normally do – cook.'

'I don't think I know how, Christy.' Alia's voice had a tinge of objection to it.

'There's always a first time for everything. Come on. We're not going to sit around and mope about – we're going to cook,' Christy said enthusiastically.

Alia began to relent a little and in a low voice said, 'I really liked that paella you cooked for us, two or three times.'

'Is there any seafood?' Suddenly Christy realised the ridiculous question she asked. 'What am I saying? Of course there is!'

As they approached the kitchen, an array of baking aromas wafted deliciously by in the hallway and both women quickened their pace to reach it. They entered and the staff was astounded to see them there and flustered about in their curtsies and bows of the head. Alia felt this intrusion required an explanation and said, 'Would we be in your way if you gave us a small corner of the kitchen to cook a paella.'

'Your Highness, we can cook it for you,' replied Daisy quickly.

'Thank you, Daisy, but the point is that my friend Christy and I want to cook it ourselves. This will be my first, but not for my friend. So I will be her pupil today.'

'Very well. Write out all the ingredients and utensils you need and I'll get them out for you.' Daisy looked over at Christy and she handed her a writing pad. 'We should have everything you need here and you can use this section of the kitchen, there. I don't think anyone will be using it right now.'

Christy didn't take long to write out all the ingredients she required and noticed that a deep thick skillet was already out for her use. A kettle for boiling water was placed at her disposal and soon all the ingredients were on the counter ready to be cooked. The seafood was left in the fridge until the last minute to be dropped into the pan, but more importantly, the fish stock and white wine made an appearance on the counter and they were set to start. Christy placed two cups of arborio rice in a sieve and asked Alia to wash it. 'Just use your fingers and let all the whitey starch be removed. That'll give a light separated grain texture rather than a gluggy, sticky rice and when you finish doing that, chop this brown onion. Cut it in half. Yes, that's right, remove the skin, slice it in narrow strips and cut them in the opposite direction so you get thin chopped onion. Yep, that's good. How's the eyes, Alia?'

'You didn't say anything about tears,' Alia complained.

'That's okay. It's good for the sinuses.' Christy made light of it and both smiled. 'While I'm cutting the fish and squid, add a couple of tablespoons of olive oil in the pan. Good. Heat it up, gently. Lower the heat. That's right. Okay, I think it's ready to place the chopped onion in the pan. Stir, but don't let it brown. Add the rice to the onion while it's still translucent.' Christy looked down at the fish. 'I think that's enough of those. Do you like mussels? Good, we'll add those too. Here are the chopped tomatoes –add those too. Before that, add the saffron to the water and pour over the rice – add the fish stock, wine and cook uncovered for about ten to fifteen minutes. If I remember well, Alia, you don't like it too spicy with paprika, so I'll add just a touch of it.'

'I'm concentrating so hard here, all I can do is nod or shake my head,' Alia stated emphatically.

It did not take long to complete their task. 'Look at this Alia, a work of art and all it took was about thirty-five to forty minutes.'

'I'll get it served for late lunch or early dinner.' Alia placed her hand on Christy's shoulder and in an earnest voice said, 'Thank you, so much. I enjoyed cooking with you.' She then thoughtfully added, 'Cooking is very therapeutic, isn't it?' Christy simply smiled at her. After thanking all the kitchen staff for their indulgence, they left and together made their way towards the dining room. On their way they found Alex coming down the staircase. 'Alex, will you join us in the dining room. Christy and I cooked paella.'

'Did you say, *you* cooked paella?'

'Yes, I did. Believe it or not.'

Alex came close to Alia and placed his arm around her waist 'That's my girl.'

Alia and Alex sat next to each other, while Christy sat opposite them. The paella was served up by one of the staff and chardonnay poured in crystal glasses, compliments and comments about the taste of the food were given. As they quietened during the process of eating, they could faintly hear Basco's hollow whining in the distance. Alia toyed with her food in the plate and suddenly did not feel hungry at all. She continued to separate the rice from the seafood and vice versa, but not a morsel of sustenance entered her mouth. Alex noticed how she tinkered with the food and used the fork as an absent-minded distraction. He could not say anything to her, and he too slowed down the process of eating. Christy's heart went out to her friend but she felt helpless to do or say anything. She remained motionless with fork and knife in each hand poised just above her plate as she silently watched Alia's ache affecting her daily life.

Abruptly, Alex placed the cutlery he held quite noisily on his plate. 'Right,' he said as he stood and pushed away his chair. 'I, for one, can't stand to hear Basco whining like this. I'm going out right now and I'm bringing him inside,' and with that he left the dining room leaving the attendant to push his chair back into place and get new cutlery to replace the one on the table and the other which fell onto the floor.

'I'm glad he's going to bring in Basco. The poor thing, he's been like this since … since Stephan disappeared,' Alia mentioned in a lamentable voice.

'I think it's a great idea. How old is the dog?'

'I'm not sure … but, four I think … or perhaps five … not sure,' Alia muttered.

Christy endeavoured to keep up a conversation just to take Alia's mind off Stephan's abduction and sometimes she thought it was working and other times she'd lose her friend in impenetrable thoughts that claimed an important space in her head.

Outside, Alex walked towards the stables and heavily plodded in the snow until he reached the stalls. The door was slightly opened, and he pushed it out further so he could fit through the space it made. As he entered, there was a body warmth that exuded from the stalls, which gave a sense that there was life within. Each stall with polished wood and brass had the name of the respective horse, which snorted and some neighed, while Alex trod towards the back of the stable where an office was located. 'Tom,' he called out. Again he shouted his name. At last Tom appeared from the office door.

'Dr Glandore, this is a surprise. How can I help you?'

'I want to take Basco out from the kennels – now,' Alex demanded.

'Yes, sir. He hasn't been happy.'

Together they laboured through the snow and Tom took the key out and opened Basco's area. 'Shall I give you his lead?'

'No, there are extra ones in the palace. I'll let him run a little' Alex leaned towards the dog and, holding his collar, spoke to him sympathetically. 'You're all cooped up in here, fellow. Come on, stretch your legs a bit.'

'Thanks, Tom,' and then he turned to the dog and released him. 'Okay, off you go.' Alex was surprised at the strength and energy with which the dog unleashed himself from the constraints of his collar. He ran away so fast that no amount of shouting from Alex to come back could entice him. Tom noticed what happened and he shouted as well, but to no avail. They both saw he was heading towards the front gate. 'I'll get my car, Tom. Come with me.'

34

As they approached the electronic gate, the attendant began the process for the gate to open ready to allow the car out. Alex pressed down on the accelerator and came to a sudden halt with no sign of the dog. Basco was crouching beside bushes and the minute he saw the opportunity to escape, he dashed out so quickly the gatekeeper hardly realised what it was that sped by him. Alex got out of the car instantly and went to the gate. 'Did you see where he went?'

'Who? The fox?' asked the gatekeeper.

'No, Basco, the dog,' shouted Alex.

'Was that him? Sorry sir, he ran so fast ... I wasn't sure. I couldn't stop him.' The gatekeeper looked at the dejected face in front of him. 'He knows the way... he'll come back.'

'It's okay – nothing can be done right now. You can lock the gate again.' Alex hung his head and as he trudged towards the car, he couldn't think how he was going to tell Stephan that his dog got lost. One calamity after another.

'I've lost him, Tom. What are we going to do?'

'What I know about dogs is that they'll always want to come back home.'

'I hope so. I *really* hope so.' He sighed deeply and thought 'I'll have to go in and tell Alia, as if she hasn't got enough to think about.'

35

The morning arrived with quite a commotion. All that everyone talked about was the news in Cumbia. It became something of a distraction in the palace as staff huddled together to read the newspaper and those who could watch the news on National Broadcast did so. Alex decided to go to the gym and work off some frustration before the arrival of his friends, Dave and Isi, and partly because he couldn't concentrate on his work or anything else. Upon sighting Alex, the staff immediately dispersed from the attention to the news and went about their work. It happened a couple of times on his way to the staircase and towards the gym.

At last, he had to ask Parkinson what in the world was going on and what was the interest? Parkinson found a newspaper and showed Alex the front-page heading: *Cumbia, Close to Full Scale Revolution*. Instead of going to the gym he went to one of the lounges downstairs and began to read a full account of events in Cumbia:

Overnight in the capital city of Gralem, students from University of Gralem and The Polytech College went on a rampage and set up blockades in the streets of the capital city, fighting off police and special combat forces.

The students armed themselves with whatever they could lay their hands on: baseball bats, hammers, some raided the gym rooms and made away with dumbbells and anything that they could remove from any of the equipment. Other students tore up cobblestones and either threw them at the police or used slings to catapult them. Writing desks, gym mats, the Dean's leather-top desk and several other furniture, which residents promptly donated for the students' cause, were thrown on top of the barricades wherever they existed.

Police used hoses and propelled water against the students, which caused some damage to the barricades and necessitated some students to be hospitalised.

By early morning, the military was called in to quash the anarchy in the streets. Several students and police officers were injured and taken to hospital. Various reasons were reported for the revolt. One American student, P J Gilchrist, spent the evening behind the barricades with the students from Cumbia and reports that there was a great deal of anger from the students who said that the constraints on the syllabus did not allow liberal learning which they were used to and the University fees spiralled to heights unknown before.

An unusual twist of events occurred at the docks, which

was reported to be a spin-off from the students' rebellion. The workers at the wharfs and their Unions called an indefinite strike for higher wages and an eight-hour working day. In the last two years, the workers at the wharfs had worked ten hours a day without any extra pay or explanation.

It appeared that the students' revolt inspired the dock workers who were now demanding their right to strike. It had been also reported that some of these workers joined the students behind the blockades, offered crates, planks from the dockyards and even joined in the fray of the stand-off with the police who used tear gas to try and quash the insurrection.

The capital city of Cumbia, Gralem, all but shut down completely. Shop windows were smashed in tiny pieces, cars overturned, and spray-painted in all colours. Shopkeepers bolted down their doors and windows in the hope of some protection to their properties.

In the words of the United Nations, Universal Declaration of Human Rights: 'Everyone has the right to freedom of opinion and expression: this right includes freedom to hold opinions without interference and to seek, receive and impart information and ideas through any media and regardless of frontiers.'

Students and workers often voiced their discontent with the suppression of their opinions which resulted in the shutdown of the monthly Uni magazine and the Anchors Away pub where many wharf workers congregated as *a meeting place and to socialise. The lack of freedoms that perpetuated in Cumbia over the last few years had frustrated its population and resulted in the current repercussions of a people in despair.*

Was Victor's Café fire and blast in Castelneuf, Rubinia, the ignition to the revolt that had gripped Cumbia? If so, who was extinguishing the flames? Where was Cumbia's Prime Minister? Where was King Gregory? Not a single broadcast was made to appeal to the people of Cumbia for patience or peace. Noted Syndicated Journalist: Nick Matthews.

When Alex finished reading the article in the newspaper, he sat there for several minutes and thought about what he had read. It did not surprise him to see Nick Matthews' name as the journalist for the article. Alex never did get the chance to speak to him, but he showed his tenacity and insight through his writing. He continued to ponder the events in Cumbia. So, it had started he thought. Was this going to be a domino effect like the nineteen sixty-eight revolts that spread through Europe indiscriminately in protest of social, political, military, and bureaucratic repression? What's to stop it infecting Rubinia and causing havoc in its wake? The freedoms in this country, the working conditions, and the institutions for recourse of unfair treatment of employees were strongly embedded in the traditions of Rubinia. Citizens' freedom of speech, to write and worship according to one's own beliefs, were as much a part of Rubinia as the monarchy to which he now belonged.

He had his own suspicions and thoughts about this sudden revolution that had rocked Cumbia, but first he needed to speak with Bob.

As he sat there in a contemplative mood, Parkinson appeared to inform him that Mr Malloy had arrived. Parkinson eyed him up and down and then asked, 'Sir, do you wish to change your clothes? I'll be happy to entertain Mr Malloy.'

'Thanks, Parkinson, but Mr Malloy and I are old friends and I don't think he'll mind my wearing a track suit.' As Alex walked past him, he said in a low voice, 'I'll change later.'

He found Dave Malloy in the entrance hall looking a little lost among the splendour that surrounded him. 'Hey, Davo. Good to have you here.' The two friends shook hands and embraced each other as old friends.

'Mate, I just couldn't believe when I read about Stephan in the news. How's Alia taking it?'

'Not too well. We tried to contact you and tell you ourselves, but with you being in Peru it was a little hard to do that.' Alex explained.

'What's being done to find him? Have they any clue where he might be?'

Alex couldn't bring himself to answer his question. 'Come on, mate. You must be exhausted after your trip. Do you want a shower or freshen up in your room? Parkinson will show you to your room – it's the usual one.' He turned and motioned to Parkinson to come. 'Will you take Dave to his room?' He then looked at his friend and said, 'Breakfast in the dining room – twenty minutes?'

'Plenty of time, mate, see you then.' Parkinson went up the staircase and Dave followed.

Alex also made his way to his bedroom for a change of clothes and was concerned he had not heard from Bob for some time. He knew he spent a few hours at the plant to make sure that everything there was tightly secured, but Alex needed him here at the palace. The recovery of his son should be prioritised.

As he began to descend the staircase, he found Dave at the bottom of it waiting for him and together walked towards the dining room. When they entered, they found Alia and Christy pouring tea at the table. Alia stood immediately as she saw Dave and went towards him. He was taken aback at how distraught and thin she looked. He opened his arms and they both embraced. 'Alia, are you looking after yourself? I know it's a very hard time you're going through, but you must take care.'

'Thank you, Dave ... I'm trying. I'm pleased that you are here. You know Christy.' Alia looked in her direction as Dave went around the table to greet her.

'How can I forget Christy? A woman, one in a million.' He embraced her as well and then asked, 'How's Isi?'

'He should be here shortly.'

'So, the old gang together again ... under sad circumstances.'

'Come on Davo, help yourself to some food – buffet-style,' Alex appealed to him. Together they saw an appetising array of food at the buffet table and Dave could not help but notice what a small amount of food was on Alia's plate. No one brought up the topic of Stephan, and Dave felt it was not his position to do so. The conversation was polite and just too polite for Dave. He wanted to wait until after everyone had eaten and then broach the topic of the abduction.

After dining, Alia suggested that they should go to the Blue Lounge for coffee and sweets to which all agreed. 'I don't think I've been in this lounge before. It's a beauty, Alia.'

'Thanks Dave. I like it here, too. There's a sense of peace and I don't know whether it's the cool colours used in this room that make it so, or I just feel comfortable here.'

When coffee arrived with a delectable range of pastries, everyone felt relaxed while they spoke of the old days at university. Dave felt he was patient enough and he now needed to ask about Stephan. 'Alia, I want to ask about Stephan. Will this upset you too much?'

'No, Dave. I'm glad you brought it up. We were hoping you might contribute something that can help us to retrieve our son.'

'Perhaps, Alex, you can tell me what has happened.' Dave's request was genuinely from the heart.

'Right you are.' Alex took a deep breath and began. 'Stephan, our little boy, was abducted from the palace grounds by a supposed bodyguard by the name Vanda Zendelli. He and our kennel keeper, Hans Bergenson, teamed up to take Stephan. Not that I think it was their own plan. There are higher minds behind the heinous crime. Have you heard of the WSO?'

'As a matter of fact, I have. When I was consigned to work up in the alps, a co-worker kept raving on about it, saying that everything will change and that we'd better be ready for it.' Dave gave a low gruff sound. 'Hmm, I dismissed it as a load of rubbish ... but obviously I was wrong.'

'Very wrong, my friend. They've been working towards their goal for ... at least twenty years. Their system is to get Heads of State to join as a member, hand over twenty percent of the Gross Domestic Product and in return each member nation will be offered protection with a military so efficient and modern that no other nation will be able to touch them. One way or another, they'll get you to join through cajoling methods, threats, and if that doesn't work, then action. They'll hit you where it hurts the most.' He paused there and drew his fingers through his hair. 'As you can see, our most precious son in all the world has gone.' He continued with some effort. 'The police have found a four-wheel drive at the bottom of St Anna's Pass. Helicopters have scouted the entire Pass, but nothing can be found. The extra fall of snow has not helped either. This is the third day, Dave, and we're nowhere near finding him.'

'St Anna's Pass you said.' Dave appeared to be in a state of recollection. 'A few years ago, a team I organised was halfway up St Anna's Pass working on environmental research of the area. We arrived in autumn and as we were to remain there for a few months, we built a hut enough to take four cots and a small tank of water in a makeshift sink. With all this snow, it's probably covered over. I think we should take another closer look at that part of the Pass.'

'Dave, you're God-sent, mate. I bet he's up there,' Alex stated energetically.

'Do you think he might be up there, Dave?' Alia suddenly rallied as she spoke.

'Now look, don't get your hopes up too high, I'm only supposing, I don't know for sure.' He then spoke in a more compassionate manner. 'I don't want to disappoint you.'

'You can never do that. It's something we haven't explored. I must contact Bob.' Alex had already taken out his cell phone. Bob was not answering.

As the small party of friends suddenly found hope, the atmosphere brightened a little and Parkinson was pleased to see that when he entered the room. 'Sir, Mr Isaiah Cumberbatch is here.'

'Bring him in, bring him in.' Alex spoke with pure enthusiasm and put his cell phone away.

As soon as Isaiah appeared in the doorway, all his friends and his wife rushed to welcome him. 'I'm so glad to see such a jolly group.'

'Isi, honey, we've just got some great news. Dave might have discovered where Stephan was taken.' Christy spoke enthusiastically to her husband.

'Now listen, mate, I'm just not sure about that. All I know is that he *may* be halfway up St Anna's Pass.'

'Well, that's great news. What's our next step?' Isi asked with some hope.

With his arm around his friend's shoulder, Alex said, 'Isi, my friend, I have to contact Bob and let him know.'

'Well, let's do it.' Isi encouraged him.

Alex was on his cell phone immediately and the anticipation of Bob picking up his call was unnerving. 'Come on, pick up,' he thought. 'Bob, at last. Listen, leave whatever it is you're doing and get to the palace as soon as possible. We have important news about the whereabouts of Stephan.' He switched off the phone and said, 'He's on his way.'

'Isi, are you hungry? Do you want a sandwich, a steak, pastries, coffee? – anything you want.' Alex found it hard to contain that small seed of hope that was spreading in his chest and towards his awakened heart.

'A cup of coffee will be just fine.'

36

Bob arrived at the palace with a sense of expectation and found the group of friends in the Blue Lounge. There was an air of optimism in the room as if they discovered the lost treasure where the X marked the spot. It was time for fresh information, just as he was beginning to think there was nothing else they could do.

'Your Highness, Dr Glandore, what's the news?'

'Bob, my friend here, Dave Malloy, tells me that some years ago his environmental team built a hut to house and sleep four people. Could it be possible Stephan was taken there?'

'But sir, we've scouted the whole area and couldn't find anything.'

'Yes, Bob, from a helicopter, but no one went down to walk and inspect the Pass closely at ground level.'

'That's true, because there was nothing to be seen down there.' Bob paused to think for a few seconds. 'I can get a helicopter organised within one hour, while it's still light. Three in the back and I'll be in the front.'

'Now you're talking.' Alex looked at Dave and Isi and knew they needed thick parkas, snow boots, and pants. 'I'll organise the clothing.'

'You better bring something for Stephan, should we find him.' Dave's instinct strongly indicated that if they did take him up St Anna's Pass, he could be nowhere else but in the hut. What he couldn't understand was why it was not visible from the helicopter.

'Bob, get a helicopter that's big enough for all of us ... plus somewhere for Stephan to lie down,' Alex strongly suggested.

'It's done.' Bob took out his cell phone and began the process. 'I want an air ambulance within an hour and Dr Fenton on board. How soon can this be organised? No, no. No paramedics, just the doctor. Pick us up in the front of the palace grounds.' He faced everyone and he could see the concerned faces, especially Alia's. 'I think, ma'am, Mr Malloy might be right. We have to be prepared for anything and everything.' Then in a consolatory voice he said, 'This might be our lucky day. The copter will be here shortly, let's get ready.'

The men left to get into warmer clothing that could repel the icy-cold sting, and Alex carried an extra set of clothes for Stephan. They all waited impatiently in the entrance hall and Alia placed her arm around Christy's and held fast on to it. In the midst of uncertain tension, the queen appeared among them.

'What in the world is going on here?' She looked perturbed as her brow formed furrows of concern.

'Mother, I'm sorry we didn't say a word to you. Everything happened so fast. The men are going up in a helicopter to check St Anna's Pass once more. Dave thinks Stephan may be in a hut halfway up the Pass.'

'But helicopters have searched the Pass many times and nothing could be seen.'

'I know ... I know ... but we must try *anything*. We can't give up, we just can't.'

The Queen could sense her daughter's pain and simply said, 'Yes, my dear, I do know.'

The helicopter arrived on time and Alia moved to her husband's side, kissed his cheek and whispered, 'Please, please find him.' Alex hugged her tightly to him and as he saw everyone else moving out towards the helicopter, he parted quickly and followed suit.

As the helicopter gyrated its blades and emitted that deafening noise all around them, the men crouched and were careful to head towards the centre of the copter. Bob waited until every man got in and lastly settled himself next to the pilot. The headphones and belts were appropriately worn, and they saw with amazement the capacity it offered for a patient. There was complex digitalised machinery with lights that beeped and winked to let the operator know exactly what the patient's vital signs were. To the side of the machinery were two transporter beds for patients and a couple of seats. A man sat in one of the seats with the belt fastened and looked seriously at everyone. Alex leaned forward and poked Bob on the shoulder, 'Is that Dr Fenton in the back there?'

Bob turned and yelled out with a wave of the hand, 'Hi there, Doc,' and he responded with a nod of his head to acknowledge Bob.

Within minutes the helicopter came to the start of the Pass. Bob turned and faced Dave. 'Look out the window and tell us when we get to the hut.'

Dave stuck up both thumbs and looked out of the window very carefully but could not see any sign of the hut. He leaned forward, 'Bob, can the copter fly lower? I think we've come up too high on the Pass.'

Bob spoke to the pilot and soon he turned around the helicopter and retraced its flight. There was nothing he could see. His heart sank, but Dave was determined. 'Bob, once more up the Pass.'

This time the pilot brought the copter even lower and as it began its search again from the bottom up the Pass, a few minutes into the flight, Alex yelled out. 'Look out here. Something's down there. Look!'

The copter got closer and an image began to form against the snow-canvassed backdrop. As the pilot brought the helicopter directly above the object, it became obvious that it was a dog, not any dog, but Basco. They could hear his continuous barking and the pilot circled a couple of times to find somewhere to land. There was a clearing nearby and very slowly the helicopter touched down on soft snow which lay on top of hard ice going deep down towards the ground.

Bob commanded everyone to stay in the helicopter as he jumped out with an automatic weapon in his hands. How he came by it, or where he had it hidden was beyond everyone else in the helicopter. He slowly approached what appeared to be a mound of snow and Basco dashed ahead of him and disappeared through an opening. Carefully he inspected the outside in case someone was hidden in waiting. He noticed the dog had stopped barking. He also realised why they couldn't see the hut from the helicopter. It was covered over with many large cut branches and the snow did the rest covering it with three days' layers of thick snow.

Eventually, he saw the opening which was at some stage a door that was obviously pushed down and left half-broken on the hut's floor. There were four cots in the hut, two on each side and one of them had a young boy on it lying flat on his back with the upper part of the dog's body on top of him licking his face. The astounding scene was beyond Bob's comprehension. He ran out and waved frantically for everyone to come. 'Bring the stretcher,' he yelled.

Alex was the first on the scene. He rushed into the hut and there he saw his son and Basco licking his face. He knelt beside him and gasped his name over and over. 'Stephan, Stephan,' he called and took his small hand into his and rubbed the frozen skin and kissed it and rubbed time and time again.

The doctor arrived with some of his equipment and sharply told Alex to move, but he seemed insensible to his command and continued to hold onto his son's hand. The dog remained motionless in the same position and persisted in licking the boy's face. Bob approached, took Alex by the arm, and forced him to leave Stephan's side. Dr Fenton placed some of his equipment on the floor and yelled out, 'Who knows anything about medicine?' Isi approached and said, 'I've a senior first-aid certificate.'

'That'll do.' Dr Fenton's stethoscope was plugged into his ears and without disturbing the dog placed it on Stephan's chest to see if he could hear a heartbeat. The doctor called out, 'I want absolute quiet.' He didn't say whether he could hear a heartbeat or not, he just asked to remove now the dog.

Alex walked towards Basco and taking his collar calmly spoke to him. 'Come on boy, you've done enough good work,' and slowly detached him from Stephan.

Immediately the doctor began cardiopulmonary resuscitation and all that anyone could do was to helplessly look on. Again, the doctor placed the stethoscope on Stephan's chest. Suddenly he raised his voice, 'Quickly, someone place the boy on the stretcher.' As fast as they could the doctor and Isi wrapped the boy with bubble wrap and once more his voice urgently came across, 'Come on people, let's get this boy somewhere warmer.' Alex and Isi carried the stretcher and as fast as they could go, plodded through the snow and managed to place the stretcher into the helicopter.

Bob and Dave looked over the place and a few metres away Dave noticed a dark object projecting up from the snow. 'Stay back. I'll go and investigate.' As Bob advanced carefully towards the object, he realised it was a black leather glove. He picked it up with his gloved hand and smartly retrieved a zip-up plastic bag from one of the pockets of his jacket. Dave wondered at the man's unique forethought and preparation. Together they trod towards the helicopter and got in.

Alex sat in the seat next to the doctor, Stephan had a drip hanging in mid-air and Basco refused to leave his master's side. He remained on the floor of the helicopter for the rest of the journey. Its destination was the Queen Sylvia Hospital where there was a well-established children's wing patronised by the queen herself. Alex turned to the doctor and asked, 'Dr Fenton, is my son going to live?'

The doctor glanced at him and surmised a father's agony for his son – he ought to know. He lost his son in a hiking accident when he fell through a crevice and was soon covered with the force of an avalanche and died. He did not want to assume this young boy was dead, for he knew that with severe hypothermia one breath may occur only per minute and the heart rate could be less than twenty beats per minute. Although he could hardly hear any breathing or heartbeat, he knew he had to tell the father something. 'I have to be honest with you. Your son's condition is very serious. In reality, he should be dead now,' and in a low deep voice added, 'but you can thank your son's dog if he survives this calamity.' The doctor felt this was a small measure of hope, rather than none. He wasn't sure if the father knew exactly what he was saying, so he continued. 'Do you understand what he did? These Saint Bernards have got a very acute sense of smell and they can track down people buried in snow, dig up the snow with their paws, lie on the injured to give them body heat and lick their face for warmth, then bark until someone hears them. Usually when they're on a rescue mission the dogs are sent out in pairs. When they find the victim, one lies on top of the body and the other goes back to get help.' The doctor hesitated for a second or two and then quipped, 'And we think we're clever!'

'Thanks, Doctor – for everything. I didn't know that about the Saint Bernards.' Alex reached over and touched the doctor's hand on the arm rest.

As the helicopter landed on top of the hospital building, an emergency care unit was at hand with a bed, nurses, doctors, and bodyguards everywhere. All the passengers disembarked the helicopter and while Bob went over to the secret servicemen, Alex stayed close by his son, and Dave and Isi walked beside their friend. Dr Fenton remained in the helicopter and as it orbited off, Alex looked up and waved while they waited to get into the elevator to take them down to the children's ward.

By the time Alex dropped his hand to the side of his body, the elevator was up onto the roof with a small bell-like noise to indicate the doors were going to open. The bed on roller coasters went in first and everyone else packed themselves in quickly. Down to the third floor it went and again the doors opened, and the second they got the bed out with its patient, it was rolled along the hallway so fast, the nurses and doctors accompanying it kept calling out intermittently, 'watch out,' 'make way.' Basco began to bark and if Alex had not held him by the collar, he would have run after the bed.

One of the doctors remained behind to explain to Alex what was going to happen to his son. 'All of our endeavours will be to raise his body temperature, slowly but surely. It's obvious the boy has gone through malnourishment and we will use a drip for nutrients. This is going to be a waiting game.'

'Look, doctor, I want to remain here all night. I can't leave him alone.' He then looked down on Basco. 'The other thing is this dog belongs to my son, who has probably saved his life. He will not move away from his side. I know for hygiene and other purposes the dog may not be allowed to stay in the hospital. All I can say is, I promise I'll tend to him. Please … if Stephan can sense his dog is with him, it will give him courage to survive.'

'Normally, we don't allow dogs in the hospital.' He peered at the father with some compassion. 'But we're dealing with a life-and-death situation here, so … we need every bit of help we can get. Okay, just take care of the dog.' The doctor looked around and noticed Dave and Isi. 'Are you all staying overnight?'

Alex came to some consciousness and added, 'Guys, you don't need to stay here. Really. Go back and talk to Alia and Christy. They'll want to see you.'

'There's no way we're moving away from this spot without you and without seeing Stephan getting better. I've rung Christy and she understands, and I know you've rung Alia, so they'll not be expecting us at all.' Isi was completely resolved with his decision.

'Listen, mate. All of us have seen this thing through together and we'll see the rest of it together. Got it!' Dave looked around the room and added, 'The room is perfect ... there are a couple of armchairs there, better still, a bed in that corner and comfy chair here. We'll be fine.' He stared at the clothes they were wearing and said, 'The only thing we need to do right now is change into something more comfortable than these snow overalls and jackets. It's so hot in the hospital.'

'You're right Dave. We've all got our normal clothes under all this, don't we?' Alex suggested.

The men shed the heavy overalls down to their own clothing and the only thing they could not remove were the snow boots, but that was fine, there were thick socks on their feet and if need be they could take the boots off for comfort. 'I'm going to buy some food and especially for this dog. He probably hasn't eaten anything for a couple of days. Isi, coffee or tea?'

'Coffee will be fine.' Isi observed Alex slumped in the chair with a look of abandonment and weariness. 'Alex, we must have faith that Stephan will pull through. He's a strong young lad and he's in good hands here at the hospital.' Alex made no reply, so Isi continued. 'When we think of how Stephan was found, how the dog ran off to find him and helped him to keep warm — that in itself is a miracle. Things don't happen randomly, there's a purpose to everything. You had chosen that particular moment to get the dog out from his kennel. Had it happened a day earlier, the dog might have been killed by the thugs who took Stephan.' Isi paused a moment. 'All I'm saying is let's have hope and be positive that all will turn out well.'

'Thanks, Isi. I just wish I was as sure as you.' Alex's anguish felt as if his heart was being torn apart.

'To have hope, Alex, is for things we cannot see as to how they'll turn out. No one is sure, we just hope and pray.'

'Please pray for my son. I'm totally spent. I don't think I can do anything right now.'

Isi's response to his friend's request was to close his eyes and remain like that in one of the armchairs — until Dave burst into the room with the food.

'Okay, you guys. Have you both gone off to sleep? I've just spoken to the doctor. I ran into him in the corridor. He said he's very hopeful for a more positive outcome, now.'

Alex suddenly became more energised and stood to face Dave. 'What else did he say? Has he opened his eyes, is there a better heartbeat? What about his breathing?'

Dave placed the parcels of food on the portable overbed table that was in the corner of the room. 'Now, hang on, mate. He just said he was hopeful and positive. Let's not jump the gun. It's early days, Alex, early days.' Dave placed his hand on his friend's shoulder and added, 'Come on you guys, dinner's served.' Isi walked up and sat on one side of the bed, but Alex sat back in his chair. 'Okay, I see I have to serve it to you.' He took a pack with a cheeseburger, chips, and Coke and placed them on his lap. 'Perhaps I should put the Coke on this table.' Alex nodded his head. Isi was already eating. 'Last but not least, fellow, this is for you.' Dave took out a whopping big burger and gave it to the dog. He gulped it down in no time. 'How hungry was he? I think he needs water ... I'll go and ask a nurse.' Dave returned post-haste with a bedpan filled with water. He placed it in front of Basco and he slobbered most of it down.

Even Alex had something of a smile on his face when he viewed the scene. Dave looked down at a contented dog and announced, 'I think I'll need to take him out after all this food.'

'I'll take him out next time, Dave.' Isi was used to pets; there was a menagerie of them at home.

'First, you'll have to get past all the security outside this door – and Bob. I couldn't walk anywhere alone. There was someone shadowing me all the time.' He pondered a moment at what he said and added, 'At least you feel safe.'

37

While the Casteler family was experiencing their worst nightmares, King Gregory had his own problems to contend with in Cumbia. The upheaval in his country took on unexpected twists and turns which spread throughout the city and in country towns. Shopkeepers closed their stores, took up banners, and protested fiercely at the rise of tax on goods, which at times exceeded a rate of thirty-five percent. Tractors on farms bore exorbitant prices, not only to purchase, but their daily running costs increased radically from fuel to engine repairs and normal maintenance. However, their farm products were now sold to Government Co-operatives which brought in an income of thirty percent less than a couple of years earlier. Farmers who were being forced off their land and bought out by the government discovered they had to find jobs to survive, and often it was working their own land as labourers.

The people of Cumbia had no recourse for their woes other than to revolt. Big industry was quickly being usurped by government takeovers. The uranium mines in the alps of Rubinia, which were leased to individual companies from Cumbia, were confiscated as property of the Progressive National Party. There were no elections held for this new Government in Cumbia, which seemed to pervade Parliament, private industries, energy companies, free press in the form of newspapers, television, internet, and social media. People began to notice the change just over four years ago. It started slowly and accelerated to this, with such an insidious speed and force that the people's revolt saw the presence of military in the streets of Cumbia. This, of course, revealed to the world a rule of dictatorial tendencies.

There were also rumblings of discontent in neighbouring countries. Not to the same degree as in Cumbia, but certainly the constraints of freedom in the media, where editorial opinions were muffled with inexplicable arrests and threats became the norm on a daily basis. It was not, therefore, surprising that the spread of student and workers' rebellions, on a smaller scale, visited several other countries in Europe, within a short space of time, as if one incident enflamed another like an intermittent fire cracker thrown in different directions.

In Rubinia, a lot of the problems were activated quietly in the background and lacked the force in the leaderships to make a noticeable mark in politics or the daily workings of the people's lives. Many perceived it to be due to the democratic policies and the strength and support of the monarchy. It was a longstanding institution with traditions that stretched back to nine hundred years or more.

It was well known that this modern royalty endeared themselves to the people of Rubinia through their hard work and loyalty to their nation. They brought a sense of stability in government and gave people balance between monarchy and Head of State. Over the centuries of rule there arose in the last one hundred and fifty years, through law and parliamentary sanctions, a Constitutional Monarchy. Apart from this, the establishment of royalty in Rubinia brought in a yearly national income of nearly a billion dollars in tourism.

In the Palace of Rubinia, Queen Sylvia and Princess Alia waited for news of Stephan's recovery with an anxiety that could not be broached without giving licence to further emotional pain. 'Mother, I must be there with my son. This waiting and not being able to see him is torment.'

'Alia, you're not well yourself. You are hardly eating ... you have lost so much weight in these last few weeks. I think your presence there may cause some upheaval in the hospital.' She peered at her daughter as she sat next to her friend. 'Perhaps, Christy, you can persuade my daughter to eat something more tonight.'

'I will try and do that, Your Majesty.' She glanced at Alia beside her. 'What if I go to the kitchen and cook something for both of us?'

'I'm not really hungry ... something light,' suggested Alia.

'A bruschetta with anything you like on it. What do you say?' Christy encouraged her friend.

'Yes. As long as I come with you and we'll do it together.'

'That sounds a lot better,' replied Christy. 'Would you like me to make something for you, Your Majesty?'

'No thank you, Christy. I am going to watch the news in the private lounge and, no doubt, there will be something there to eat.' The queen stood away from the armchair and approached Christy and softly said, 'Please, make sure she eats something tonight.'

She nodded her head and together with Alia, who was a little in front of her, made their way to one of the kitchens.

The queen settled in the lounge room and used the remote control to switch on the television. Rubinia's National Broadcasting station was, at most times, comprehensive and endeavoured to be objective. What Queen Sylvia watched was disturbing on many levels. The rebellions were not just contained in Cumbia, they were enflamed and contagiously catchy in other countries of Europe. Rubinia, it appeared, was right in the middle of this extraordinary revolt. It was only natural for her to think that her country might have lost its immunity against such upheavals that surrounded it; for all it needed was a spark to light the fuse of insurrection and anarchy. Her resolution was to definitely speak with Mike … and Bob when his duties from the hospital allowed him to do so. She picked up the phone and asked to see Mike as soon as possible.

Within ten minutes he was in her presence. 'Take a seat, Mike.' She waited until he was comfortable after offering him tea or coffee. 'Tell me, what are the chances of this chaos reaching our borders and heart of our nation?'

'Ma'am, all I know is Rubinia is as secure as ever. Bob made sure of that and I believe your communication with the President of America did not go amiss in directing extra force and protection around Rubinia. The Lockheed U-2 with its high-altitude reconnaissance and the F-22 Raptor has total stealth superiority in the air. Very few would dare to come face to face with them.'

'So, you are aware of my communication with the President. Is nothing sacred in this fiasco world we live in?'

'Ma'am, I can guarantee you that apart from Bob and me – no one else knows.' He knew he had to reassure her. 'Your Majesty, we needed to know this so we can direct our operations according to the knowledge we have. They're aces up our sleeves.'

'I understand that. I just wish I knew what these "operations" are exactly.'

'At times such as this, ma'am, we all need to pull together to save what we've got.'

'I am aware of that too, Mike ... just keep me informed ... whenever you can.' She felt keenly the awkward situation.

As if Mike had penetrated her thoughts he added, 'We've never had to deal with anything like this before – certainly not in the last fifty years or so.' He paused, but the queen did not respond to his statement, so he continued. 'This is new for all of us and the experience of it all will be immeasurable.'

'It can be viewed in that way. But much of this is manipulated and modified to suit us. I cannot see my enemy.

I know who it is, but his image escapes me. This is a warfare with which I am not familiar and I've good knowledge of two World Wars whose aftermath touched our people's peripheral lives. I can see it cannot be resolved in any other way – technology has played a big part in this.' The queen sighed and stood, and Mike immediately took his cue by being upstanding. 'Thank you, Mike, for the care you have given us and especially the protection of our precious culture and traditions we hold so dear.'

'Yes, ma'am. I would give my life for that.' He turned and walked in the direction of the door and carefully shut it as he left the room.

She stood transfixed as her mind replayed scenes from her conversation with Mike. Promptly, she was brought back to the present moment as the cell phone rang incessantly. It was Alex. 'Ma'am, Stephan has opened his eyes ... he's still weak, but he can see us ... he tried to move his hand ... I can hardly believe it.' His voice was racked with emotion and relief at the same time. 'I couldn't get Alia, tell her to ring me.'

'Yes, yes, Alex. Go back to him. I'll tell Alia.' She endeavoured to contain that feeling which was exploding inside of her to shout through the roof and let everyone know. Instead, she quickened her pace and held onto the banister, lest her feet went flying down the staircase ahead of her body. As she reached the bottom, Alia and Christy were coming towards her holding a tray each with what appeared to be food and immediately saw Her Majesty and sensed the urgency in her step.

'Mother, what's wrong? Are you all right?' Alia gave the tray to Christy and rushed towards her.

'Stephan has opened his eyes. I think he's going to be fine … Alia, I think he's better.' Alia quickly went to her mother and held her so tightly that she couldn't remember the last time her daughter ever did such a thing.

When she recovered a little, Alia distanced herself slightly and asked, 'Who told you?'

'Alex. He's been trying to get a hold of you, but you were not answering. He wants you to ring him.' The queen uttered her words with a sense of calmness, which belied the glow in the vicinity of her expectant heart.

'Oh no, I must've left my phone in the Blue Lounge.' Without another word she dashed to the lounge and quickly retrieved her cell phone. As she scrolled down it became apparent that he had tried ringing her several times. The continuous sound of a phone ringing could be faintly heard as the queen and Christy stood in the entrance hall and heard her say, 'Alex, I can't believe it,' then her voice disappeared into the lounge room as she softly closed the door.

Christy had placed the two trays on the table in the middle of the entrance hall and slowly walked towards Her Majesty. 'Ma'am, I can imagine how happy you must feel. I know my heart feels like bursting out of my chest.'

'Christy, you've been invaluable to us all – especially to Alia. Thank you.'

'Ma'am, I'd do it all over again for Stephan and all of you.'

Alia emerged from the Blue Lounge room and as she

approached her mother and friend, they could see the red-rimmed eyes and tear-stained cheeks. She directed her steps straight towards Christy and both embraced and teared some more. 'I will go tomorrow and see Stephan. Will you come with me, Christy? Mother, are you coming?'

'You go first, Alia and I will go a little later. It's important that you see him first.'

'Thank you, Mother. I love you.' She was surprised at the words that slipped out of her daughter's mouth.

As Alia glanced around the hall, she noticed the two trays of food sitting ever so lonely on the table. 'We went to a great deal of trouble to cook this food, so let's go and eat it. Mother, come and join us.'

'With all my heart.' The queen followed the two friends towards the dining room, and she felt an elation in her heart and a lightness of foot.

38

Alia was up early the next day. She dressed warmly and could hardly wait to go to the hospital and see her son. Christy accompanied her while Nat and one of his junior assistant bodyguards escorted them to the car driven by Trent. The queen was upstairs and as she heard voices outside in the front of the palace, she saw her daughter wearing a red coat and beret to match and long black boots. A secret smile settled on her lips for she knew whenever her daughter was excited and happy, she wore bright colours. Christy's woollen navy coat with its synthetic fur collar was accompanied with a white angora scarf which was practical yet looked smart on her slim body. Together they made a convivial couple of friends looking forward to what the day had to offer.

As the car approached the hospital it was noticeably cordoned off with yellow police tape to caution people and Trent stopped the car, got out and approached the policeman manning the area. He produced a driver's licence to satisfy

38

all queries and soon removed some of the tape for the car to sidle up to the kerb and allow his passengers to disembark in front of the hospital. The driver was promptly out and automatically scanned the place with astute eyes, while he helped the ladies out of the car. Alia and Christy were amazed at the hundreds upon hundreds of flowers and toys outside the hospital. The media also made its presence known in no uncertain terms. The clicking of cameras, the broadcasters, the vans, and the heavy equipment appeared to be a setting for some Hollywood movie that made itself comfortable to remain on the lot for the long haul.

The two bodyguards, one in front and one behind their charges, entered the hospital and walked towards the elevator. As people began to recognise who the visitor was a spontaneous cry of comfort was heard in the corridor of the hospital. 'Happy for Stephan, ma'am,' 'God bless him, Your Highness,' 'So glad he's well' and similar sentiments were continuous and Alia was quite overcome by the kindness people showed towards her son and herself. She stopped, shook hands, spoke to each and every one who approached. One little girl holding a teddy walked straight over to the princess and held it up to her. Alia crouched down to her level, 'This is for Prince Stephan. I'd like him to have it.'

'But this is yours, isn't it?'

'Yes, but he's sick and he might like to cuddle it. I'll give it to him.'

'What's your name?'

'Marie.'

'Well, you're very kind Marie. I will definitely give this to Stephan.'

Alia went up to Nat and asked him to get the little girl's full name and address from her mother, who stood in the back ground looking on, so Stephan could send her a thank you note when he was well. As they all entered the elevator, Alia waved to quite a crowd that had formed in the corridor. 'That was a heart-warming thing, Alia. I believe people do love you and I dare say the whole monarchy. How wonderful.'

'You know, Christy, it's very humbling when a child such as Marie gives up her own toy for someone else. Heaven knows if she has another one ... it doesn't really matter even if she does, it was done from the depths of her heart,' exclaimed Alia.

'Yes, a lesson for all of us, I think.'

'Quite right.' Alia took her friend's arm and together got out on the third floor, followed, of course, by the bodyguards. They walked towards Stephan's room where several secret security males and two security females were outside the door and there were others up and down the hallway. They were informed that some of the surrounding rooms were taken up for security and bodyguards to use.

Nat held the door open and Alia stepped into the room quite tentatively. She didn't want to make too much noise in case Stephan was asleep. Alex was immediately by her side and they embraced each other. 'He's sleeping right now, but you can sit in this armchair – it's quite comfortable.'

'I want to sit near his bed in that chair,' Alia pointed to the chair and holding her hand, Alex took her there.

Alex then noticed Christy who was standing by Isi on one side and Dave on the other. He went over and greeted her warmly. 'So good of you to be here, Christy. I don't know how we would've done it all without you, Isi and Dave.'

'I'm glad to be here, Alex.' They all settled in their seats and spoke softly so as not to disturb the patient.

A little time later, the magic word was spoken. 'Mum.'

'I'm here, my darling boy. Mummy's here. How are you feeling?' She placed his small hand into hers and brought it to her lips. 'I love you so much,' and kissed his hand several times.

'I'm okay, Mum ... I want to go home. Can I come home with you?'

'We'll have to ask the doctors and see what they say.' Alex stood to the side and observed his wife and son. Alia looked up at him and asked, 'What do the doctors say, Alex?'

'They haven't done their ward rounds this morning yet. We can ask them and see what happens.'

Just as Alex finished speaking, in came a group of doctors and the head of the unit came up to Alia. 'Your Highness, I'm sure Stephan is very happy to see you here. He's done very well since he was brought in.'

'When do you think he can come home?' Alia enquired eagerly.

'All his vital signs are returning to normal ... breathing, heartbeat, temperature and most importantly his cognitive signs. I think tomorrow, if he's a good boy, and I know he has been, you may go home then, Stephan.'

While the consultant spoke to Alia, his two registrars began to examine their young patient while the intern looked on. They spoke to the boy and laughed and asked about his dog and the games he played with him, but mostly they were able to make an assessment of his ability to comprehend and respond to questions. He needed to meet certain requirements before being discharged the next day.

'You see, Mum, I'll be home tomorrow ... and Basco, too.'

'An amazing dog, ma'am – amazing.'

'Yes, doctor, I've heard what he has done. He's inseparable from Stephan and vice versa.'

'I can see that. So, Stephan's appetite is slowly returning, and tomorrow will be fine, as long as a physician attends to him every day for the next week. I believe Dr Schultz is your physician. We will send all of the equipment that's required for Stephan to be placed in his bedroom, so the physician can monitor his recovery every day. We don't normally do this, but in this instance, he will recover better and faster being around people who love him.'

'I think so, too. We will make sure everything happens according to your recommendations.' Alia shook hands with the doctor and thanked him.

She spent the rest of the day with her son as did Christy and the three men. They played board games, checkers, chess, and snakes and ladders, and everyone took it in turn to play with Stephan who naturally won all the time. He walked slowly around the room and up and down the hospital corridor to strengthen his legs. Most importantly, he also needed to sleep and rest. So, towards mid-afternoon, Alia and Christy made their farewells.

Alia leaned over and kissed her son on the cheek. 'You know grandmamma wants to come tomorrow, but what do you say we surprise her by you coming home.'

'Grandmamma rang me, and I told her I wanted to come home tomorrow. So it won't be a big surprise.'

'That's fine. She will be so pleased to see you – she can't wait.'

'She told me that, too.'

Alia blew a kiss to her son and waved goodbye. 'I love you as far as the moon and back.'

'Me too,' Stephan replied blowing kisses to his Mum.

Christy also made her goodbyes and Alex escorted them to the waiting car outside, but not before trying to convince Isi and Dave to go back to the palace with the ladies. They would not hear of it. 'We came all together, we leave all together,' they insisted. There was nothing else Alex could do but accept their decision.

At the palace, Queen Sylvia was almost at the front door before Parkinson. As the two women came up the front steps, the queen stood in the doorway and urgently bid them to come in. 'It is freezing out there.' She embraced her daughter and gave Christy a kiss on the cheek. 'Now tell me, how did you find Stephan?'

'He's such a little trooper. Improved enormously. He was laughing, playing board games and trying to eat. Hasn't got his full appetite back yet, but he's getting there.'

'He rang me just before you came and told me he is coming home tomorrow. He was so excited.'

'I think we all are. I can't wait either.' Alia turned to Parkinson, who stood by, and instructed him to tell the staff that Stephan is well. She could see Daisy peering around one of the doors, and the personal assistants stood at the top of the staircase waiting to hear the news about him. 'Parkinson, please tell Daisy to make all of Stephan's favourite food tomorrow. I want his appetite to return and it will help if he sees food that he likes.'

'Of course, Your Highness. Daisy will be very happy to do so. I'll go and tell her and the rest of the staff that Master Stephan's returning tomorrow.'

'Do you girls want to have supper in the private lounge? There should be some food there.'

'Thank you, Mother. Yes, of course. Christy, come along with me.'

'I certainly will. I was thinking ... maybe we can put up some streamers and balloons to welcome Stephan home.'

'That's a very good idea, Christy. I'll ask Parkinson to have it organised.'

The queen and the two friends made their way towards the lounge in a most amiable and congenial atmosphere.

39

It seemed everyone in the palace had a very early alarm clock. By six in the morning Daisy's kitchen abounded in aromas which tantalised the olfactory cells and tempted everyone to taste everything that was cooking. By six-thirty Alia and Christy were dressed and followed their noses in the direction of the kitchen.

'Daisy, this smells absolutely divine. Oh look, Christy, chocolate croissants. Stephan's going to love them.'

'You may have one, ma'am, and your friend,' Daisy smiled broadly at both of them.

'Daisy, this is my very best friend Christy. She comes all the way from a little town called Histon in England.'

'Ma'am, I know it well. In my younger days I was a cook in a tavern in Impington, not far away from Histon,' Daisy recollected with pleasure.

'They're very close. These two villages are only separated by the A14 road,' Christy added and quickly placed a mouthful of fluffy pastry and warm melting chocolate into her mouth. All she could say in between each crunch was 'Hmm, hmm.'

Alia had already gobbled down one and was on her second croissant. 'At this rate we're not going to leave this woman any to serve up when Stephan arrives.'

'Don't worry, ma'am, I'll make enough for your breakfast and Stephan's return. We're all so happy to have him back in the palace.'

'Thank you, Daisy.' She looked askance at Christy and added, 'We'll go and see if Mother's up,' and then had a bite of the croissant. 'Hmm, what a mess I've made. Look at all the pastry flakes. I think I better finish it off here or I'll leave a trail of it right up to the dining room.' As she bit into the last of her croissant, she turned to Christy and stated, 'I'm ravenously hungry. Shall we go?'

'I'm with you all the way.' Christy smiled to herself at the extraordinary change in her friend.

There were streamers and helium balloons in the main entrance hallway and a very large colourful sign which read WELCOME HOME STEPHAN *and Basco*. By about midmorning, the sound of a returning vehicle was heard with Stephan slowly climbing the steps holding onto his father's hand and followed by Dave and Isi. The main door was opened and there stood Parkinson with the biggest smile that spread within an inch between his ears, and as he looked down on the young boy he happily said, 'Welcome home, Master Stephan.'

Stephan stretched his neck to see Parkinson and said, 'Thank you.'

39

As he walked into the main entrance hall, his surprise was beyond him. 'Wow, wow. Look at all this.' His face looked upwards and read out aloud the sign and then took the string of one balloon and turned to Basco, 'Look Basco, it's for us.' Basco was too busy chasing some balloons that were on the floor. When he overcame the initial surprise of his welcome, he found his mother's face and naturally made his way to her. She crouched, opened her arms and he went straight into them. She squeezed his small body to her chest and held him for a while. Then she rounded his face with her hands and kissed him on the cheek. 'You know how much I love you?'

'Yea – to the moon and back,' replied Stephan.

Alex came and stood next to his wife and held her hand, and every so often he brought those delicate fingers of hers to his lips. Isi was next to Christy and as he looked on the scene, his gleaming smile reflected his joyous heart. Dave stood next to Isi also and every so often he'd slap his friend's back with his broad hand and emit an exuberant chuckle as he continued to repeat, 'That's just great, mate, great, isn't it?' To which Isi always replied, 'Yes, mate, it is.'

Stephan then saw his Grandmama and immediately walked in her direction. She encircled her arms around him and after a moment or two, she asked, 'And what do you think about all of this?'

'Did you do all of this, Grandmama?'

'No, it was Christy's idea and Parkinson organised it all. Do you want to go and say thank you to everyone?'

Stephan had a hug ready for her and said, 'Thanks, Christy.' Then he turned his face towards Parkinson and with a lilt in his voice uttered, 'I love all the balloons. Thank you.'

In the corner of his eye he saw Robert Glandore step inside the entrance hall. He walked as fast as his little legs could carry him and called out, 'Grandpa, I missed you.' Robert collected him into his arms and held him tightly to his chest.

'Stephan, I'm so glad to see you, my boy,' and again he pressed him to his chest. 'I missed you too.' He held his hand warmly and together went to greet everyone else.

'Look at Basco, Grandpa.' The dog was chasing balloons that bounced on the floor and floated intermittently in the air. Together they went closer and observed Basco while Susanna joined them to make sure Stephan didn't overdo his excitement. Soon she took him into the dining room to enjoy his favourite food and the entire family sat around him as did their good friends.

Susanna insisted that Stephan must go and rest before the physician arrived and much to his discontent he was taken to his room, wherein a story was read to him and one generally tried to calm his excitement. The doctor, of course, found him in good spirits and his condition generally a lot better, but he still needed rest and attention. Both Alex and Alia were in the room while he was being examined and they were pleased with the outcome.

Their three friends had organised to leave that evening with Dave returning to Peru, while Isi and Christy would be going back to their family and congregation. There were hardly any words to express their heartfelt thanks to all of them. Alex was determined to donate to Dave's environmental charities and to Isi a donation towards the building of a church hall and a sizeable amount for the "Poor Box" that was always in need. Although he was met with much protestation, his mind was made up. As he said to each one of them, 'No amount of money that I donate can ever cover your acts of kindness and your loving friendship in helping to find and bring my son back home. So, please, accept this small token of appreciation.' There was nothing else to be done but accept it graciously.

By the end of the week and with the physician's approval, Stephan felt strong enough to return to school and was also allowed to bring Basco with him for the first day. Alia found her desk wanting of her time and she and Jillian were hard at work to respond to the mail that had accumulated. Alex was keen to see the progress at the company and although he occasionally took a call from his CEO or Manager, he felt his presence was essential, but before he could start his work once more, he wanted Bob to bring him up to date with various issues that needed to be sorted.

The minute Alex stepped into his Aerospace Engineering Centre he came across Lars Gilmar. 'Alex, good to see you. We're all happy about Stephan. How is he?'

'He's back at school, but the physician is still monitoring his health. He's a resilient kid and I'm sure he'll be fine. Now, how are things with the new computer systems?'

'I think you'll be happy with the computerised technology in the prototype plane. Mack was really pleased. Should any one system fail, there is a booster system to see the plane fly for a half hour extra. That means it could save pilots, personnel and passengers on board.' They continued to walk in the direction of Alex's office. 'As for the general company's computer systems, I think you'll like what I've done. I'm just finishing off my report on all areas I've worked in. On your desk in ... a couple of hours.'

'Thanks, Lars. Come into my office a minute.' As he entered his personal assistant's office, Ebba stood and welcomed him back, but not without saying how happy she was about Stephan's return. 'Thank you, Ebba. Come in, Lars.' He closed the door behind him and sat at his desk. 'Take a seat.' He looked squarely into his face and said, 'I know that you were approached by the WSO to join them and reveal everything you know about this company and especially the computerised electronics. I want to congratulate you for resisting them, considering the pressure they applied.'

'Thanks, Alex.' His face had a most puzzled look about it. 'How in the world did you know that? I never told a soul about it.'

'That doesn't matter. It's your strength, loyalty, and ethics, firstly, to your own beliefs and secondly your resolved commitment to this firm. I know that your employment is part-time until you finish this job, but if you are interested in a full-time position, let me know.'

'Well, Alex, that's terrific. I might take you up on that. I'll let you know soon.' They shook hands and each man went about his own business.

Before he could settle in his chair, Ebba was on the phone. 'Jacob Einheimmer is on the phone for you.'

'Put him through ... Mr Einheimmer, how can I help you? Yes, I can do that. What about at eleven this morning? Good, I'll see you then.' He picked up the intercom phone and asked Ebba to come in. 'Mr Einheimmer is coming in today at eleven. Now, I have a lot of work here on my desk. Is there anything you need to tell me before I start?'

'No, sir. I've emailed you all the letters I was able to answer and others sent you emails, and all the postal letters are on your desk. If there is anything you want me to change, I'll do that.'

'Nothing at present. I'll let you know as I press on with what's on my table and computer. Thanks.' The amount of mail, both hard copies and electronic, was overbearing, but he meticulously went through all of it. He was surprised to see the amount of work he was actually able to accomplish in two hours, and this helped him to receive Einheimmer with a calmer disposition.

Mr Einheimmer was directed into his office and soon they sat facing each other.

'What was it you wanted to see me about, Mr Einheimmer?'

'I'm sure you recall our deal when you bought out my company. In lieu of some cash payment I received an equivalent of shares in your engineering company. I feel my time in Rubinia is running out. I have a house in Kent, England, and an opportunity to work as a consultant with an engineering firm there. But, for this to happen seamlessly and without any hiccups I need to be cashed up. So, how would you feel if you bought out all of my shares in your company? I ask you first, because I know you can do it and I also need this to happen as soon as possible. Today won't be too soon. So, what do you say?' Einheimmer appeared relaxed and receptive for discussion.

'Leave it with me and I will get back to you by the end of the day.' Alex stood to indicate the meeting was over.

'Make sure you do. It's important to me,' emphasised Einheimmer.

'It's important to me too. When I say I will do this, then I do it. You will hear from me by the end of the day.' Alex stared at Einheimmer and continued, 'Goodbye and I wish you well with your endeavours. I'll be in touch.' He saw him leave his office and sensed that he paused for a moment or two at Ebba's desk. Alex was already on to his sharebroker to get the latest share price for his company. He was told that the shares had gone down, due to all the unrest around Rubinia, and this was the ideal time to buy. Alex did just that and waited until he received all the paperwork and confirmation from his sharebroker before contacting Einheimmer. He would wait towards the end of the day and ring him then.

By one o'clock in the afternoon, Bob arrived to see Alex. 'Right on time. Come in. I hope you haven't had lunch yet. I've ordered some for here.'

'I'm quite hungry. I've spent the day down at police headquarters and the secret service. I'd like to go through my reports, which I've already emailed you. I have them here on my iPad, as well. Dealing with the arrests, there were several more made. We were able to take fingerprints off the black glove which I found outside the hut, and they matched that of Blake Crowley. He is in custody, but apart from that, Hans was picked up on the border of Switzerland and Vanda was identified trying to board a plane for Brazil. Both were brought to the police station where intense interrogations cracked their resistance and they spilled a gutfull of information.' Bob took a deep breath and continued. 'In the end, Hans was more willing to tell us all he knew than Vanda. Between Hans and Vanda and the antiquated CCTVs they were able to bug and cause havoc all over the palace and grounds. Hans had been recruited by Vanda with the promise of being a Captain in the WSO military and money on top if he helped with the abduction.'

At that moment two people rolled in a tea-trolley with platters of food, which ranged from grilled salmon, venison meat, baked vegetables, a salad, and crème de caramel for desserts. 'Oh, good it's here. Set everything up on the coffee table. Thanks, guys.' Alex motioned to Bob to come and sit down around the coffee table. 'Tuck in. Are you comfortable to eat and talk at the same time?'

'Not a problem. I can do that.' Bob chose the meat and filled the rest of his plate with some of the baked vegetables. 'Vanda took direct orders from Crowley and they made their way to the hut with Crowley's private helicopter. That's why there were no visible tracks or traces of a vehicle on St Anna's Pass. The helicopter landed near the hut and the snowfall took care of that.' Bob cut a sizeable amount of steak and part of a potato. 'Hmm, this is really delicious.' He swallowed and continued. 'You might like to know that Crowley boasted he had contacts high up in your company and when he was pushed to the limits he confessed.' Bob glanced at Alex who searched Bob's face for some clues. 'It's your CEO – Gustof Fischer.' He noticed Alex's shocked expression. 'He was also graphic about Stephan – do you want to hear? Let me see if I can remember word for word – "That little brat, kicked and scratched and bit me. He's an untamed animal ... not a prince, but we soon quietened him down." When Vanda was asked, why did they leave the hut and the boy behind, he said that Crowley came with his helicopter and told them to get out because there were rumours that the big boss had left the country for Cuba and he wasn't going to take the rap for kidnapping the kid – and not just any kid. They closed the door behind them and just left your son there, drugged up, to freeze to death.' Alex involuntarily winced as he thought of what could have been. 'Little did they know that the dog would come and pound the door down with his paws and body weight. Fortunately, the door was worse for wear and fell quite easily and the rest we know.' Bob hesitated for a while to allow Alex to recollect his emotions.

Alex was more than willing to change the subject a little. 'Now what about this guy, Gunter?'

'He's a volatile man, quick to anger and physically shows it. He eventually broke down, especially when we told him that Gregory was on his way to Cuba and soon gave us the exact positions where his military was hidden in the alps. We were astounded at the numbers that had joined. We had to bring in reinforcements and after a few exchanges of bullets and grenades, they could see it was a losing battle. Fortunately, we commanded the air and took them by surprise — they could not regroup quickly enough. What did astound us was the immense stockpiles of munitions, equipment, combat essentials, and tanks.'

'How in the world did they accumulate all of that?' Alex asked incredulously.

'Over twenty years a lot can be bought and stored.' Bob placed the last mouthful of meat in his mouth.

Alex noticed it and added, 'There's more if you want any.'

'No, I'm hanging out for the dessert ... I forgot to mention that Prime Minister Yallenski of Borovia was cited in some statements that he too was a member of the WSO, but he's denying ever knowing the WSO. He's just clutching at last straws.' He looked over at Alex and saw he was getting ready to start on the crème caramel and Bob took the depleted dinner plates and placed them on the side of the coffee table to make room for the dessert. 'You may also want to know about Ms Barbour – the teacher. She's been charged with pernicious political activities, but I think she will probably get away with a hefty fine – it depends on the judge.'

'According to the news, much of the uprisings have

simmered down, but every so often they ignite sporadically. What concerns me is that they might spread to Rubinia. What's your inside information tell you?' Alex's concerns were genuine.

'You have no fear of that. If it was going to spread, it would have done so at its height. It'll all be under control shortly. Politicians in Cumbia straining at the leash to be re-elected are promising to reverse the harm that has occurred in their country and promises of new national elections are on the horizon. There are promises all over the place. Many of the people's liberties that had been confiscated will be reinstated and in a short while all disturbances will cease. I'm fairly sure.'

Alex interrupted Bob's account of the insurrections and said, 'Why do I feel that a lot of this has been planned and strategically worked out?'

'Sir, the politics of nations is a very strange thing. There are many influences that sway the pendulum – one minute it's left, next it's right. What is being done here is to find a median of the political line.'

'With some outside persuasion, I suppose,' added Alex.

'Look at it this way, Dr Glandore. What would have happened if no one had stepped in and took hold of the reins? Can you visualise that?'

'Not a very pretty picture on a personal level and political level.'

'This was a massive international effort. It may have been secret, but then secrecy gets quick results.' Bob rounded up his commentary.

'Ah, speed! We live in a world where everything needs to be done in microseconds to satisfy technological inventions, and now it seems insurrections as well.' Alex sighed and brought his outspread arms up to shoulder level and let them fall to his sides. 'And the sad thing is that I'm not precluded from it, at all.'

'No, Sir, none of us are. It's a tech world and it's here to stay.'

Alex changed the subject and regarded Bob for a moment. 'Thank you for today, Bob. I presume Her Majesty has been briefed on all you've told me.'

'I'm on my way from here to the palace where I'll inform Her Majesty of everything, although I know Mike would've had a few things to tell her. I'll make sure she's up to date with all the latest happenings. And of course it will include Princess Alia as well.'

'Of course. Do that. Thanks again for everything.'

As Bob was about to leave, he stopped at the door before opening it and said, 'Oh, just one more thing. Cumbia has exiled the monarchy, except for King Gregory who's in hiding or slipped through to Cuba.'

'What has happened to King Gregory's parents? I remember them as decent people,' Alex asked with interest.

'They were shipped off to England — the destination for most exiles as seen over history.'

'It's sad to think how different a son can turn out compared to the parents,' Alex pondered this inevitable turn of events that had left profound markings on the annals of modern history.

Alex's day was spent between his office and the workshop. He was pleased with the way things were shaping up with the prototype plane. He thought hard about Gustof Fischer and he could not delay it any longer.

Lars Gilmar's contribution with all the computer electronics were brilliantly conceived and constructed. His enquiries from Mack about him were very positive and going with what he knew and saw, he concurred with Mack. He still didn't know why Einheimmer was against Lars. Perhaps, he thought, Blake might have influenced Lars to work towards his company's collapse. Whatever it was, the final result spoke for itself.

Towards the end of the day he received a call from Gilmar. 'Lars, good to hear from you. How can I help you?'

'I've thought about your offer of work and I want to accept it.'

'Great. When can you start?'

'Any time you want me to.'

'How about tomorrow? I'll have all the paperwork ready for you to sign at nine. See you then.' Alex swiftly pulled the door open to see if Ebba was still there. 'Oh, good, you're still here. The paperwork for a new employee – will you print them out with Lars Gilmar's name on them. He'll be in tomorrow morning to sign them. Bring the paperwork into my office. I'll need to speak with you.'

'Yes, sir, of course.' Within half an hour the forms were downloaded and printed with the right name on each sheet. She knocked and pulled the door open. 'This is all the

39

paperwork,' and left it neatly on Alex's desk.

'Take a seat, Ebba. As you can see, Lars Gilmar is starting work with my company and as a new executive, he'll need someone to support him as his personal assistant. How would you like to work with him rather than me? It's going to be a big task ... a challenge, in fact. Are you up for it?'

'Sir, whatever you think is best. I'll work with Mr Gilmar. I don't have a problem with that.'

'Good. Then that's that. I want you to move all your things in the office which Bob occupied and help Lars to settle in. You know the running of this engineering firm better than most. Let me get young John to help you pack and move.' Before Ebba disappeared into her office, Alex exclaimed, 'Just one more thing. This new move will come with an increase in your salary.'

'Thank you, sir.' Ebba was surprised, but she had an inkling as to the reason for her well-paid new position.

As Ebba left his office, he picked up the phone and rang the area in which John worked. He made a quick smart arrival at Ebba's office. Alex could hear the clanging of things and banging of books into the carton boxes. He had the common sense to bring a workshop trolley with him, so everything could be transported without any fuss. Alex made a mental note to follow this young man's work ethic and see where it would lead. When all the extraneous noise was silenced, he leaned back in his chair and thought *Who am I going to choose as my PA?* More importantly, he racked his brain about his CEO. This must be dealt with immediately. He rang Gustof Fischer himself and asked him to come and see him right away.

Soon he heard his knock and called out, 'Come in Gustof ... take a seat.'

Gustof looked around him and eventually sat in the chair directly in front of the desk. 'It has come to my notice that you were a member of the WSO. Tell me, why did you join?'

Gustof appeared shocked and as the blood rushed to his face, he placed his hand to his cheeks, mouth, and chin as if he could wipe away the redness imprinted on his skin. He could feel the dryness in his mouth, but he needed to recover his composure and asked, 'How do you know that?'

'It's irrelevant how I know and don't deny it. That's just going to make matters worse.' Alex paused momentarily and studied closely his CEO. 'I'll ask again. Why did you join?'

He eventually yielded and answered, 'The WSO sounded exciting and I wanted to be part of this new Order. In truth, I really didn't know much about them.' He then began to fiddle with his tie and collar in a nervous movement of his fingers as he swallowed hard.

'Did the WSO coerce you to give them information about my firm?'

'Yes and no.'

'It's either yes or no. Did you give them any information?' Alex insisted firmly.

'No.'

'Did you sabotage the prototype plane?' Again, Alex asked forcefully.

'No.'

'Did you video the prototype and pass it on to the WSO?'

'No.'

Alex continued unperturbed. 'Tell me then – how did this video end up in your cell phone?' He opened the middle drawer of his desk and Alex produced Gustof Fischer's phone. He clicked the gallery button and immediately began to play the video detailing the prototype plane's engine.

Gustof instantly and with great speed endeavoured to find his phone in his jacket's pockets and back pocket of his trousers, without success. 'Give me that,' he yelled at Alex. He tried to lunge at the phone as Alex pressed a button under his desk.

Bob opened the door with a gush of noise and swiftly restrained Gustof's hands with handcuffs behind his back. 'I think it's time for you to come with me.' He then turned to Alex and asked, 'Are you okay, sir?'

'Yes, Bob. Just get him out of here.'

Half an hour later Alex got a call from Alison Melroy, Fischer's personal assistant. 'Sir, there's a man here and he's just packing all of Mr Fischer's things and is ready to walk out the door.' Her voice was quite alarmed.

'Alison, come and see me, now, please.' The phone went dead and within five minutes Alison stood in front of her boss. 'I just want to let you know that Mr Fischer will not be working for this firm anymore. You are not to receive any calls from him or have any interaction with him whatsoever, now or anytime.'

'Of course, sir.'

'Now, how would you like to be my personal assistant?'

'Yes, Dr Glandore. I'd like that very much,' Alison replied with a smile.

'Move all your things over to this side as soon as you can.'

Between the change of the offices and the reorientation of Alison, the end of the day had announced itself. 'The transfer over was as smooth as possible. Thanks, Alison, and how are your two kiddies?'

'Oh, they can be little terrors sometimes, but I love them.'

'As parents we know all about that. So, thank you again and goodnight.'

'Good night, sir.'

He went and checked what Alison had done in her new office. He could tell her efficiency was smart and minimalistic. He liked the rearrangements she made.

40

Christmas was approaching, and as the tradition was to celebrate on Christmas Eve, they all looked forward to cutting down the Christmas trees and then decorate them. There were always two trees in the palace. One in the entrance hall and the other in the drawing room. The boxes of Christmas decorations were brought out to begin the joyous act of placing some of the most interesting and beautiful ornaments on the tree. It was traditionally always for the queen to place the angel on top of the Christmas tree and then everyone chose their own decorative piece to adorn it, but before this actually occurred, Alex was given the task of positioning the lights around the tree. That was fine except the lights were so tangled that it became incumbent upon one and sundry to straighten out the cord without getting twisted in the process. This gave Alia the bright idea to take the cord and wrap more of it around Alex, while he exaggerated his attempts to untangle himself. This, of course, only had the effect to cause more laughter and hilarity.

In the end, Stephan was given the honour to switch on the tree lights and many 'Ahs' and 'Wows' were heard as they stood back to admire the trees. Stephan went to the piano and began to play *Silent Night* which cued many voices into song. The only thing missing were the presents below the tree which undoubtedly were going to appear miraculously that evening.

As the time drew near, Stephan scampered down the staircase as quickly as he could, while his parents and the queen looked on and shared his excitement. Soon they were joined by Robert Glandore and Jill. Robert was delegated the task to hand out the presents. Each gift had its own reward and Stephan's new bicycle was on top of his list. He couldn't wait to go outside and try it out, but he was patient for everyone else to get their gift as well. Alex's present to Alia was a miniature carving of the resort on the Greek island where they spent their honeymoon. Alia's gift to Alex was the last to be received. It was in a small square box and when he opened it, he looked at it curiously. As he pulled it out of the box and continued to stare at it, the object became clearly recognisable as a ceramic cradle with a baby in it. He gazed at Alia's face for some cognitive explanation. Her response was to place her arms around his neck and smile at him. 'Is this what I think it means?' Alia nodded her head and then placed two fingers in front of her husband's face. 'What, do you mean twins?' Alia nodded her head again. Alex couldn't contain himself. He shouted for the world to hear. 'We're going to have twins.'

He lifted her up into his arms and kissed her face and lips over and over again.

'Alia, you're pregnant. How wonderful. How far advanced are you?' Questions were thrown at her from everyone.

Eventually, Alex put her down gently and all gathered around with congratulations and pats on the back and kisses and lots of hugs. Stephan approached timidly and asked, 'Mum, are you going to have a baby?'

'I'm going to have twins, Stephan. Maybe two boys, or two girls or one of each,' Alia confirmed.

'Wow, when's that going to happen?

'In August next year.'

As she held her son closely to her, Robert Glandore approached and gave his congratulations. 'You'll make a wonderful mother of three,' and then hugged his daughter- in-law.

Alia's sense of elation was so exquisitely deep that had Gregory walked into the room that very moment, she would've forgiven him for everything. She was glad for the distraction when the call for breakfast was made and as they all sat around, still discussing the arrival of the new twins, Alia shined the focus elsewhere. 'Robert, when are you and Jill getting married?'

'I think probably in May. Isn't that right Jill?' Robert looked towards his fiancé as she nodded her head and beamed at him. Alia wholeheartedly proposed that she should organise a wedding shower which surprised everyone and resulted in a grateful acceptance.

Eventually, when the young couple moved out of the dining room towards the staircase, Alex paused just at the bottom of the steps and asked, 'So when did this all happen?' Alia smiled up at him without a response. Then with clarity as clear as crystal, he said, 'Ah, my apartment.' He continued to look at her with a twinkle in his eye.

'Oh, come on, you.' Alia punched his upper arm with her fist. 'Help a pregnant woman up these stairs.' She wrapped her arm around his and step by step went to the top of the staircase.

'Have you been to the doctor, is everything all right?'

'Yes. He just wants me to eat more and gain a bit of strength. It's no wonder I couldn't eat a thing. I felt nauseous all the time and I didn't know why. Never felt like that when I was pregnant with Stephan.'

'Look, Alia, I want you to take on less responsibility and look after yourself. I'll try and take on some of the burden from you.'

'You will?' Alia asked with surprise.

'I'm going to try. I can cut a ribbon and make a pithy speech and shake hands with people. Not a problem.' He waved his arm with ease to suggest the simplicity with which he could perform these tasks.

'Come here, you.' Alia lifted her arms towards Alex, and he leaned over and planted a kiss on her lips.

'I think you should go and have a rest. I'll walk you to your room.'

Just as they opened the bedroom door, Helena arrived

to give her assistance. 'Ma'am, would you like to lie in your bed?'

'Not right now. I think I'll just sit in my armchair and read a while.'

Alia glanced at Alex and asked, 'Are you happy?'

'I'm ecstatic,' and with that he left his wife's bedroom, knowing she was in capable hands.

She settled in the armchair and regarded Helena as she moved effortlessly around the room and then her gaze naturally fell across the opposite wall where she noticed the hairline crack. 'Helena will you please let Parkinson know that we need a plasterer to repair the wall over there,' and pointed with her finger. 'It's just a faint crack line, but it needs to be fixed.'

'Yes, ma'am, I can see it. I'll let Parkinson know.'

41

In the eight months that lapsed Alia felt and looked ready for delivery of her two babies. The media kept second-guessing day by day as to when the twins were due. Alex was on constant alert as was the rest of the palace household. In particular his driver, Trent, who needed to be ready at a moment's notice. As it turned out, the babies decided they were in a hurry to see what was outside of the warm and comfortable womb and arrived two weeks early. The doctor was notified, the hospital on geared alert and Alex, with some nervous energy, accompanied his wife to the car, where Trent patiently waited. The queen was at the door, as Parkinson held it open for her to wave goodbye.

Alex waited anxiously with his father by his side until the twins were born. The surgeon came out to the private waiting room and told them that everything went well, and they could go and see Her Highness now. Robert allowed his son to enter first and gave him a few moments to be with his wife and new babies. 'I'm so happy, Alia. You look fine

41

and the twins ... what can I say ... I'd forgotten how small they could be.' He picked up his son first as he stood nearest to him and looked straight into his red and wrinkled face. 'What are we going to call him?'

'I thought, Frederick Johan Robert Glandore. What do you think?'

'That's just fine.' He placed him by his mother's side, then went around the other side of the bed to pick up his daughter. 'She's so beautiful ... she looks just like you.' He couldn't stop staring at her. 'Have you found a name for our daughter?'

'What about Marianne Sylvia Adelaide Glandore?'

'Where did Adelaide come from?' Alex asked curiously.

'She was a most amazing British queen with a loving heart for children who were disadvantaged and helped to set up orphanages. I've read her story and I really like her. Are you happy with that?' Then she thought again. 'We can give them other names if you want.'

'No, they're just all perfect.'

Alia suddenly noticed her father-in-law standing a little further back. 'Robert, come and meet your grandchildren.'

'Come on Dad, they're beautiful.'

Robert smiled and nodded his head and said to his son, 'I thought the same thing about you, when you were born.'

Alia remained in hospital for less than a week and when she was ready to leave with her two children, the entire medical crew of obstetrics and gynaecology were out to see the Princess, her husband and their new babies drive away to their home. The media was out in force and many people lined the streets to get a glimpse of the princess and her new babies. The cathedral bells rang, and they were still faintly heard when the princess and her young family all arrived at the palace. Alex took his son in his arms and Alia held her daughter as they went up the steps towards the door. When they entered the palace, Stephan approached his mother and father rather tentatively and stared down on the two little creatures that were still quite red and ready to cry. 'Stephan, you can touch their little head and if you like let the baby hold your finger.'

Stephan placed his forefinger near his brother's hand, and he gripped firmly. 'Wow, he's strong.'

'Try doing that with your sister,' Alex urged him.

'She's just as strong.'

'Stephan, your sister's name is Marianne and your brother's Frederick.' His older son was too busy playing with the babies' fingers to concentrate on what his father was saying.

Alia noticed her mother as she looked on the family scene and said, 'Mother, come and pick them up.' Queen Sylvia went and picked up Frederick first and smiled down upon him lovingly.

'Let me pick up Marianne.' She gave Frederick back to Alex and then cradled her granddaughter in her arms. She was mesmerised by her. 'You know, she looks exactly like you, Alia.'

'That's what I told her too,' Alex boasted.

Then the queen placed her granddaughter on her arms so

the baby's head rested comfortably in the palm of her hands and Marianne's eyes were facing her Grandmama. She lifted the baby closer to her face and, broadly smiling at her, said, 'And you darling girl, you can grow up and be *anything* you want to be. Yes, sweet girl, even a *surgeon*.'

Alia suddenly stared at her mother with a quizzical look and asked, 'Mother, where in the world has that come from?'

'Oh, it's a long story, my dear.' The queen paused and peered directly at her daughter. 'One of these days, I'm going to tell you.'